LOATHE
AT
FIRST
SIGHT

ALSO BY SUZANNE PARK

The Perfect Escape

PRAISE FOR
LOATHE AT FIRST SIGHT

"*Loathe at First Sight* bursts with humor, heart, and great energy. I loved it! Park is a hilarious new voice in women's fiction."

—Helen Hoang, author of *The Kiss Quotient*

"Hilarious and poignant, Park's debut sparkles as a great addition to the new voices of the rom-com renaissance."

—Roselle Lim, author of
Natalie Tan's Book of Luck and Fortune

"Park gives us the story that only she could create. It's hilarious, smart, and the rom-com we need!"

—Alexa Martin, ALA Award–winning
author of *Intercepted*

"Park has created a wholly original, smart, fierce heroine (with a hilarious inner voice) who takes on an industry hell-bent on underestimating her. . . . Just like the 'entertaining, fresh, snarky' video game she conjures in her novel, Suzanne Park has written a fast and fun debut, putting females in the lead."

—Amy Poeppel, author of
Musical Chairs and *Small Admissions*

"[A] punchy adult debut set in the world of video game design. . . . Park . . . makes tough topics go down easy by couching them in wry humor and lighthearted romance, and her fierce, snarky heroine is irresistible. This smart rom-com is a winner."

— *Publishers Weekly* (starred review)

"Melody's characterization and voice sparkle throughout. . . . Smart, punchy, and memorable."

— *Library Journal*

LOATHE AT FIRST SIGHT

a novel

SUZANNE PARK

AVON

An Imprint of HarperCollinsPublishers

This is a work of fiction. Names, characters, places, and incidents are products of the author's imagination or are used fictitiously and are not to be construed as real. Any resemblance to actual events, locales, organizations, or persons, living or dead, is entirely coincidental.

HarperCollins books may be purchased for educational, business, or sales promotional use. For information, please email the Special Markets Department at SPsales@harpercollins.com.

FIRST EDITION

Designed by Diahann Sturge

Chapter opener illustration © bioraven / Shutterstock, Inc.

Library of Congress Cataloging-in-Publication Data has been applied for.

ISBN 978-0-06-299069-3

20 21 22 23 24 LSC 10 9 8 7 6 5 4 3 2 1

For my family
(Mom and Dad, sorry again for all the cussing)

CHAPTER ONE

The group of developers gaped as I barged into the almost-empty conference room. The wrong conference room. With beads of sweat on my forehead and upper lip, I panted, "Is. This. Tolkien. Room?"

"Wrong place. This is the George R. R. Martin room." A thin guy with mouselike, pointy facial features shrugged as he bit into his sandwich.

"We booked this! It's ours!" His lunchmate, a thirtyish-year-old man with an eastern European accent, glared at me as he stabbed his pasta and forked it into his mouth.

The other two Asian guys in the room looked at me, then whispered to each other in Cantonese and laughed. Whatever they said, I knew it wasn't *She seems very smart and cool—we should cut her some slack and be really nice to her.*

I couldn't figure out where I needed to be, and the meeting started over five minutes ago. I slammed the door shut and kept hustling down the hallway. Sorry! No time to apologize. Could I get fired for extreme lateness?

After a couple of left turns, I found myself on a dark and cavernous part of the floor. I tried to read the name on a door of a nearby meeting room, but squinting and leaning in didn't help me make out the letters. Instinct led me to flip a light switch, which turned out to be the emergency lighting panel override for the entire area. All our quality assurance team, who happily played and tested games in the dark even on the sunniest of days, screamed as the artificial lights blinded them, like vampires being stricken by sunlight burns.

So many pasty-white, hairy forearms shot in the air, temporarily protecting these men's eyes from death by fluorescence. So much cursing! So much yelling! As the QA guys adjusted to the light situation, over a hundred pairs of dilated eyes scanned the room for someone to fixate on and persecute. With my feet frozen to the floor like a tree rooted near the light switch, I stood in shock by all the pandemonium I'd caused.

Finally, one of them walked up to me, shot me a look condemning me to a death by a million paper cuts, and turned the light back off with a swift palm strike. I had no doubt that these QA vampire guys would be—no pun intended—out for my blood after that incident.

With nothing left to lose, I asked, "Can someone please point me to the Tolkien room?"

"It's the corner one," a cubicle dweller grumbled, pulling his noise-canceling headphones from around his neck and placing them on his ears.

My cheeks burned as I headed back to the reasonably lit section of the floor. I double-checked the name etched on the conference room glass before entering. TOLKIEN. *Thank god.* After my whirlwind of panic, I took in a deep breath. *Chin up, Melody, you're just as smart and capable as everyone in there.* The door, slightly ajar, creaked as I pushed it open. I grabbed the nearest seat, and after hunkering down into the chair with a relieved exhale, my left armrest clanked to the floor.

Ian MacKenzie, the game studio's CEO, looked at the armrest, and then glared at me. The other ten guys in the room gave me icy stares too. Ian's inset, cold blue eyes locked with mine.

"Who are you?" he barked.

"I . . . I'm Melody Joo, the new production assistant." I couldn't hold his stare, so I looked down at his shoes. Brand-new pair of white Toms. To match his gleaming white, gritted teeth.

Someone's chair squeaked while we waited for Ian, the company's messiah, to say something. He turned his cold eyes away from me and gazed at the whiteboard scribble. Holy hell. What an intense stare.

I had only been at this game company a little over two weeks, but I could tell that most people had a visceral reaction to Ian. A handful of people loved him, but most of the staff didn't. The company's board of directors had hand selected him for his role because of his gaming industry pedigree. I spent most of my first day at work researching him online: he had been an executive creative director at Shazam! Game Studios and had one hit triple-A title under his belt. He was the creative mind behind *Undead vs. Undead vs. Undead*, the fastest-growing console game in the last decade, unexpectedly popular in Canada. Yes, Canada. Somehow his third-generation Irish brain figured out what would make Canadians become addicted to this type of shooter game.

Ian had left Shazam! just days before a Korean Canadian family in Calgary sued the company on the grounds that the game was so addictive that their sleep-deprived son ended up with urinary tract disability because he frequently held his pee for eighteen hours a day. The parents filed a lawsuit against Shazam! for millions of dollars. Some industry conspiracy theorists believed that Ian had hidden subliminal messages in the game to intensify gaming addiction, but no one could prove it. When asked if any of the allegations were true in a recent interview by a famous gaming journalist, Ian replied, "What can I say? Gamers can't get enough of my genius." Assuming everything I read online about this lawsuit was accurate, Ian seemed like a total asshole.

I couldn't say too much about Ian's lucky career success because getting my production assistant job had been a stroke of luck, which never usually happened for me. The board wanted more "entrepreneurial-minded" women at Seventeen Studios, and I fit the profile.

The company offered decent pay, and trying out a new career path in video games was on my professional bucket list. And to be honest, my ten-year high school reunion would be here before I knew it and I wanted to impress everyone. For the first time in my entire life, I was in the right place at the right time, and I carpe diem'ed that shit.

"Damn it!" Ian slammed the dry-erase marker on the conference table. "We need a new name for our studio. I don't like 'Seventeen Studios.' It's so . . . pedestrian. Let's start throwing some ideas out there." Ian repeatedly capped and uncapped the whiteboard marker in his hand. *Click. Snap. Click. Snap.*

"I thought this was a product brainstorm, not a studio-naming exercise," said a female voice from the other side of the room. It was Kat Campbell, one of the senior designers at the company. I silently sided with her on this one. The name of the meeting in our calendar was "NEW PRODUCT BRAINSTORM" in shouty all-caps.

Ian said to Kat, "This meeting is whatever I decide it should be. Any other questions?"

Nope, no other questions. This meeting was now a studio-name brainstorm.

And thirty minutes later, all the ideas we had collectively come up with were up on the whiteboard, and they were terrible.

A lanky, freckly guy said, "How about 'Hemlock Studios'? It's funny because of its toxicity."

Ian's head shook with disappointment.

Another freckle-covered bearded dude wearing a tattered

Pokémon shirt asked, "How about 'Catastrophic,' with two Ks instead of Cs?"

Ian made a finger-down-throat vomiting gesture. "How about 'Epicenter Games'?"

As he gushed about how brilliant the name was, I googled it. "Um, it looks like there's a gaming studio in the Bay Area that already has that name," I squeaked.

"Okay, so who cares if that name is taken?" Ian's stare-glare made my arm hairs quiver in fear.

Kat chimed in. "I'm sure their lawyers would. It's probably trademarked."

Ian's icy glare shifted to Kat. "What if we made ours different, instead of 'Epicenter' we called ours 'EpicEnter'? That wordplay takes our company's meaning to a whole other mind-blowing new level." He made a head-exploding gesture with his hands.

Changing the syllable emphasis didn't matter. We would have the same name as another US gaming company, and that violated trademark law.

Ian asked me, "Hey, noob, why are you frowning?"

I stammered, "Th-th-there could be a trademark infringement issue, and—"

He cut me off before I finished talking. "Here's the problem with people like you . . ." he began. Excuse me, *people like you*?

"Looking up legal jurisdiction during a brainstorm is stifling and narrow-minded," he argued. "You're artificially constraining my creativity and vision! We can't elevate this company to a higher level if every genius idea gets shut down. Honestly, I should fire you for this negative attitude of yours, but I can't, because you're one of the few GIRLS here other than HER." He pointed at Kat and then went back to glaring at me.

I assumed my days in the cutthroat advertising industry had prepped me for a male-dominated work environment. This place? It might even be worse.

Ian barked at us, "Does anyone else like the name 'EpicEnter'?"

When no one answered, Ian threw his marker down. "I can't believe this. Never mind! This meeting is adjourned." He flung the door open with such force that the door handle dented the lime-green wall. I had just witnessed my first forty-five-year-old man tantrum.

Ian MacKenzie, our company's visionary, our fearless leader, had just stormed out like a sulky toddler.

Pokémon-shirt guy muttered, "Well, at least it's Booze Day Tuesday. If anyone needs me, I'll be at the beer cart." He slung his computer bag on his shoulder and left the room.

Yes. At least we had that.

Welcome to the gaming industry, Melody Joo.

CHAPTER TWO

The battering rain made crossing the 520 bridge a nearly impossible task. Even on the highest setting, my windshield wipers couldn't seem to keep up with the buckets of water dumped from the sky. I had lived in Seattle for a couple of years, and while the rain and dreary weather got me down at first, I didn't really mind it anymore. I grew up in Nashville, but went to college in the Midwest and stayed there for nearly seven years. My slight Chicago snobbery had worn off (or was washed away) and I loved my life here. With its outdoor beauty, amazing restaurants, and laid-back lifestyle, this city had grown on me.

As I pulled into my gated, rain-free garage, my phone buzzed.

Oh no.

Mom.

Damn. I hadn't called her in two weeks. I braced myself for the imminent onslaught of Korean mom guilt. Bullets of sweat sprouted on my forehead as I tried to cram my Nissan Sentra into the only parking spot available in my apartment building's garage: a compact parking spot between an Escalade and a Honda Odyssey. I pulled in and backed out about fifty times. WHY did these fools park so close to the lines? Well, because they parked their fucking enormous cars in compact spots, that was why. None of my doors could open wide enough for a person to get out, so I had to climb out my passenger-side window.

While I shimmied out and banged my head on the metal window frame, Mom texted, *Melody why you nOT CALL US? YOU WORKING TOO HARD YOU CANNOT FIND TIME FOR US. OR TO FIND HUSBAND.*

For years, my mom and dad had pressed me so hard about getting married. I was only twenty-seven, for god's sake! I had plenty of time to settle into a good career and could still wait on marriage. But to them, twenty-seven was too old to "play around" because I wasn't, in their words, "a springing chicken anymore."

Mom texted again. *Never mind don't boTHER CALL US WE are fINE!!!!!*

My mom was like a really old teakettle on high heat: when in her low-boil stage, I needed to make contact before she became too hot to handle—because then the deafening screeches would annoy the hell out of everyone within earshot.

I unlocked my apartment and unloaded my computer bag and purse next to my shoe rack. As usual, it was dinner-for-one that night. I threw a lasagna brick in the microwave and poured myself a glass of cheap white wine. I liked my quiet nights in with my Lean Cuisines and Bagel Bites. And Chef Boyardee's Beefaroni was so bomb. And cheap!

After I'd eaten a few bites of delicious microwave fare, I called my parents' home phone. Mom picked up after the third ring.

"You calling too late. We are tired," she said.

"Mom, I just got your text about five minutes ago."

"Yes, I text five minute ago but I waiting for you calling many days."

I sighed. "I'm sorry. I had back-to-back meetings today and I haven't had time to do anything except work, eat late dinners, and go to sleep. I was planning to call you this weekend." Okay, so that was a lie. I had no plans to call her. My girlfriends and I were heading to Portland on Friday night for a tax-free shopping jaunt, but maybe my white lie would make her feel better.

"I thought you go to Portland this weekend. You mention it in Instant-gram photo post and I like it with heart picture."

Damn it.

Another lie? "I was going to call you on the drive down there."

A few seconds passed. Would she hang up on me? She'd hung up on me before for calling her to wish her a happy birthday a day too early. It wouldn't surprise me.

Instead, she said, "Your dad is here and want to talk to you."

"Melody? It's Dad." I tried to stifle a laugh. *Thanks for clarifying you were my dad, Dad.*

"You upset Mom. She very worry when you not call."

I sighed again after taking a bite of lasagna. "Yeah, I know, I know. I should have called. Things got superbusy at work. I promise, I'll be better at checking in with you guys more often."

He said, with a hint of disappointment in his voice, "When I was twenty-one, I came to United States with no family or friend. Not much money. And I still have time to write letter and call my home in Korea."

Ouch. They threw down the Korean-Immigrant-American-Dream card. I had no doubt in my mind that they'd had a harder life than I did.

Apology time again. "I'm sorry, Dad. Can you put Mom back on the line?"

"Mom? I thought she go to grocery store. Call us this weekend."

Click.

What had just happened? They had nothing urgent going on in their lives and probably decided to call me out of sheer boredom. Well, at least this time our conversation didn't escalate into yelling, or silent treatments, or hurtful commentary about how I had no future because I wasn't married. You know, our run-of-the-mill Korean parent-daughter exchanges.

My phone buzzed.

Mom: DID DAD HE TELL YOU WE GO TO ITALY? I WENT TO STORE TO BUY hiM CARNATION *instant breakfast for our trip.*

They were going to Italy? What? I had wanted to go to Italy since I was ten years old and found out that Chef Boyardee was Italian. I had never been, but now my parents were traveling there. Without me.

I texted back. When are you going?

Tomorrow. We gone for a month.

Well thanks for inviting me.

No immediate reply. I texted again. Do you want me to do anything for you when you are gone?

She wrote back. *Find boyfriend.*

Did she think her haranguing about dating would help conjure up a guy who'd bend down on one knee and tell me he would love me till death do us part? None of my past boyfriends—okay, there were only three—passed the parent test. Mom and Dad had Mensa and Navy SEAL–level criteria. Gareth Hinman wasn't ambitious enough (back in eighth grade, mind you). Patrick Garcia in high school was too chubby ("that mean he too lazy"). Jimmy Han from college was premed and Korean but turned out to be gay. My parents knew this, yet still asked every once in a while if he was available. Basically, aside from Jimmy, no one would be good enough for my mom and dad.

Mom called me just as I polished off my glass of wine. "You

sure you don't want to meet Philip Kwon? He graduate Yale and is tax lawyer in Seattle."

Her voice sounded distant even though she was shouting.

I asked, "Uh, Mom, am I on speakerphone?"

I heard shuffling, and a bunch of beeping, and then the airy background sound disappeared. My mom continued. "Philip Kwon need a wife. He very nice, serious man. He lost lot of hair on head but he have very nice, expensive house. He is also very quiet, but maybe he like your too-loud voice."

All the Korean guys she picked out for blind dates had excelled academically and reaped financial rewards as a result, but her curated selection of men were usually incompatible with my personality. Every single time I carried the entire conversation and eventually we'd disagree about something major, like he didn't own a TV, or he hated cup-of-noodle ramen. Every. Single. Time. I had a long, heated argument with an accountant about Rolos. I loved them. He couldn't stand soft caramel. WTF.

Financially speaking, I didn't need a rich guy. I had made a decent salary as a copywriter and had nearly finished paying off my student loan debt. I gave myself an A in frugality and budget management, too. If I had listened to my parents and become a miserable corporate tax lawyer, I would have worked eighty-hour weeks and never seen daylight. My vitamin D deficiency would be even worse than it already was.

My mom said, "If you marry Philip Kwon, you have big

house for big family. You can marry and have many boy children."

"You mean sons?"

"Yes. Sons. Something I never have." Here it was. A typical moment when my mom would remind me that she could never bear any more children because of me. When I came into this world, according to my mom's folklore, I pulled her uterus out with me. "A childbirth placenta tear," the doctor told her, but the way she told the story you'd think I had been born with my two little baby fists holding on to the inside of the uterine walls with all my might, clenching tightly, refusing to come out without bringing my placenta and lots of my mom's other innards along with me.

I changed the subject. "So why are you going to Italy? I begged you guys so many times over the last few years to travel to Europe with me and you refused."

"Excuse me! I need chocolate breakfast, not the ba-nilla one."

"What?"

"I talking to grocery man. No chocolate Carnation instant breakfast at this store. Daddy will be upset. He need that in case he can't eat the Italy food. And then he die from starve to death."

"Mom, you shouldn't joke about that. You might jinx him."

"I not joke. He need chocolate instant breakfast. If he upset, the blood pressure go way up and then he shout at everyone. And maybe he die from the too much stress. His poor stressed-ful heart."

I asked again, "So why did you choose Italy?"

"You don't have chocolate kind? Chocolate malted kind be okay. No strawberry. He hate strawberry. It taste like air freshener."

"Mom, it's hard to talk to you because you keep talking to people at the store about breakfast food."

"If you call me back earlier, I not be at the store. I am home with peace and quiet." She grunted. "We go to Italy with church group. They have a mission trip."

She had finally answered my question, just as my thumb hovered over the hang-up button. "I don't understand. Why would you go to Italy on a church mission trip? Aren't there other places in the world that aren't as holy that need help? The pope lives in Italy. He should have that country covered."

She blew a puff of air into the phone and changed the subject abruptly. "I forgot ask. Any Korean guy working at the toy company?"

"You mean the game company?"

"Yes, did you see any Korean boy?"

I snorted. "No Koreans at all." Amazing. I admired her single-mindedness. "Oh wait, there was one Asian guy who might've been Korean who worked in the HR department. A fresh college graduate."

With a few seconds of silence I could tell my mom struggled to do basic math. I helped her out. "That means he's five years younger than me, Mom."

"Waaaaa! Five years? New generation it is okay for woman

to be much older than husband. We see all the time in Korean drama. Men die earlier anyhow."

I scarfed down the last of my dinner, scraping the corners of the black container for every ounce of sodium-filled sustenance. Still hungry, I opened the fridge and stared at the barren waste-land. Old jars of pickles, shriveled apples, and almost-raisin grapes were my tastiest options. Or rather, my only options. I shook my head and shut the door. "I need to go to the grocery store, Mom. I need to restock my fridge. Send me your trip information so I know how to contact you if there is an emergency."

"You never call anyway. So just call in month when we back." *The Korean mom guilt, back in full force.*

"You're really leaving tomorrow? Like, you mean in less than twenty-four hours?"

"YES. I said tomorrow many time."

Damn. They'd be off on a jumbo jet soon, and even though it made zero sense to accompany them to pope-land for a church mission trip, my heart hurt with abandonment.

I sank into my couch and rested my head back. What a long day.

My mom asked, "Melody, can you do Daddy favor? Can you buy chocolate Carnation instant breakfast? There is none here. Name is called 'Carnation breakfast essential, rich milk chocolate.' You can still ship tonight so we get before our trip. FedEx and UPS still open till nine o'clock."

Was this a test of my unwavering devotion to my dad? A

test to prove to my parents that despite me not calling, they were still the highest priority in my life? Okay, maybe I did feel guilty about not knowing their plans to embark on a huge overseas journey, so I grabbed a granola bar for dessert, put on my raincoat and boots, and headed back to my car.

Damn it. I had forgotten all about the nonopening doors situation. The Odyssey and Escalade were still there, blocking my access. As I shimmied into the passenger-side window while pressing onto the side of the Honda to provide balance, the goddamn minivan alarm went off, and the headlight flashes pulsed to a steady beat.

HONK!

HONK!

HONK!

HONK!

The incessant car alarm continued blaring as I contorted my body through my window. While scrambling over the gearshift, my knee banged on the steering wheel. Tears welled in my eyes from the pain as I peeled out of the garage, my shoulders finally relaxing as the minivan honking sounds remained trapped in the confines of the garage echo chamber box. I checked my rearview mirror to see if anyone tailed my car. Would anyone really follow me for allegedly burgling a soccer-mom-mobile? Seriously, who would bother to follow me anywhere?

The Fred Meyer megagrocery store down the street had the best chance of stocking gross, processed chocolate breakfast

CHAPTER THREE

The office manager stopped by to tell me I'd be moving from the cubicle I'd been assigned a month ago to an interior shared office on the other side of the floor, closer to the executive team. They needed my work space for an intern, who also happened to be Ian MacKenzie's nephew. Kicked out of my spot because of good ol'-fashioned nepotism.

After stacking my office belongings into a precarious pile on my laptop, I headed to my new home. I had only been at Seventeen Studios a few weeks, not long enough to accumulate the dozens of bobbleheads, figurines, and other promo merchandise that other game veterans had littering their work spaces. The tchotchkes ranged from cute, marble-eyed animals to red-eyed, flying demon aliens with bloody razor teeth. Some of the QA testers and marketing people had so much crap in their cubicles and offices that it looked like a toy store's unwanted Black Friday inventory had exploded all over their desks and shelves. A few senior people on my team were among the first employees at Seventeen Studios, and on their fifth anniversary, they were gifted real company-issued samurai swords and metal battle shields engraved with their names and their company start dates. These swords and shields were heavy as hell: I tried to lift one of the swords with two hands and nearly threw out my back.

Once I unpacked, the only thing missing was my coffee mug. The one with "$C_8H_{10}N_4O_2$," the atomic structure of caffeine, written on it in big bubble letters. A going-away present from my coworkers at my last job, and the only thing I had brought to work with any sentimental value. Other people had framed photos of dogs and babies. I had my nerdy mug.

I passed by my old work space on the way to the bathroom. A new minifridge, Keurig coffee machine, decorative lamps, and an $800 Aeron desk chair made the transformed space unrecognizable. There was an actual red carpet runner rolled out from the footpath to the cubicle entryway.

On the desk, the intern even had better pens than everyone else. And nonyellow Post-its cut into cool shapes. And a brand-new MacBook Air. My eyes narrowed as I read his name on the frosted cubicle wall.

NOLAN MACKENZIE

I pulled out my phone to find out more about Nolan. Fucking. MacKenzie. There were older pictures of him online shaking hands with famous politicians. Images of his worldly travels to exotic destinations. Recent photos of him with a woman deliberately cropped out. Someone with wavy blond wisps and a very tan left shoulder. I rolled my eyes and tried not to think about how unfair all this was.

One of the finance assistants came up to me. "You got booted from your cube already? Didn't you just get settled in?" He glanced at the nameplate and raised his eyebrows. "Oh. I heard about that guy."

"What'd you hear?" I asked, mirroring his eyebrow action.

"It's Ian's nephew. Some hotshot MBA guy. He's probably just like his dear ol' uncle. Sorry he stole your work space." He walked away shaking his head.

One "silver lining" about my office move, though: the room had skylights and fit two desks plus a preinstalled small sofa. The not-so-good news: I'd share the office with a TBD employee, not of my choosing. But the absolute worst news? Five life-size cutouts of busty anime Japanese women in bikini armor littered the entire space. They were the "Kaizen Five," and each possessed a unique battalion weapon. Yoshi and Toshi, twin warriors, carried identical AK-47s, which seemed physically impossible to strap and shoot over their 36DDD chests.

The scrawled signature across the breasts of these giant cardboard characters read "Created by Ian Mac*Kaizen*." They were promotional relics from one of Ian's blockbuster game launches, so tossing them into a dumpster was not an option. But was my office a storage closet? I refused to stare at these women all day long. They were distracting, not to mention grossly offensive. How was this even here, in the post–#metoo era?

While Ian went out for his typical two-hour lunch, I dragged all five cutouts into his office. They were his, after all. Those ten boobs took up a lot of space, but in Ian's spacious corner office he'd likely not notice the new decor. Plus, what heterosexual man wouldn't want a boob shrine? It wasn't until after I headed back to my desk that it crossed my mind that Ian could fire me for this. If I wanted to stay at this company and launch my game production career, I had to cool down my snarkiness, stat.

When I got back from a postlunch budget meeting, the cardboard cutouts were back in my office and placed in a semicircle around my desk. The attached note read:

FROM THE DESK OF IAN MACKENZIE

Maybe these badass ladies can inspire you to gaming greatness. —Ian

---

I rolled my eyes and let a frustrated sigh out my nose. How'd these five offensively sexy Asian women even get housed here in the first place? Did the office manager think to himself, *Well, here's the designated Asian woman room, let's stick Melody in there?*

Rather than obsess, I made a sign on my door that read

KAIZEN SIX! in slanty letters. Male coworkers passed by and chuckled. A few passersby even gave me two thumbs-up.

I HOLED UP in my office until late into the evening uploading projects and tasks into our studio's workflow tool. Near dinnertime, my stomach growled so loudly that it sounded like a wounded yeti was trapped behind my belly button, yelling in its native language, *Time to go home!* I walked out my office door and smacked into a new life-size cutout: the buxom body of one of the Kaizen girls with my photocopied face on top of it. Okay, it was a little bit funny because the grainy picture came from my name badge photo from our company intranet page, but it was also extremely vulgar and grossly unprofessional.

I dragged my customized Kaizen cutout into my office and decided to let this joke run its course. Complaining to senior management or HR would likely get me labeled as someone with no sense of humor, or worse, someone "anticommunity." Seventeen Studios clearly had blinders on when it came to inappropriate conduct. But I wasn't about to take these hits without fighting back my own way.

With a quick rifling-through of our trade show closet, I found what I needed: a floor display of one of the most-hated characters from our studio's UFC games, Maverick "Chile" Morita, the tattooed, insult-hurling, hypermuscular cage fighter. I dragged it back to my office, printed out a copy of Ian's face, and taped it onto Chile's bulbous head, then faced new-and-improved Ian out toward the hallway for everyone to see. I kept the office light on so he could be easily visible to anyone passing by.

WHEN I GOT into work the next morning, all the cutouts had been removed from my office. No more Kaizen Six. No more UFC cage fighter Ian. The lights were turned off, with no signs of retaliation.

Yeah. That's right.

Good game, bishes.

CHAPTER FOUR

I'm Asher. My bros call me Ash." My new officemate barely looked up from his computer screen when he introduced himself. Apparently, I wasn't worth his wholehearted attention. While I grabbed lunch and ran a quick errand, this guy had moved in and rearranged the entire office, pushing my desk flush against the wall. His toy-covered desk stood in the center of the room, and he still had boxes strewn all over the floor, overflowing with what appeared to be hundreds more tchotchkes. And what did he mean by *My bros call me Ash*? That only friends called him that, or that only GUYS could call him that?

I heaved my desk flush against his so we faced each other. "I'm sorry, who are you again?" Because I couldn't believe this guy was in my work space confines, I hadn't paid attention to his uninspiring introduction.

Asher sighed as he stood up. He easily cleared six feet tall and was a weird mix between nerdy and fratty. He had the sort of body that suggested he used to be athletic, and then he met beer and pot.

"I'm Asher—I'm an assistant producer who worked my way up through QA. Who are you?" He had to be a foot taller than me and definitely used his height to intimidate.

Neither of us feigned any excitement about being office roomies. Within the first few seconds together in the same room, we knew instantly that we despised each other. Insta-hate, for both of us. His massive presence would suck up most of my available oxygen with his 230-pound body. And he'd jack up the office temperature with his substantial amount of body heat. This did not bode well for me.

"I'm Melody. The person who had this office first. The person whose name is on the door. The person whose shit you moved around without permission."

He laughed and held his hands up, like he was simultaneously surrendering and pushing away my crazy. "Look, I don't want to start anything. Ian told me yesterday he'd get me an office, and this morning he sprang the news that I'd be sharing it with some new chick—uhhhh—person, and that I should move my stuff here today. I had high hopes."

Ian didn't say a word about any of this to me, though. Bastard.

Asher asked, "Are you an artist or something?"

Nearly all the women I'd met at my company worked in

marketing, in HR, or in the art department. I couldn't fault him for assuming that.

"No, I'm in production, too. I used to be a copywriter at an ad agency. I managed a creative and production team to develop a few game apps and also did a lot of localization stuff . . . now I'm here."

Asher said flatly, "Huh. I've never heard of someone getting into game production with your background. You've never actually worked in the industry." He pressed his lips together and stared at me.

"Well, it's hard to break into gaming if one of the prerequisites is already having game experience under your belt. How do you get gaming experience if no one will let you get a job in the first place?" Game companies complained all the time about needing more women in the industry, but at the same time, the job requirements precluded women from actually being able to get those positions. At my first company happy hour last week (Booze Day Tuesday!), one of the women in recruiting explained to me that upper management white dudes tended to hire other like-minded white dudes. And since women didn't fit in the white dude demographic, well, they had trouble finding women for key positions here.

Asher shrugged and went back to rapid-fire typing. Maybe, just maybe, Asher wouldn't be so bad after all. He'd been on the testing team and had clearly been at the company a long time given the massive number of Seventeen Studios collectibles he had amassed. Maybe he could help me. Maybe we could help each other.

The clicking of the keyboard stopped. He asked, "Wait, are you that girl who flooded the QA team with fluorescent lights a few weeks ago? All those testers were so fucking pissed."

Oh my god. How'd he know?

"Yeah, I did that," I said coolly.

Asher tossed his head back and belly laughed. "That was pretty fucking embarrassing. Almost as bad as that anonymous idiot who tripped over the power cord in the war room this morning. Did you hear about that?" That idiot he referred to was also me, but I had escaped without anyone seeing my face.

Tripping on the main power supply in our war room where we tracked all online game activity took down our monitoring system. Because of the blackout, our ops guys didn't see there was a problem with our game servers, which pissed off millions of players worldwide when the network went down for a few minutes. I shouldn't have even been there, snooping around in the dark, but the door was propped open with a magazine and curiosity got the best of me.

Neither of us had anything more to say. I went back to reading email, he went back to his machine-gun typing. As minutes ticked by, Asher's office coexistence became suffocating, quite literally. Our office had poor air circulation and the one air vent was on top of him, blowing Asher-diffused, unshowered air into our small room. Looking up from my laptop and seeing his smug face was punishment that was too much for anyone. I needed coffee breaks. Lots of them.

THE LINE FOR coffee in the kitchen was ten people deep.

"You'd think they could spring for at least two coffeemakers, right?" The guy in front of me had these tortoiseshell, bookish glasses that gave me major spec-envy.

I smiled. His curly brown hair, navy-blue-checked button-down, and new tan cords gave him a Corporate America vibe, but his vintage Air Jordans threw me off. Unlike Asher, it looked like he showered recently.

Someone in the front of the line yelled, "New batch brewing! Another two minutes!" Mr. Spectacles turned around again to continue our conversation.

I should have been taken by his lopsided smile and warm brown eyes. But all I could focus on was the $C_8H_{10}N_4O_2$ caffeine mug in his hand.

My mug.

In this random dude's hand.

I'd never shifted to MUST KILL HIM mode so quickly in my life. "That's *my* mug!" I growled. "It's been missing and it was a gift! Where'd you get this?"

His face fell a little. "It was on my desk when I got here. It matches my coffee shirt." He pulled open his shirt to reveal a heather-gray tee with "BUT FIRST, $C_{25}H_{28}N_6O_7$" scrawled on a coffeepot decal.

Then he had the nerve to smirk at me. "I'm the new MBA intern, helping out with inclusivity initiatives."

Inclusivity initiatives? This guy? "But you're not just an intern. You're Ian's nephew, Nolan Fucking MacKenzie." *Oops. Should have censored that.*

His wide-eyed look expressed both horror and humor. "Some people probably call me that. Most people call me just Nolan, though." I grabbed at the $C_8H_{10}N_4O_2$ coffee cup in his hand but he held on to it tight.

He pleaded with his words and his puppy-dog eyes. "If you take this, what am I supposed to use?"

I yanked it toward me. "Why do you even need this coffee? I saw your Keurig."

He pulled it back. "I don't like single-use disposables. Landfills and all that. Also, Keurig pods are expensive."

I tugged again. "Go raid your uncle's office—he's probably got a ton of them sitting in a drawer. I bet your dear uncle would even expense the specialty flavored ones for you."

Sighing, he asked, "It's just a mug. Not worth beefing with me, right? Can I just borrow it today? Please?"

It seemed like a reasonable request. I was a reasonable person. I loosened my grip just as he yanked hard. The mug slipped out of my hands and flew out of his grip from sheer yanking force.

If the concrete floor had been carpeted, the cup might have been saved.

"Oh, shiiiiit," he muttered, grabbing two fistfuls of his hair.

He knelt down to pick up the shards. One of the handle pieces had slid under the counter, completely unreachable by hand.

Too stunned to move, I offered him no assistance. Nolan Fucking MacKenzie had broken the only personal thing at work that actually meant anything to me and "Oh shiiiiit!" wasn't an apology. He could pick everything up himself. Plus, my denim pencil skirt wasn't too forgiving.

"I don't have time for this." Glancing at my watch, I left the kitchen in a hurry. I didn't have to be anywhere, but I could feel hot tears welling, and crying over a coffee cup in front of the CEO's nephew was immature and unprofessional. No way could I let anyone see me like that. Especially not the intern.

With no afternoon caffeine running through my veins, punching through the postlunch slog through minimum awakeness was no easy feat. My insomnia caught up with me and by three P.M., I'd hit a wall. I cleared my calendar and made the decision to sneak out and head home early. Asher came into the office and noticed me fishing around in my purse.

"Hey, are you headed down to the café to get coffee? Could you grab me one, too? I can't believe Ian just sent out a five P.M. meeting invitation. Very uncool. I'm gonna need some caffeine to keep me going, and I hate the new chargrilled fancy coffee they ordered for the kitchen. Thanks, roomie!"

Well, there went my three P.M. departure. The only chance I had to make it through that five o'clock meeting would be to take a quick power nap in my car, but that would happen after I got two drip coffees for Asher and me. A caffeine boost to supplement my power nap would hopefully keep me awake during the meeting. Plus, the kitchen coffee did taste a little more burnt-roasted than usual, and there I ran the risk of running into that intern again. Maybe getting Asher a cup of caffeine could be the first step toward office peace and harmony.

THE CAFÉ WAS crowded, no doubt a direct correlation to the inferior coffee product brewing in only one coffeemaker in our kitchen. Behind me in line, two barely pubescent engineers giggled as they stared at something on an iPhone. I glanced over their shoulders and immediately regretted my snooping.

These two guys were watching porn. One of them said to the other, "We need to adjust our bouncing to make our boobs more realistic. Like this." He pinched the screen and widened for a better view. At least they had the courtesy to have the sound off.

Behind me, a familiar female voice called out, "While you two are diligently researching, can you improve your male jiggle physics, too?"

The one holding the phone cocked his head. "Wh-what?"

Kat appeared by my side. "I'd love to see better male pectoral movement in our games, and of course, improved dick physics."

A snort escaped me as she explained. "We definitely need more realistic and natural movements of male body parts, too. Ignoring our male body parts and only focusing on boobs would be sexist. I can set up a meeting where we brainstorm ways we can maybe even weaponize them, like have a swinging cock of death."

I chimed in. "Helicopter cocks could lift the player to safety."

Kat fought a laugh. "Maybe we can make it large enough so it could be its own character or player. Co-op game play. Player two, penis."

Still stunned into silence, the two engineers' mouths gaped open. One of the engineers said to the other, "Are they serious?"

Kat looked at him square in the eyes. "I'm dead serious."

The line moved up and the two engineers scurried away. And to think my mom thought my future husband could be somewhere among my work peers.

What a joke.

A wide grin spread across Kat's face. "Oh my god, did you see their faces? I'm Kat, by the way. Your drink's on me." She held out her hand.

"I know who you are. I'm Melody, and I'm thrilled to finally meet you," I said, enthusiastically pumping her hand. "Don't worry about it, I need to buy a coffee for my officemate, too."

While we waited for our orders, I examined her physical features and admired her go-against-the-grain beauty as she made a quick call. She had brown, short mousy hair, cut asymmetrically, and she had so many ear piercings that it made me think her lobes had more holes than skin. She was also rail thin—an aspiration of mine, but not feasible given my atypical Asian bone structure. I maintained average weight (by American women standards), but elder Korean friends and family insisted my beauty lay hidden underneath all my fat. I was comfortable keeping my beauty nestled and protected.

Kat put her phone in her back pocket. "Everyone here actually thinks they're doing women a favor by making games with sexified female heroines. Like Ian's *Kaizen Five*. Such a noble act of feminism, don't you think?"

I laughed as my order appeared on the counter. "I just thought of a funny idea for a shooter game that women like us would love." I took a sip of my coffee before continuing. "As you know, there's a huuuuuge growing female gamer population continuing for the next decade." I gave a sweeping gesture with my right hand, pointing upward. "Now picture a satirical game targeting the growing female demographic: a group of male strippers find themselves in the apocalypse, facing every world-ending nemesis you can think of: zombies, vampires, aliens, and evil robots. The ultimate apocalypse. These stripper dudes basically run around topless with giant guns, both the arm-flexing kind and the weapon kind, fighting and shooting up and stabbing all kinds of shit to survive. Women warriors would exist, too, but they're not 'damsels in distress' types. They save those strippers' asses time and time again. This game has dollar signs written all over it! Sexiness sells, right?"

A smile spread across Kat's face. "And what if you get accused of sexism the other way around, where you are dehumanizing and debasing the male body by having the guys be, you know, strippers?"

What a good question. But I had a rebuttal. "I have a scientific reason why these guys need to be topless."

Kat raised her eyebrows. "Go on."

"The virus that causes the zombification of the world also alters human DNA, and the virus needs to find hosts who have a vitamin D deficiency. And the main source of vitamin D is the sun. So the more surface area exposed to sunlight for our protagonists, the better."

Kat shook her head. "Melody, that is so absurd."

"Look, I didn't set the precedent on this stupid shit. You know that game *Metal Gear Solid V*? Kojima, the creator said his female assassin runs around in a chain mail bikini because she breathes through her skin through photosynthesis! At least my case for seminudity sounds a teeny bit more scientifically plausible. We can even have characters hunt for vitamin D supplements in the game. Or power up by purchasing vitamin packs."

Kat burst out into a fit of giggles. "That's some crazy-ass shit you made up. You're not even drunk or high or anything. I love it."

"Ladies, mind if I scooch around you to get some sugar?" Ian stood just a few inches behind us with a smirk on his pompous face. How long had he been there?

Kat sighed. "Good talking with you, Melody. Swing by my office sometime. I have a stack of game production books I can loan you. Too bad our conversation got cut short." The

look she threw Ian was a cross between disappointment and
revulsion.

Ian cocked his head coyly. "Hey! Don't mind me, I just wanted
a quick cup of coffee. You ladies can continue talking about your
game ideas." He grabbed a sugar packet and tore the corner.

Kat looked at the wall clock. "Time for me to get back and
work on some character designs. Bye, all!" I said goodbye, too,
and marched a few feet behind her with my drinks, leaving Ian
standing near the coffee accoutrements all by himself. Most people would jump at the opportunity to chat with the company's
CEO one-on-one, but not me. I couldn't wait to get out of there.

As the café door closed, Ian bellowed, "Keep those ideas
flowing, ladies!"

I CLEARED A spot on Asher's desk for his coffee next to his cy-
clops alien miniatures and headed to the parking garage. Even
though the coffee helped, I still needed that nap.

No one else was there. My car was near the main entrance
in between a Subaru wagon and one of Ian's many luxury
cars, a bright red Porsche Classic, which had the vanity plate
"KAIZEN5."

I slipped into my car without being seen. I reclined my seat
to a horizontal position and let out a yawn so wide that my
watery eyes spilled tears that leaked into both ear cavities.

So. Tired.

Wet ear canals.

And . . . finally . . . sleep . . .

"Hello?! Are you still there?! I can talk now! I canceled the five o'clock meeting so we can discuss everything." Ian's booming voice from next to the Porsche shook me awake. "I'm in the garage because my office walls are so goddamned thin. No one is here, though." I couldn't see his exact position, but judging by the sound of his megaphone-like voice projection he was standing only a few feet away, very close to my 180 degree–angled body.

Ian again?

Shit. Shit. Shit.

Please don't see me. Please don't see me.

Drawing in slow and deep breaths, I tried to imagine playing a corpse on television. My heart thumped so loudly I bet Ian could hear it, like Edgar Allan Poe's telltale heart, but much worse because there was no mystery or intrigue surrounding my situation. I was simply a fucking idiot taking a nap in a car when I should have been upstairs, working.

Ian had paused to let the person on the phone talk, but it was now his turn. "We have some amazing game concepts that are in various stages of ideation and development." As I lay there barely consuming oxygen, it became clear that I had to pee. But moving wasn't an option.

Ian sighed. "You want that info now? Uh, we wanted to present these ideas to you and the rest of the board sometime next month. I'm not really prepared right now to pitch but there are a few games I know you'll love."

More muffled yelling passed through the phone. "I see. No, we're not hiding anything from you, Doug. Okay, so you already know we have more of those zoo games in the pipeline, and that franchise is our studio's biggest cash cow because of all the merchandising." I heard a tinge of defeat in Ian's voice. He had admitted he needed these games Kat had designed for the business to stay afloat. I almost felt a little bad for him, but then I remembered he was a sexist asshole, and that empathy went away quickly.

More barking through the phone. Ian sighed again. "What women gamer group protests?" More muffled man yelling. "Well, we actually do have a pro-woman game that is being led by a girl . . . I mean female employee. Its working title is, uh, *Ultimate Apocalypse.*"

Oh. My. God. He was pitching my game idea!

My satire/joke/parody game idea. I almost popped up from my seat to yell at him, NOOOOOOOOOOOO! but my circumstances were precarious at that moment. What good reason did I have for why I'd been in my car with the seat fully reclined during work hours?

"I loved the idea when it was pitched to me!" Ian exclaimed. "It's a shooter game, but it's an all-male team of, um, strippers, fighting off zombies, vampires, aliens, and guys like Kim Jong-un. We want to get more women playing shooter games, and we think sex appeal is the way to do it. We may make it a mobile game instead of a console game, to help us diversify."

The yelling subsided and the man on the phone talked for

a while. What was he saying? Hopefully he was giving Ian a *sorry, it is with mixed emotions that we need to fire your ass* speech. Pitching the world's most absurd game idea to a key member of the board out of sheer desperation could be grounds for termination, right?

"You think the other board members will go for this strategy, too? We want to diversify, for sure, especially if it draws in a bigger female audience. I'll make sure we have our female producers lead this effort and get some good PR out of it. Thank you so much for calling. We can't wait to get started! Goodbye!"

After a few seconds of silence, Ian screamed, "Shit! Fuck me! Fuck-fuck-fuck!," which echoed throughout the garage. He paced around his car a few seconds and cussed all the way to the elevator. It dinged open, and Ian's grating voice finally faded away.

Well, fuck me, too.

The only good thing to come of this was that I wasn't tired anymore.

THE FIERCE, HAIR-TANGLING wind nearly pushed me into the Belle Towne Tavern. For once, I had arrived early enough to be the one to negotiate our trio's seating situation. Belle Towne had become our regular stomping ground because it had everything we wanted: Candace had her complimentary serving of truffle-salt popcorn, Jane got a wide selection of top-shelf imported vodka for her martinis, and I got what I wanted most out of a bar experience: half-price happy hour till nine P.M. And bonus, they had five stalls in the women's restroom. For me, just this warranted an automatic five-star Yelp review.

The hostess seated me near the front window at a small circular table with barely enough room to hold a tealight candle.

"This table looks a little small for three people. Any chance we could get seated over there?" I asked, nodding my head toward the side of the room with several empty booths.

She glanced in that direction and then looked back at me. "There's less ambiance there. And it's dark."

I didn't think I looked like an ambiance kinda girl. I grabbed the tiny tealight. "This'll help. I can bring it over."

She shrugged. "Suit yourself. You'll get less action in a booth. But the seats are more comfy."

Before I could ask her why she thought I needed some "action," Candace breezed through the door and chirped, "Oooh, good job on the booth!" while Jane slid in across from me.

Candace and I had gone to college together and were best friends then, and had been since. Jane was Candace's childhood friend and former postgraduation roommate, which was how I had come to know her over the years. Jane was like the Anti-Candace, an ice-queen-triathlon-foodie-juice-cleanse type who worked at an investment bank. Candace, whose cheery demeanor and warmness made you feel good as soon as you saw her, took Jane under her wing and over the years had managed to soften her to the point of tolerability. We were all three just so different. We probably looked like a band of misfit superheroes whenever we walked into any downtown bar.

We peeled off our wet coats and the hostess handed us dinner menus. "Could we have the happy hour ones?" I asked.

She shrugged apologetically. "New owners, new hours. Happy hour ended at seven."

I looked at my watch. It was 7:01.

Before I could protest, Jane said, "We've been coming here for, what do you think, two years now?" She glanced at Candace, then me, then at her Cartier watch. "I'd love to continue our frequent girls nights out here. Could you please ask the new owners if they could stop by our table so we could introduce ourselves?" She pulled out her Gucci wallet, leafed through a few hundred-dollar bills, and pulled out her business card from one of the slots next to her visible AmEx Centurion card.

Jane was one of those friends I hated at first and thought I'd never like. She exuded beauty, success, and good fortune. She had a world-renowned doctor boyfriend. Her job paid more than double my salary. But over the last few years, she'd proven to be a reliable friend, even though my pendulum of feelings toward Jane usually swung between modest like and extreme dislike. I hadn't seen her in a while despite the fact that she had moved into my apartment building last year, so my current like-to-hate ratio for her was about 80:20, which was an all-time high.

The hostess swept her hand toward us. "Oh, you know, that

won't be necessary. I'm sure we can squeeze in your happy hour drink order. I'll send over your server and let the owners know you stopped by this evening." After she took off, I realized that she never even got our names.

A new-on-the-job waitstaff took our happy hour orders: Candace had a Moscow mule, I asked for a half carafe of red house wine (an indeterminate pinot-merlot-cabernet-zin blend). Jane requested a hibiscus dry martini.

When the drinks came, we toasted and took our inaugural sips.

Actually, Candace and Jane sipped. I glugged.

Jane eyed Candace's copper mug. "You've been drinking Moscow mules since I've known you," Jane scoffed. "Do you drink that with your PR clients, too?"

Candace smiled into her brass mug. "I like my mules. Not all of us want to drink overpriced thrice-distilled paint thinner." She took a sip. "Although this tastes bitter and too sweet. Ew."

"You want some of this?" I lifted my small carafe and tilted the rim toward her.

"Nah, it's okay, I'll tough it out. So how's the new job?"

Ugh. Job.

I shrugged. "Eh. It's worse than the last one. But the pay is better, though I work longer hours so maybe it's a wash."

"If you hate the job, why don't you just quit?" Jane asked, pulling out the hibiscus flower from her drink and placing it on her cocktail napkin.

Candace nodded. "I'm with Jane on this one. You shouldn't

stay there if you hate it so much. And you're probably doing what you always do . . . you take on everything by yourself, keep piling on responsibilities, and then burn out in the process."

Jane took a slow sip. "You could use some beauty sleep, too."

Thanks, Jane.

I sighed out of my nose. "Look, I have to do a lot of things myself, or it won't get done. I'm in a new industry now and want people at work to respect me. The only way that'll happen is if I don't look weak." It did beg the question, though, why I gravitated toward careers where I was always sprinting against an escalator always set on "down."

Just as I thought this *let's grill Melody* conversation couldn't get any worse, Jane asked, "So are you actually dating anyone?"

Midswig, I coughed, and red wine burned the inside of my nose. "Nope."

Not reading into my one-word, curt reply, she continued with her line of questioning. "No one? Isn't there that cute guy on the first floor who just moved into our building? Or maybe someone your mom can set you up with? Or anyone at work maybe?"

I shook my head. First-floor guy was gay. Mom's blind date setups—ugh. And the guys at work? Big nope. Asher was flat-out gross, and Mr. Nepotism Nolan—oh hell no. No elitist jerks. I'd only run into him that one time in the kitchen, and trust me, that encounter was plenty. "My parents are still traveling, probably scouring the planet for a suitable husband for me. And definitely no one at Seventeen Studios fits the bill."

Jane and Candace exchanged glances.

"Well, maybe before you get too overcommitted at work, you should find time to, uh, get out there more," Candace said in a concerned tone.

"And not be so picky," Jane added, her judgy eyebrows peeking over the rim of her wide-rimmed martini glass.

"Hey, I'm *not* picky!" I practically yelled. "First of all, guys never ask me out. Ever. Never happens at the gym. Or at a bookstore. Or at parties"—I counted to three on my fingers. "So it's not me being picky when no one's interested. And before you ask about online dating, that's not gonna happen. I don't like the idea of my photos or personal info floating around on the internet."

I drank the last of my wine directly from the glass carafe. "And I'm always working because if I wasn't, I'd be at home all alone, drinking cheap rosé, watching Shark Week reruns in my pajamas."

Candace giggled. "That sounds pretty amazing actually."

This torture needed to end. "Look, if a suitor comes around and he's halfway normal, I promise I won't say no to a date. And maybe I'll even ask him out instead of waiting for him to do it. I'll be more open to opportunities. I swear."

They exchanged looks again and nodded in approval.

The server came over with a small platter of appetizers. The smell of Belgian fries made my mouth water. "I call dibs," I said, rotating the plate so the potatoes were in front of me.

Candace wrinkled her brow and looked around for our wait-staff. "We didn't order this. Let's send it back."

I'd already eaten two fries before she finished talking. I chewed and gulped. "Sorry. I'm starving."

The hostess stopped by our table and said, "Well, looks like you're truly VIPs here. The chef sent this over, free of charge."

Jane and Candace dug into the hummus and pita while I shoveled more fries into my mouth. When the server came back, she said, "How's everything tasting?"

I nodded enthusiastically while the other two said in unison, "It's great!"

Jane said, "We'll take another round of drinks." After glancing my way, she added, "And one more order of fries, please, so Candace and I can have some."

Candace said, "Actually, no drink for me. I still haven't finished mine."

When the new drinks came, we clinked glasses again. "To new jobs and new beginnings," Candace said. Translation: *Let's toast to Melody's new gaming job and us convincing her to keep her dating options open.*

Cheers, ladies. Too bad I had no options.

CHAPTER FIVE

That night I slept a full nine hours and still woke up early enough to make breakfast and an iced coffee. The three-or-more-cups-a-day java habit that had befallen me the very day I moved to Seattle cost me hundreds of dollars a year. Money that could be going toward saving for a house, or toward a fancy-schmancy coffeemaker. With my home brew in hand I took the elevator down to my apartment parking garage and turned the key in the ignition.

And . . . nothing.

I tried the key again.

More nothing.

Damn it. No more Starbucks for me, I needed a new car, stat. And I didn't even have time or money to shop for one. Getting to work early was a top priority in case Ian had more news about the *Ultimate Apocalypse* game launch during our nine A.M. all-hands meeting. Walking to work in the torrential rain wasn't my favorite option, though, so I opted to use

Liftr instead, a ride-share service that specialized in short urban distances and flat fees by zone numbers. I ordered my car and waited near the garage entrance for "Paul, 4.7 rating" to show up.

Within thirty seconds a tricked-out Honda Element with a Liftr sticker on the passenger-side window pulled up next to me. I never understood how any Honda executive ever approved the design of those ugly-ass, Kleenex box–shaped cars in the first place.

I entered the back seat and said a quick hello. Paul, dressed in a trucker cap and '70s-style wire glasses, turned around and held his stare a little bit too long. He looked more predator-like than hipsterish. *Could he be deciding if I'd be today's murder victim?*

"Melody Joo," he said quietly and turned back to face forward. OMG, I was totally going to die. He knew my name, address, and possibly my credit card information. Ohhhh fucking shit. And I was going to die in a fucking Honda Element.

He put his car into gear and drove me down the hill toward Elliott Bay, thank god, in the direction of work. He was transporting me, and not murdering me.

"Sorry if I spooked you. I wanted to figure out why you had such a low passenger grade."

A . . . what? "Sorry, I'm still half asleep this morning. What's a passenger grade?"

"You know how you rate the driver when you end your ride? Well, drivers rate passengers, too." He glanced at me in the rearview mirror. "I'd normally not pick up someone with a really low score, but right now there isn't a lot of demand for rides for some reason, even with the downpour."

"Uhhhh, how bad *is* my score?" He glanced at me again in the mirror, this time with a look of worry. Maybe he feared I was going to murder HIM.

"Do you ride a lot?" He adjusted the news radio station down a few notches.

"Like once or twice a month," I muttered while swiping through my previous passenger history on the Liftr app.

He whistled in a way that sounded like an atomic bomb dropping. "Well, given your score, more than one driver gave you bad ratings."

"How bad is it?" I asked with a tinge of unhinge in my voice. Even I could hear it.

He pulled up to my office building and said, "Well, the worst score I've ever seen was for a guy who begged me to drive him to Mars. Your score was a little higher than that guy's. Come to think of it, your score may be the same, actually. Looks like we're here. I hope you enjoyed your ride! Have a great day!"

Hard rain pelted from all directions and I sprinted to my building's main entrance. I arrived just in time for the morning meeting and sat down in the back row, next to Kat. She leaned over. "You look a lot better today."

"Thanks, I finally got some sleep," I said, peeling off my raincoat and hanging it on the back of my chair. "But apparently I might need a new car." I jotted "fix/buy car" on the gajillion-item to-do list in my notebook. It was something I needed to solve quickly before I got kicked off Liftr.

Ian strode to the front of the room and looked right at me as he made his big game announcement. "Everyone, I have big news! *Ultimate Apocalypse* is a new feminist game concept recently approved by the executive team and the board." As the crowd chatter faded to silence, he explained that I would be taking on a big role by assisting Maggie (the only female senior producer at this company) on this "brilliant female-friendly game that is destined for greatness." He also named Kat as a core member of the team. I tried to feign surprise as he disclosed the news to the entire company that we'd be developing a game featuring shirtless male strippers while every other person genuinely looked shell-shocked. Those whose mouths were not hanging open in incredulity murmured in hushed tones to one another about how this game would no doubt be an epic failure.

The dude sitting to my right whispered to his neighbor, "She's gotta be sleeping her way to the top."

First of all, gross. Ian and me?

Second, how sexist! I shot my neighbor a look so deadly it could castrate him. He held my stare a couple of seconds but then looked away. How was this my fault that the board wanted female leadership and I was one of the only two females on the production team at the company?

Ian fiddled with the button on his shirtsleeve, answering questions as if this new project had been in the works for a while, and was not, say, an absurd joke mentioned in passing on a coffee break by two women making fun of sexism in gaming. Plenty of naysayers sat in this meeting, but no one dared to openly speak out in dissent. But at the same time, people weren't nodding along as usual, like Ian had spoken the word of God himself. Ian had instantly lost credibility with this male-dominated crowd, and it would be hard to gain it back.

Ian fixed his stare on me. "Melody."

I gulped. What else could he spring on me?

"The quarterly board meeting is coming up. I'll need budget projections and preliminary revenue forecasts of *Ultimate Apocalypse* from you as soon as possible. Consider this your number one priority."

I shook my head. "I'm in production, budget projections and revenue numbers belong to those guys." I pointed to Jagger the clueless product manager and John the schmoozy brand marketing lead. Two guys that talked a good game but did absolutely zero when it came to work. Ian loved them, of course.

Ian's eyes narrowed. "But I'm assigning this to you."

"It's not part of my job responsibilities," I replied.

Crossing his arms, Ian growled, "Your *job* is to be a team player, Melody."

I cocked my head. "So you're telling me to make the revenue and finance projects my number one priority, and to also get this game launched on time as my number one priority. Which is it then? I'm perfectly capable of doing all these projects, but that won't get *UA* released on time if I'm busy with forecast and budget assignments."

Match point. Melody.

He balled his fists and his lips pursed to a thin line.

No one in the room dared to move. It was like everyone collectively held their breath to see what Ian was going to say next.

He panned the room to look at everyone's faces. Jagger and John looked down at their notebooks, feigning an attempt to look busy. Avoiding eye contact so they wouldn't get called on to actually do any work.

Ian inhaled a long, deep breath. "Nolan," he said on the exhale.

His nephew straightened his posture. He had on a red-checkered shirt today, making him look like a picnic basket. "Yes?" he gulped.

"You're good with numbers. You'll work on this and Melody will supervise."

Nolan's laser beam glare shot right at me, which I returned at double intensity. *Hey, I wasn't happy about this either, Mister Intern.*

Ian moved on to other lengthy and boring announcements before I could ask any questions. As soon as the meeting ended, Ian sped away to his next appointment.

The room vacated instantly, and Nolan shot me one more glare of death as he stormed out. Kat walked over to me. "Congratulations, I think?"

"Thanks, I think?" I shrugged. Being on the production

team on a game originally conceived as a joke wasn't exactly something I envisioned in my five-year plan.

People who were there for the next meeting streamed in and one of them handed Kat a notebook. She flipped through it and tucked it under my arm. "It's yours, it's got a bunch of budget and monetization notes in it for the new game."

Opening the notebook, I pored over the detailed notes on budget and forecast assumptions and ideas for how to present the information. Small and neat penmanship, a few hand-drawn doodles and quick calculations in the margins. This notebook belonged to a quant whiz. Someone smart, confident, and fun. Was it weird I found this sexy?

"Hey! That's mine!" A large hand snatched the book from my hands. Glancing up, my terrified eyes met Nolan's narrowing ones.

As he held his notebook tight against his chest, heat flushed to my face.

While I struggled for words, he continued. "You know, this is actually worse than the alleged mug theft. This is intellectual property you stole."

I placed my hands on my hips. "Hey, at least it's still intact, you BROKE my mug, remember?" This intern really knew how to get under my skin. "Someone found your notebook and thought it was mine, so don't flatter yourself and go blaming me for stealing *your* stuff. Stop kicking a dead horse while it's down."

He burst into laughter. "I don't think that's how that saying goes." Amusement flickered in his warm brown eyes, momentarily distracting me from annoyance.

Deep breath, Melody. "Okay, whatever. I'm sorry for reading it. You can flip through my notebook if you want, but there's no valuable IP there. It's got some messy meeting notes and a to-do list the length of a football field."

He raised an eyebrow and held his hand out. I handed over my spiral and crossed my arms.

"Wellll—" He pulled out his glasses from his shirt pocket and adjusted them so he could peer down like a distinguished librarian. "It looks like you desperately need a new car. Your 401(k) forms should have been turned in a month ago. And you really shouldn't put your computer and network passwords on a Post-it note in here. Shady people at this company steal notebooks." He smirked as he handed my spiral back to me. "I'll send you a meeting request to go over the budget. Yet another thing to add to your to-do list."

Nolan's phone buzzed. "Crap. It's Ian." He texted while speed-walking out the door, cutting our conversation short.

Rude.

Just when I thought he wasn't so bad, his climbing approval rating took a nosedive.

Waiting outside the conference room were a few midlevel guys I remembered from the meeting. They formed a circle around me, in a nonthreatening way. Some were even smiling.

One of them took a step forward. "Those things you said in there, when you called out John and Jagger . . . those two loser guys always steal people's work and get credit for it. On behalf of all of us, thank you." He fiddled with his hoodie zipper as he stepped back in the circle with the others.

The entire group murmured and nodded. I could hear phrases like "dead weight," "CEO's pet," and "lazy mother-fuckers" emerge from the chatter. And I agreed with all of it.

"If you need our help, let us know," another guy said to me. "But maybe you'll have enough help from Ian's pet intern." The crowd dispersed quickly, like an anti–flash mob.

A slow smile spread across my face with the realization that I'd just won support from a few important players in the office. A huge win in my book.

CHAPTER SIX

I had just put on my flannel pajamas and poured myself a glass of white wine when Jane unlocked my apartment door and walked in, as if she lived there.

My jaw tightened. "Hey! I gave you those keys for emergencies only. You're not supposed to come in here anytime you want. I don't waltz into your place with your keys."

Jane paused at the door, and for a second she made me think she cared about what I said.

"I forgot to bring my new set of keys for you. I changed my locks a few months ago." My keys to her apartment wouldn't have worked anyway.

She plopped down on the sofa next to me and examined the half-empty bottle of wine on the coffee table. Lifting the wineglass out of my hand, she sniffed its contents and took a gulp.

Her current like-to-hate ratio was about 65:35 and getting lower by the second.

"Wellll, did you notice anything?" She held out her left hand without giving me a chance to actually guess. *Holy fucking shit, she had on an engagement ring that looked like a very luxurious Ring Pop.*

"Oh wow! You're engaged! And the ring is so . . ." I couldn't think of the right adjective to describe that honking diamond ring without sounding like an asshole. Once you hit a certain size of diamond it went from pretty to gaudy superfast. I needed to say something.

Your diamond would make a beautiful paperweight.

You could cut a lot of glass with that sucker.

It could set forest fires with the right sun angles. Be careful.

"Your ring is so . . . perfect for you!" *Bam. Best words ever.*

She beamed at me. "Thank you, Mel! That's so sweet." She'd never done that before, made a comment so outwardly kind. My stomach tightened, knowing something unsettling was about to happen.

"I was wondering, Mel, since you've been such a wonderful friend the last few years . . ."

Oh no. Jane's asking me a favor. Oh no.

". . . I would love it if you'd be my maid of honor."

Her maid of honor? But . . . we'd hated each other for more than 50 percent of the duration of our acquaintance. I couldn't handle a prima donna like Jane. Being her maid of honor would be a nightmare. How could I get out of this? In general, I hated weddings (except for the cake). I'd never been in a wedding party before.

"Oh, that's so sweet that you thought of me. Wow. What about Candace, though?"

"I already asked her. She declined because she committed to being maid of honor for her cousin and for her best friend from high school. She said she wouldn't be able to give me the attention I deserved."

Well, hell. I wasn't even first pick. I tried to think of something to free me from this obligation. I couldn't think of anything. Not a single thing! My mind drew a complete blank. *Damn you, stupid blank mind!*

She looked at me with earnest eyes, like a puppy at the animal shelter needing a home. Other than the fact that she would drive me absolutely crazy and we might end up not on speaking terms after her wedding, I had no genuine reason for declining her request.

"I have some ground rules before I accept. And some boundaries. But . . . maybe?"

Her eyes widened. "Oh? You do? Like what?"

I tried to think of things that didn't make ME sound like the lunatic in this arrangement. "Like, maybe, if we go over a certain budget for the bachelorette party, or for buying bridesmaid dresses and stuff like that, you could help chip in?" Jane had a taste for opulence. No way was I going to spend thousands of dollars for a wedding that wasn't even mine.

She nodded. "Deal." She cocked her head a little. "Anything else?"

"Uh, well, money was the biggest thing. Um, and dress

shopping . . . I'll go with you and stuff, but my taste is different from yours so don't expect me to know what you'd like."

She nodded again. "That's true. I'm more Valentino and you're like . . ." I could see her searching hard for the next adjective. "Like, not Valentino."

Well, that was better than her insulting me. "Okay, one last question, how many bridesmaids are we dealing with?" I pictured myself in Vegas herding a group of drunk, stiletto-wearing Jane clones.

"Well, it's just you, and Candace said she'd be in the bridal party." She went from engagement giddiness to instant sadness. "You two are my only real friends." Her lip trembled as she took a sip of wine.

Oh wow, she just tore out my heart and handed it back to me. I had to say yes. I was no monster.

"It would be my pleasure to be your maid of honor!" I hoped my sudden perkiness made up for my previous jerkiness.

"You'll do it?! Thank you!" She hugged me and walked to the door. "I'll call Sean, *my fiancé*, oh my god . . . I have a fiancé! He wants to get married sooner rather than later, but it all depends on what places are available, but you'll be the first to know the date. Sean and I are going to have a bridesmaid and groomsman get-to-know-you dinner in a couple of weeks, so you can all meet each other."

She paused as she turned the knob. "Oh, a quick warning. The best man was Sean's fraternity brother and is kind of a dick. But you'll only have to deal with his shit on the day of the wedding. Sean's doctor friend is the other groomsman. He's married." She crinkled her nose and shrugged. "But you're not really his type anyway."

And there was the tactless Jane I hated.

"So what's my first duty as maid of honor, Your Royal Highness?" I debated whether to confiscate her keys or not.

"First we'll go look at wedding dresses together. Then shoes. Then bridesmaid dresses." She looked me up and down. "I might choose a halter in a beigey-champagne color, but that will definitely wash you out even more. If we do a summer wedding, do you think you could get a tan?"

I nudged her out the door. "Sure, maybe I'll get Botox, too, while I'm at it."

She squealed, "Oh, maybe for your crow's-feet on your left eye!" I mumbled a quick "Bye!" while grabbing my apartment keys from her hand. I locked the door behind her and scurried over to the bathroom to stare at my face in the mirror. Ugh. In plain sight, small wrinkles on the outside of my left eye, but not my right.

Signs of aging. Or stress. Or both.

Damn it.

Jane texted me as I went back to the kitchen for more wine. *I'm definitely doing halter dresses. I have some arm weights you should borrow.*

Did she mean to type "*could* borrow?"

No. No she didn't.

Then it sank in. How did I end up Jane's maid of honor?

CHAPTER SEVEN

Asher already had his EDM music blaring on his shitty, tinny computer speakers early the next morning. It didn't matter when I arrived at the office, Asher always made it there first. With his goddamned Starbucks.

I cleared my throat and angrily tapped my laptop keys. "Hey, uh, the music? Do you mind? We're at work, not a five A.M. spin class."

I expected him to comment on that. Instead, he asked, "So what do you have on Ian?"

"What do you mean?"

"Look, it's pretty obvious that you are grossly unqualified to produce video games. So that means you have something on Ian. Or maybe you two . . . you know." He raised his eyebrows up and down.

I glared. "I know what you're insinuating, and Ian and I do not have some kind of arrangement. I pitched a game to him and he liked it. It's that simple."

Ash-hole shot me a look of contempt. "I need some air. Your presence is suffocating." He rushed out of the room, leaving a trail of his Asher dude smell in his wake.

A loud knock on the door made me jolt upright.

"Is this a bad time?" Nolan MacKenzie stepped into the room carrying a brown paper grocery bag with handles.

Pinching my brow, I asked, "Whyyyy are you here?" A deep, impatient sigh escaped me. Mr. Intern needed to leave ASAP because I had fifty unread emails labeled "urgent" and Asher would think Ian was playing favorites because I knew Nolan. "Don't you have intern things to do?"

He said flatly, "I'm here to go over the finance and revenue assignments." He plunked the bag on my desk. "I brought you something. A peace offering, since we have to work together." He reached in and pulled out my mug. Specifically, my broken caffeine mug, with riverlike cracks running down and across it, held together by poor Krazy Glue craftsmanship. "I found all the pieces and tried to fix it, but as you can see, it's not the same."

Nope. Not the same.

He cleared his throat. "I got you another mug from the pharmacy downstairs. It's temporary until I get you a real replacement. I haven't had much luck finding the same one online, but don't worry, I'll find it."

Out of the bag came mug number two. "World's Best Grandma." I broke my stoic demeanor and snort-laughed.

He smiled in return. "Okay, good. At least you're not glaring at me anymore." Our eyes met as he handed the grandma mug to me, along with the "repaired" one. "On my honor, I will get you a replacement mug. And trust me, no interns would dare steal either of these, so you're safe."

This was a cease-fire gesture, I got that, but I just wasn't in the mood. And I didn't want him still here when Asher got back, last thing I needed was incessant chiding about Nolan. "I really need to get back to work."

He frowned. "You won't accept any of my meeting requests and we need to get our assignments done before the deadline. I looked on your shared calendar, it's not blocked out right now."

Jumping to my feet, I nodded my head toward the door. "Sorry, but you saw my to-do list with your own eyes. I'll find some time later this week. Now go."

He wouldn't budge. "We can't do later this week. Ian stopped by my desk and said, quote, 'Goddamnit, Nolan, this was due yesterday!' End quote."

Asher's laugh echoed nearby. I needed Nolan out of here.

Without thinking, I nudged him toward the doorway by pushing his back. Nolan scoot-stepped along a bit, but then dug in his heels at the exit. His trim, strapping body gave a ton of resistance.

"Thanks for stopping by." With a light shove, I pushed him into the hallway, straight into Asher.

Nolan, being the smaller of the two, ricocheted off Asher's chest and right arm and bounced back to me. He opened his mouth to say something, but I cut in.

"Nolan was just leaving," I said, shooting him a stern look. "Thanks for the reminder about our meeting."

Nolan pursed his lips and scooted past Asher.

Asher smirked as he took his seat. "In-ter-es-ting. Did I interrupt a spat? A lovers' spat perhaps?"

God-fucking-damnit. It didn't help that my face burned hot from embarrassment. Or maybe exertion—pushing Nolan out the door was harder than it looked. That guy had serious muscles packed under that checkered shirt.

Asher opened his desk drawer slowly and rustled some papers. "Ah, here it is. The employee code of conduct." Clearing his throat, he read, "'Employees are strictly prohibited from engaging in any physical contact that would in any way harm another employee.'"

I glowered at him as he rubbed his upper arm. "Your intern really did a number on me. I hope this doesn't bruise."

Staring hard at my laptop screen, I tried to ignore his distractions, but he was getting to me.

"Oh, here's an interesting HR tidbit. 'Personal relationships, including romantic and-or sexual, between individuals in inherently unequal positions, where one party has real or perceived authority over the other in their professional roles, may be inappropriate in the workplace and are strongly discouraged.'" He tut-tutted and continued. "'If such a relationship exists or develops, it must be disclosed immediately.'"

He shoved the pages back into the drawer and closed it. "Just let me know when you're ready to tell me, office roomie. It's cute that your boyfriend brought you gifts. But not gonna lie, they're pretty lame. Maybe it's a MacKenzie family inside joke."

As if I'd paged him, Ian waltzed into our office with Kat trailing a few steps behind him. Kat shot me a look that I couldn't decipher. It looked like . . . pain? Pity? Appendicitis?

Ian sat on my desk and smiled at me. I didn't like that.

He announced, "I wanted to get the dream team together here for a quick morning stand-up. Melody, there's been a small change. Maggie, the senior producer who just came back from sabbatical and was assigned to lead your project, is leaving the company to work at Riot Games, so you'll be transitioning with Maggie until she leaves, which will be in three weeks."

"Wait. Then what happens when she's gone?" My posture stiffened and a bout of nausea permeated through my body.

Ian yawned, like he was bored with this conversation already. "Well, you'll basically colead with Maggie until she leaves. Then you'll be interim lead producer until we find a replacement."

Asher sputtered Starbucks venti coffee onto his desk. "Shit, I'll report to Melody then?"

I gasped and said, "What do you mean by interim?"

"Well, *interim* means temporary. And it's only until we find a producer to fill that role."

Yes, I knew the definition of "interim," asshole Ian, but to him "interim" probably meant I'd be paid the same salary to fill bigger shoes, and then when I got used to that job, he'd take it away from me with his new producer hire. And I might even have to teach that person how to do his or her job.

"The board specifically requested that we staff this game with more women, and you're our only female producer now. After

Maggie leaves, we can partner you temporarily with Rain, he's our senior producer on *Zooful Nation*, to help answer any questions, but hopefully after a few weeks you'll be running the show on your own. Asher will be on your team, too, supporting your efforts. Kat will be the lead designer. Go ahead and set up a meeting this afternoon with Maggie and Rain to work on the production schedule and deliverables."

"Before I start on a production schedule I need to know if you've got a launch date in mind."

Ian laughed. "Well, it depends if we go console or mobile." He tapped his lips with his pointer finger. "Console would be well over a year, but since we've had some success developing for console and porting to mobile, I think we go straight to mobile because we need this market ASAP. You can blame the board for that, too. So, six months."

"SIX MONTHS?" I thought that was me yelling in disbelief, but it was actually Asher and Kat screaming in unison. My vocal cords were paralyzed from shock.

Ian leaped up from my desk. "Yep. Six months till beta launch. Then full launch immediately following." He clapped his hands together. "We want to go down in history as having one of the fastest blockbuster game launches. It'll be perfect timing for a holiday push. Plus, the board will fire my ass if we don't hit our revenue numbers by the end of the year, and this game should help with that. Our end-of-the-year projected numbers weren't looking too good. Oh, that reminds me, I need those revenue projections and budget numbers pronto." Ian walked out, whistling.

Six.

Months.

Six months of working late nights. And weekends. I'd miss the rest of Seattle's beautiful summer. I'd get roly-poly from stress eating. All my free time would be spent hanging out with Jane, helping her pick out unflattering bridesmaid gowns to show off my flabby, pale, bat-wing arms. Six months of major work-life unbalance. And I hadn't even started on those stupid forecast and budget scenarios.

I crossed my arms on my desk and buried my face.

Asher said in a low, gravelly voice, "Ian can go screw himself if he thinks I'm working for *you*." His tone said everything. He hated me more than I hated him.

JUST THINKING ABOUT this game release made me feel projectile-vomity. How the hell did this game even get greenlit for production? And why entrust ME with such a huge responsibility? Sure, I had game app experience and some international localization knowledge, and I loved spreadsheets, too, but that sure as hell didn't make me qualified for coleading—and then leading—this mobile game launch. I didn't even know where to start, except to look for someone named "Rain." Maybe the right thing to do would be to let Ian know I should assist rather than lead. They needed to find someone else.

I rehearsed a short *thanks, but no thanks* soliloquy and

marched straight to Ian's office. His door was cracked a little, allowing me to peek in and see if he had any company.

He wasn't alone. The CFO and the head of development sat on his couch, sipping coffee. Just as I thought about leaving, Ian mentioned my name. And then, of course, how could I walk away?

> **Voice 1:** *That game, the apocalypse one, could make money. Think about all the added levels we could charge for: mummies, giant tarantulas, evil ninjas, '80s hair bands.*

> **Voice 2:** *It'll be good to diversify into mobile too. Our zoo games are doing well but we need to see growth in other areas. The board will fire all of us if we don't show that we can keep growing.*

> **Voice 1:** *You worried about letting* that new girl *run the whole thing?*

That new GIRL?

> **Voice 2:** *Does she even know the difference between FPS and FTP?*

Yes, I knew FPS was first-person shooter. Had to google FTP, though, when I first joined the company: free-to-play. But eff you, anyway.

Ian: *Look, don't worry. I had to choose her to run the fucking thing because of the board. That's it. No one expects it to do well. It's just a vanity PR ploy to make this company look good to all the whiny board members who keep preaching equality. They wanted more women in here, remember? Kat's working on the project, too, so we can market and promote it as "girl-friendly."*

Voice 1: *You mean* female-*friendly?*

Voice 2: *Yeah. Menstrual-friendly. Feminazi-friendly. Whatever.*

Ian: *Feminazis aren't friendly. Look at Kat.*

Laughter.

Acid bubbled from the pit of my constricted stomach. I couldn't listen anymore to those bigoted assholes. They'd given me the production lead job simply because of my gender and simultaneously assumed I couldn't do that job because I was female.

Well, screw them.

I raced to Kat's office, a few doors down. She was sketching zombies on her tablet. In her doorway I announced, "I'm making this apocalypse game, MY game, MY idea, a huge success."

She nodded. "Okay. Let's do it," she said with a grin and went back to drawing.

The three executive jackasses left Ian's office and walked right by me in the hallway, without any kind of acknowledgment whatsoever. I'd show them they underestimated me. That I would roll up my sleeves and lead this entire thing myself.

Collapsing on my desk chair, I closed my eyes to slow my rapid heartbeat. Opening them again, I focused my gaze on the mugs Nolan had brought me.

I had an idea. Grabbing my wallet, I took the elevator to the ground floor and evaluated my novelty mug options at the drugstore attached to our lobby. For a mere seven dollars, I bought Ian a present: a "World's Greatest Boss" oversize coffee cup. With a Sharpie marker, I wrote on the bottom "Juuuuust kidding!" for people to see when he drank from it. I peeked inside my brown bag and admired my penmanship as the elevator took me to the office floor.

While Ian was in a meeting, I stealthily placed the mug on his desk, with no note and no card for explanation. A few hours later, I saw him in the kitchen, sipping from the boss mug while intermittently telling one of his many rotating "glory days of gaming" stories he had in his arsenal. Employees gathered around, sniggering and smirking into their lattes, savoring their warm drinks and the shared inside joke.

A small win, but a win nonetheless.

CHAPTER EIGHT

Candace called me on the way to the Bay 55 Steakhouse, the hottest restaurant in town according to *Seattle Metropolitan* magazine. With a several-week wait list, Jane must've had some serious connections to get a reservation for a large party within a few days of becoming engaged.

"Mel! I'm going to be like ten minutes late. I had to get gas. Are you there yet?"

I would be a little late, too. I had completely lost track of time working on Ian's budget and forecast assignments and I didn't feel like paying nine bucks for valet as extra torture that evening.

After circling around for ten or more minutes and searching well outside a comfortable parking radius from the venue, I found a spot a quarter mile from the restaurant. But damn it, I saved nine dollars. Yeah, I was aware this made absolutely no sense since this logic caused me to be late all the time. I blamed my frugal upbringing for this unsound parking rationale.

My car was at the bottom of Queen Anne Hill, with the restaurant at an 89 degree angle at the very top, so not only was it far, it was also high. I trekked two-thirds the way up before my excessive panting began. I let Candace talk while capturing my breath.

She asked, "Hey, were we supposed to bring anything? Like a gift, or flowers or something?" I personally hated getting flowers as gifts, but other people seemed to like them. To me, buying them for someone was, like, *Hey, here's something that will die in a week. Enjoy.* It was depressing to see a lovely botanical specimen shrivel and wilt by day seven. And no matter if you plucked, pruned, or watered, the florae faced an inevitable death. I let her know I'd be arriving empty-handed.

She shouted into the phone. "Hey! My Bluetooth isn't working. I have you on speakerphone now. I've never been to a pre-rehearsal dinner before. For the wedding party there's usually only the rehearsal dinner beforehand. This is really unusual. But it's totally Jane, right? Doing her own thing?"

"Yeah, having a *rehearsal* rehearsal dinner seems like a very Jane thing to do." I huffed back up the hill. "I'm almost there. I'll let her know you'll be a little late." My phone buzzed with an incoming call from my mom. "Hey, I have to go, my mom's trying to do video chat."

We said our quick goodbyes and I switched over. "Hi, Mom, what time is it in Italy?"

All I could see was a peach-hued blur. As usual, her thumb was blocking her phone camera. "Early morning," she croaked.

"We having jet lag pretty bad." Dad's snores rumbled in the background.

"Are you enjoying your visit?"

"It be okay. I eat too many cannoli. Too much dairy but I eat anyway. You know, I have lactose problem since you were born."

I sighed. "I know. It's one of your favorite topics to bring up."

"Rome is nice. Florence is nice. You should come to Italy. One day, when you have honeymoon. But you need husband first."

As if on cue, the sky darkened to black, and torrential rain bullets fell from the sky. I had no umbrella, no raincoat, and for some stupid reason I'd chosen today to wear suede shoes.

"Mom, I really have to go. Have fun there and enjoy your cannoli."

"Okay. We can't buy you any cannoli because it will get rotten. But we buy you hat." Her thumb moved off the camera so she could show me a bright yellow cap with ROMA in red letters on the bill. She turned it side to side to show me the Italian flags stitched in various places along the trim.

"Wow, that's . . . something. Thanks for getting me a gift. Call me when you're back home! Have a good—"

She hung up before I finished my sentence.

I picked up my pace at the crest of the hill. According to the map on my phone, I had arrived at my destination, drenched, winded, and perplexed. I scanned the newly constructed building. Hmmm. No door handle. Or to be more specific, there was no fucking door. The only thing on the building's white wall was the name of the restaurant in tiny gold lettering.

A giant golden button on a white marble pedestal caught my eye. I looked around to see if anyone could help me. Was this some kind of IQ test formulated by Jane? What the hell was going on?

I pushed the button and waited.

A rumbling sound emanated from the inside of the building, and the slab of wall in front of me swung open at a slug's pace, revealing the bustling restaurant hidden behind the white heavy panel.

The exquisitely dressed hostess, with a perfect bun and flawless skin, walked toward me and said hello. Her gold bangles jangled as she waved me forward.

I staggered in and cleared my throat. "Hi. I'm with Jane Townsend's party."

She smiled at me with her impeccably straight, white teeth. "Of course, I just seated them in the back. I'll show you to their room."

We walked past the dozens of clients having work gatherings and fanciful dinner dates. Colorful Chihuly glass sculptures hung from the ceiling. The lighting was dim, but not so dim that you couldn't read the menu or tell if your wine was white, rosé, or red. Each table showcased miniature candelabras with teeny lit candles. Customers seated along our path smiled as they ate towers of oysters and mounds of shrimp cocktail. I loved seafood but I liked the kind of place where they tied a bib around your neck and handed you a giant Thor mallet to smash open whole crabs. This place was way out of my league.

I asked the hostess, "So can I ask you something about that really giant, slowly moving wall door? Isn't that a fire hazard or something? Do you feel like you're in the Haunted Mansion room with the hidden panel at Disneyland?"

"We have several fire exits on the premises, all have a green Exit sign overhead." She pointed to them as we walked to the back of the restaurant, ignoring my pressing Haunted Mansion question.

Toward the back of the restaurant, there was a bar filled with elegant couples and postwork happy hour meetups. On the last stool in the row sat none other than Nolan, looking at his phone with one hand while sipping a beer with his other. He looked comfortable there, with his thick brown curly hair slightly damp from the rain falling forward into his eyes. I debated whether to say hello. It was always strange to see work people out in the real world in their natural habitat. But when Nolan laughed at something he read on his phone, something inside me urged me to walk over to him.

As I took a hesitant step toward the bar, a swish of fresh blown-out golden hair swung right past me.

Nolan looked up from his phone, offering her a warm and inviting smile that I'd never seen before. With both hands, she swooshed her golden locks back over her shoulders and went in for a hug right away. He hesitated at first, but then reciprocated. Who wouldn't? I didn't need to see her face to know she was smoking hot.

After the embrace, she patted his shoulders. A ripple of jealousy pulsed through me as her hands traveled down to his chest, then down, down, down . . .

"Did you want to stop for a drink?" the hostess asked, breaking my trance-stare at the bar. "I can wait here if you'd like."

"Oh, no, thank you. I . . . I was going to say hi to someone but he's busy." I placed my cold hands on my cheeks to cool them down as we continued walking.

"Here you are, ma'am." She gestured toward a tiny private dining room lined with walls of wines. I breathed in deeply, then put on a cheery smile and entered.

Sean, Jane's fiancé, gave me a little nod to acknowledge my arrival. He gestured for me to join his conversation with a dark-haired guy with a serious look on his face.

"Hi. I'm Zachary. Sean's friend from the hospital." His stoic demeanor didn't change, even though I smiled widely. We shook hands.

I took a glass of white wine from the server walking by with a tray of them. "So are you a doctor, too?"

Still, the grave face. "Yes, I'm in OB-GYN. Sean and I go blow off steam after long shifts at work at the pool hall." It was hard to imagine anything riling this animatron up enough for him to need "blowing off steam."

Candace flurried through the double doors, peeling off her damp coat and shaking out her umbrella on the carpet. "Sorry I'm late," she said.

Sean brought her over. As soon as Candace saw Sean's doctor friend, her hand flew up to cover her open mouth. She gasped instead of saying a customary hello.

"Do you two know each other?" Sean asked. I looked at Candace, then back to Animatron. Maybe he did her pap smears?

Jane stood by the doors and clinked her wineglass with a spoon before Candace could answer. "Please take a seat, everyone."

The bride-to-be saved a spot for me by her side, a reserved seat for the maid of honor. Quite literally, I was Jane's right-hand woman.

We all sat. I sipped water to replenish all the fluid ounces of sweat I'd lost from walking up that hill. Candace whispered to me behind her menu. "I have to tell you something." She used the prix fixe insert to fan away the heat rushing to her ruddy face. It was impossible not to notice Dr. Zachary watching her from across the table, in tune to her every move, slightly more animated with his anxious glimpses over at her. When their eyes met, her gaze quickly shifted to her menu.

Was Candace cheating on her longtime boyfriend?

My pulse quickened at the thought as a familiar voice boomed into the room. "Sorry I'm late. Work was a fucking pain in the ass." I briefly suspended my Zachary-Candace surveillance detail to look up.

Asher stood in the doorway.

His eyes darkened the instant he saw me.

My eyes widened as his narrowed to slits.

Oh god, no.

Sean stood up. "You made it! Everyone, this is Asher, my best man. So good to see you!" He stood up and gave his frat brother a bro hug that ended with a two-man hair tousle. Asher found his seat next to Zachary and continued to shoot over little blasts of hateful stares. I couldn't believe that directly across the table was Satan himself.

I grimaced but tried to be friendly. "Hi, Ash-hole."

Oops.

He chugged his glass of water and continued to glare. Did he do this at work, too, while I took calls and typed? That would be pretty fucked up.

"You guys know each other?" Sean asked. Candace cleared her throat and tried to send me nonverbal questions through weird, obvious facial expressions and hand gestures, like, *Who the heck is he?* and *Why the hell are you acting so weird right now?* Like she had any room to judge me, with her strange lookie-loo stares at Dr. Zachary.

I let Asher be the one to answer Sean's question while I chugged my wine. "Yeah, we work together. She even sits in my office." He added, "I was late to dinner because she assigned a production deliverable today that required lots of overtime hours for our team. But I see *she* made it here on time."

Jane squealed, "Wait, is Melody your BOSS?" She clasped her hands together in delight, like I'd given her this intense awkwardness as an engagement present.

Candace, who had no context about this work relationship but could tell the Melody-Asher dynamics were off, gasped and cringed behind her napkin. Even she knew not to say something like that. *Why, Jane? Why?*

"He and I share an office, and we're on the same team," I grumbled.

Sean responded with a single laugh. "You go by 'Ash-hole' now? You should go by 'Hash,' like we called you at school, bro." Asher's icy glare morphed into an exasperated eye roll. So he was a pothead back in college. No surprise there.

"Hey, Melody, did you see your boy toy intern outside?" Asher shot over a sardonic smile. "I'm sad to report that he's moved on to another girl. A really hot one, too."

Jane asked, "You have a boy toy intern?"

Asher added, "Yep. The CEO's nephew, too—does she know how to pick 'em or what? But he's heading out with a hottie tonight. Lucky guy."

I coughed out my wine. "There's no boy toy. Everyone, please ignore him."

"Who's hungry?" Zachary snapped open the menu. But between Asher being here, Nolan being on a date, and this weird Candace-Zachary tension hanging in the air, my appetite was nonexistent. On top of that, my heart beat so fast it was on the verge of exploding with any more stimulation.

Candace leaned over and said to me, "Mel, I need to tell you something later. After dinner."

"Yeah, you have some explaining to do," I said in a clipped tone. Focusing on the menu was difficult, with Ash-hole's critical eyes watching my every move while he chewed dinner rolls with his mouth open. This was way too much Asher for one day.

The table chattered about appetizer options and the waiter came by with champagne. He poured generously and we all held up our glasses of bubbly to toast the soon-to-be married couple.

Jane smiled at us and then at her fiancé. "To marriage!"

Ah. Short and sweet.

We all clinked glasses (even Asher and I did) and I downed it all without taking a breath. Refill, please.

Jane asked, "Candace? Don't you like champagne?"

Candace's eyes widened like she'd just been caught reading a nudie magazine by her grandma. Candace loved champagne. "I . . . I . . . can't have any." She watched Jane with the fearful eyes of hunted prey.

Then it clicked. But Jane's brain processed things more quickly than mine.

"You're PREGNANT?" she screeched.

Candace squeaked, "Yes?" She glanced at me and then looked at Jane again.

A waiter walked by with a steaming, heaping bowl of seafood spaghetti alfredo. "Our house specialty!"

Candace yelped, "Oh god, I think I'm going to be sick!"

She bolted to the bathroom and I excused myself from the table to go look after her. Jane remained in the same motionless position, her color drained from her face, with her full champagne flute in her hand. She looked like someone had frozen her into a toasting pose. This night had been carefully planned and then . . . surprise! Candace dropped a bomb. A baby bomb. This had left Jane literally speechless, which I'd never seen before.

I swung open the bathroom door and found Candace standing over the sink, with both hands clenching the rim. A slightly green hue colored her face.

"Sorry, wave of nausea. I just found out about the baby and wanted to tell you. There's already a heartbeat! I didn't plan to announce it here publicly." She entered a stall and, leaving the door open, dry heaved and slumped down next to the toilet. Thank god the floor looked clean.

I bent down and rubbed her back. It all clicked now. "Candie, this is great news. Is Zachary your doctor?"

She nodded. "We're due in six months."

A laugh bubbled out of me. "Sorry, I was just thinking how funny it was that I thought you and Zachary were having an affair."

"Me, cheat on Wil with Dr. Robot Zach?" Wrinkles formed between her brows as she frowned at me.

"I know, it was a stupid thought. But wow, six months! My game will be released in six months, too, just before the holidays. We'll be giving birth at the same time." Stroking her hair, I added, "Jane will be fine. She's probably just worried about her foiled bridesmaid dress plans because you're preggers now. But I have to ask . . . I thought Wil was superreligious and didn't believe in sex before marriage."

She lifted her eyes from the floor to my face. "Yeah, we abstained while we did the long-distance thing, but one night we got really drunk and, well, all those years of pent-up angst blew the fuck up, and we crammed a lot of sex into a short period of time. He was so horny that we broke the—"

I cut her off before she got too pornographic and made ME vomit. "Oh geez, I don't need to hear all that. I just assumed you guys were all Puritan-like and, well, you aren't."

"Yeah, we are definitely not. Not anymore." She pulled herself upright, using my arm as leverage. "Do I look okay? Let's go back to the dinner. I'll be fine." As she washed her hands she said, "Oh, wait, I had one more thing to say."

Between Asher's dinner cameo appearance and Candace announcing her pregnancy at Jane's prerehearsal dinner, I couldn't imagine anything else surprising me.

"Wil went out and bought me a ring." She pulled a tiny drawstring satchel from her purse's inner pocket. A classic square-cut solitaire ring its only contents. Exactly Candace's style. Good job, Wil.

She continued. "I didn't put it on because I didn't want to upset Jane at her special dinner, you know how she is." It was a good plan, except for the fact that the accidental baby announcement turned out to be an even bigger deal than Jane's engagement. Our Candace bringing a human into this world? What a huge fucking deal!

"I really am so excited for you! Wil is an amazing guy. I know you'll be happy together! And that little guy or girl will be gorgeous, I bet." Wil was Chinese, Candace was Caucasian. They'd have a cute little happy hapa baby.

She smiled and hugged me. "Thanks. I . . . I know it's crazy to ask, but . . . um . . . would you be the godmother for the baby?"

What did godmothers do? Babysit? Attend all birthday parties? My only godmother context was Cinderella. And that involved ball gowns, fairies, and step-bitches.

"I guess? Could you let me know what that means? And are you getting married first?"

She nodded and sighed. "We're going to do a courthouse wedding soon, because I don't want to look huge in all the pictures. I know, it's totally shallow. But I hope you'll come to that. I can't imagine getting married without you by my side."

My eyes brimmed with tears. We'd been through so much since our freshman year of college together, and I loved her so much. Plus, she was pregnant and no one should be mean to pregnant people. "Yes, of course I'll come. And I'll be the god-mama. I would be honored."

She squealed and hugged me again so hard my arms may have bruised. "I was thinking about asking Jane to be at the courthouse ceremony, too, but I might give her time to sit with my baby news first. I think my engagement news on top of that baby announcement might be a lot for her to handle. Since the pregnancy and engagement were unplanned I'm hoping she doesn't see this as me upstaging her somehow." Candace put her ring back in the satchel. Really? We couldn't celebrate this amazing news out of fear of hurting someone else's feelings? She and Jane grew up together, and they became roommates after college. I met Jane through Candace. We'd all gone through a lot together and I had hoped by now that none of us would be trying to one-up each other.

We stayed in the bathroom a while, chatting about the pregnancy while we freshened up. When we were ready to rejoin the festivities, we walked back to an empty room. Candace asked, "Where'd everyone go?" The balloons and flowers were all removed, too. The prerehearsal dinner party had vanished. I checked my watch. We were in the bathroom for only thirty minutes.

On the table next to our purses were two silver domes on top of two plates. One where Candace was seated, the other where I had been, next to Jane. I handed Candace one of the sets of silverware in the center of the table where the orchid arrangement had been.

She lifted her dome first, revealing a small can of ginger ale, a cup of chicken soup, and a pack of oyster crackers.

Under mine? A "skinny girl" salad, fat-free Italian dressing, and a small square of engagement cake with Jane's face on it.

Classic.

"Hey! Where's my cake?" Candace moaned.

I slid mine over to her. "Baby can have first dibs."

CHAPTER NINE

Five thirty A.M. wakeup times were the worst, but I could either wake up at the asscrack of dawn or stay at work way past midnight to get the game launched on our accelerated schedule. Neither choice was good, and both were worse options than rocks or hard places. I chose the asscrack.

Already, these long days and nights had taken a toll on my body. But I had to do this. To prove to all the naysayers at work that I could handle it. Plus, with the Seventeen Studios brand name on my résumé I could go anywhere next. It had cachet like Google or Apple. AND . . . my game idea was going to be produced by ME! That was maybe the coolest thing to ever happen in my entire existence. Who cared if my life span shortened by a few hundred days because of the grueling work hours I imposed at age twenty-seven and a half?

On my drive to work I called my mom, who had texted that they were back from Italy. Eight in the morning central time was a perfectly reasonable time to call them. After all, she often called me presunrise in Seattle, presumably by accident.

Mom picked up on the first ring. "Melody-ya, what's matter? You in hospital? You hurt? Why you call so early?" Her voice was more shrill and panicked with each sentence.

"I'm on my way to work and thought I'd call you while I had time in the car. I'm not in the hospital. Oh! I wanted to ask you something."

My dad jumped on the line. "You finally have boyfriend? Is that why you call so early morning?"

Oh my god. I didn't realize that calling at an unusual time translated into me being injured or announcing I was actually dating someone.

"No, Dad, I don't have a boyfriend. I just called because I had time to check in with you."

I could feel my parents' hearts sink with their weighty silence.

"Well, at least you not in the jail." *Thanks, Mom.*

"And you not call to tell us you move back home with us." *Thanks for looking on the bright side, Dad.*

Time to change the subject. "So how was Italy? What cities were your favorites?"

"Rome. Vatican City. Venice. Very wet in Venice, you need special rain shoe," Dad said. "Too many pigeon."

"So did you have a good time, though? Did you go to a lot of museums and walking tours? How was the pizza and pasta?"

Mom chimed in. "I got sick of too many cannoli. Too much cheese in all our food. So we ask around for Korean food."

"Wait, you ate Korean food in Italy?"

Dad cleared his throat. "Most of time. We miss some tours because we looking for it."

I rubbed at my brow. "Seriously? You ate mostly Korean food there?"

"And some of your Carnation instant breakfast."

I shook my head. Time to change the subject again. "Well, I hope you had fun. Anyway, remember when I downloaded the Liftr app on your phones when you came to visit me a long time ago?"

"Yes, we have some trouble, I remember, and you help us." The trouble she referred to was when the app prompted her to enter a username, and she entered in all caps, "I.DO.NOT.HAVE.USER.NAME.SORRY." Luckily, Liftr rejected it because it had too many characters.

"Have you guys used that app recently? I got some feedback from a driver that there had been some recent passenger activity that I wasn't aware of."

"Melody! What you blame us for?" In a flash, I had triggered my mom's anger. You could hear it in her shrill, antagonistic voice, and she would soon detonate if I didn't diffuse this hostile situation right away.

"A Liftr driver informed me of some unusual activity on my account, and apparently my passenger rating is really bad."

My parents, having a muffled sidebar conversation in Korean, whispered words like *cheongmal* (really), *aigoo* (oh geez), *ssawoseo* (argue), and then in English, "black person driver." *Uh-oh.*

My work commute moved faster than the GPS had predicted. I needed to wrap up this conversation before I entered the no signal parking garage entry ramp. "Hey, Mom? Dad? I'm pulling into my building now, so I have to go. I'm going to remove you from my Liftr account today, okay? My car is dying and I need Liftr. If you want me to set up your own account, I can help you with that, but not now. Maybe this weekend."

I had every right to remove them for their questionable conduct. So why feel so bad about deleting them from my account? I was a few steps away from being banned from the service, and I needed that riding option in case of an emergency. Like my car not starting. *Nope, you will not feel guilty about this, Melody.*

Rather than raise hell, my mom said without any fight in her voice, "We don't use it much anyhow. Just few time when we going around downtown. Why you drive to work? You should walk. You need more exercise." Was this one of her proud *you need to be healthy like your dad and me* moments, or one of her *let's talk about your weight* segues? Since I'd moved to Seattle a few years ago from Chicago I'd gained about ten pounds. And she noticed, because she mentioned it every few conversations.

"I'll call you later!" I zoomed down the garage ramp and took my pick of widely available parking spot options. The only other car here? Ian's fucking new Tesla.

Before I could put my stuff down in my office, I heard Ian bellow behind me, "Melody! You're here. In my office, **NOW**."

I had been quiet, how did he know I was here? With my overstuffed computer bag, old raincoat, and worn-leather purse hanging off my arms like a TJ Maxx last-chance clearance display, I padded over to the executive corridor.

Ian scooched out of the doorway to let all my schlepped belongings and me through. On the wall monitor were my forecast and budget PowerPoint slides I had put on the shared drive the night before. Seated in one of the guest chairs was Nolan, running his hand through his wild brown bedhead hair, scrunched flat on one side, sticking straight up on the other. His gray plaid shirt was covered in "left in the dryer a few nights" wrinkles. He had a rolled-out-of-bed-after-being-with-a-gorgeous-woman-all-night look about him.

"Nolan and I have been going over the forecast and budget numbers you both prepared for the board."

I bit my bottom lip and stared hard at the screen. I never told Mr. Intern I'd be doing everything without his consultation.

Ian continued. "For the most part, it's correct. But your assumptions aren't spelled out, and most of your calculations aren't shown in detail. The board gets super in the weeds and really gets off on rolling around in data."

I waited for an apology for his crass remark. Of course, it never came. "I need you to do all of this over. Show the work this time with a bottom-up granular approach instead of a top-down one."

My brain finally woke up. "Do it all over? That took hours! I don't have time—"

Nolan leaned forward from his chair and adjusted his glasses. "Not a problem. I'll work on the number crunching, and Melody can review the final version. We'll send it to you this evening."

A grimace flashed across Ian's face. "Okay, but this afternoon we have the nine-hole tourney at the country club. Who's going to be my caddy if you're working on this?"

My mouth opened to respond, but Nolan's *no, don't you dare* glare made me bite back my words.

Ian sighed. "Send it to me by one P.M. today so we have time before the tournament to review it if I have questions." Then he shooed us away to make a call.

Once we were out of earshot, Nolan muttered, "He woke me up before sunrise so we could go over the numbers. You know, the ones you worked on yourself and didn't even have the courtesy to share with me."

"It was easier to do myself," I huffed. "I had too many meetings so I had to work on it whenever I could find spare time. Plus, I'm sure you had your hands full last night. The last thing you probably wanted was to work on budgets and revenue forecasts."

Confusion flashed on his face. "What's that supposed to mean?"

"Nothing. Never mind," I muttered. "So why does Ian want another pass at the numbers?"

He sighed. "Well, you could have had me do the work, or at least let me review yours before you uploaded it. Some of your assumptions are too conservative, and some of your revenue projections are way too optimistic. You need to clear your calendar so we can get this finished by the deadline."

"Fine." I declined all my day's meetings on my phone calendar. "Let's start now. Maybe if we finish early you can still make it to your treasured golf game with your uncle," I said flatly.

He rolled his eyes. "And I'll book a conference room for the whole day just in case. The small one at the end of the hall is usually free." It was the freezing conference room that had a wobbly table and was littered with broken chairs. One look at my facial reaction and he burst into laughter. "Look, it's not THAT bad. At least it's available. And there's no Asher to deal with there."

Well, we both hated Asher. At least we had that in common.

We walked to the always-empty Ernest Cline conference room in silence. The motion-sensor light took a few extra seconds to register our presence. When the overhead fluorescents flicked on, we could see that some evil bastard had uncapped all the dry-erase markers and scattered them on the floor, removed the rickety table, and left a graveyard of broken chairs in our midst.

Nolan inspected our seating options and wheeled a seemingly normal chair over to me. "Okay, here's one of the least messed-up ones I could find." I sat, and it hissed as I slowly shrank down to the shortest setting. "Oh, I guess the height adjustment mechanism is broken," he said, stating the obvious.

When I stood, the seat hissed again, moving the seat back up to the original position.

Nolan pushed another chair in my direction. This one also looked "normal" but didn't swivel, which was fine, given the alternatives.

For himself, he sat in one that was stained with black, brown, and white splotches. I never understood how seats could get that dirty from everyday work use. Maybe they got that way from after-hours recreational use? *Gross, Melody, don't even go there. Mind out of gutter, please.*

"Shit, we need a table." Nolan disappeared and came back a minute later with a small circular metal bistro table that he stole from the kitchen.

Asher messaged me as Nolan propped open the door. *Just saw your ex-boo N in the hallway and grilled him about that hot girl. She was a drunk hot mess when she arrived and he put her in a cab. He also said she was boring??? Idk who cares?*

I couldn't fight the smile forming on my lips.

Nolan cared.

Holding the heavy tabletop with both hands, Nolan shimmied through the door like he was holding a very large steering wheel. It was the first time I had the opportunity to take in all of his tall, athletic physique. He breathed heavily as he placed the table in the middle of the room, and I wanted so badly to push away the swath of his hair that fell onto his tortoiseshell frames. Did he notice my gaze when I followed the outline of his shoulders and chest as they strained against his button-down fitted shirt? *No, no, no, Melody. It's Nolan Fucking MacKenzie.* I distracted myself by pulling my laptop from my computer bag and signing in to the network. My cheeks prickled with heat, even though the room was meat-locker cold.

Remember, he's your intern. "Okay, let's get started," I said in a clipped, businesslike tone.

He unbuttoned his shirt a little. "That was some good strength training."

My eyes stared at where his fingers had just been.

"What?" he asked, noticing my intense interest in his upper-chest area.

My cheeks flushed with heat. "What? Oh, I was just . . . thinking I liked your shirt. Big fan of plaid." *Oh god.* "It's a good cut, too." I couldn't stop talking. "It's not too baggy."

Over our opened laptops, I peeked up from the screen and caught Nolan watching me. His mouth curved upward as he looked back down and typed.

"What?"

He smirked. "I was just thinking about how you tried to do this without me. Big mistake."

I rolled my eyes. "Look, I did these types of projects all the time at my last job, even though I was a copywriter and a creative person. People like me get stuck doing other people's work all the damn time."

He pushed away some chairs and lifted a projector off the floor and placed it on the table. Connecting it to his laptop, he turned it on. It whirred for a few seconds before a beam of light shone on the white wall.

"Well, I don't know what the standards were at your last job, but you forgot some key assumptions in your projections and budgets. I have a list of them here." A mirror image of his laptop screen appeared on the wall. Nolan typed in his password and a detailed Excel sheet popped up.

My eyes moved down his spreadsheet, taking in each of his detailed line items. All twenty-three of them.

I had only half of them accounted for, at most.

When I finished scanning, I thought I'd find a smug *I told you so* expression plastered all over his face, but surprisingly, I didn't. He leaned in closer. "Do we need to add anything else?"

I pulled up the presentation from the hard drive. "I had two others. One is for music licensing costs. The other one about whether we make an Android version."

He nodded and added those to his spreadsheet. "Anything else?"

I shook my head and updated the spreadsheet I had used for all the previous calculations. With Nolan's added caveats, my revenue projections and budgets had changed by 12 percent. Not a huge amount, but enough to probably get fired if we ever had to request additional budget or missed our financial target.

My lips pressed together. It killed me to say it, but not saying something would be wrong. Looking at my laptop keyboard, I mumbled, "Thanks for your help."

He cleared his throat to get my attention. He had his index

finger behind his earlobe when I looked up. "I'm sorry, what did you say? I missed that."

I pinched my mouth. *Damn it, Nolan Fucking MacKenzie.*

I exhaled. "Thank. You. For. Your. Help."

He beamed at me. *Arrogant bastard.* Leaning back in glory, he nearly fell because his floppy chair back was broken. I burst into a fit of giggles as he skittishly sprang up like a jack-in-the-box.

Feeling bad about my outburst, I asked, "You want to double-check my numbers before we email them over to Ian?"

Tingles of excitement passed through me as Nolan scooted his death-trap chair next to me. With him this close, I could really see how attractive his features were, with his gleaming dark brown eyes, full lips, and powerful, broad shoulders. I found myself subconsciously leaning closer, removing the distance between us. Swallowing hard, I tried to focus on the numbers on the screen and not the heat radiating from his body. Could he hear my heart thudding against my chest? *Thud-thud-thud-no-no-no-no-Mel-Mel-Mel . . .*

He tapped the down arrow key on my laptop. "I ran into Asher in the hallway. He mentioned that he was at a rehearsal dinner with you yesterday and you both saw me."

Oh no.

Oh-no-oh-no-oh-no.

Sweat sprouted in the usual places. Forehead. Upper lip. Armpits. My bra underwire area.

He shrugged. "It was the first time I'd tried online dating since I moved to Seattle."

"Oh, how'd it go?" I swallowed hard and stared at the laptop screen.

"She introduced herself by saying she had just met up with another guy earlier and they'd had too many drinks. And guess what?"

I bit my lip and looked at him.

"After I complained to your officemate about how she was twenty minutes late for our date, that she had already had three drinks and wanted to do shots with me, and then asked me flat out how much money I made, Asher slapped me on the back and asked for her number."

I laughed so hard it hurt my sides. What a classic Asher move.

He smiled and his gaze shifted from the screen to my face. "Everything checks out."

"What?"

"The numbers. All the formulas and inputs look good." Nolan took off his glasses to wipe the lenses with his shirt. When he put them back on, he lowered his head and looked at me through the top of them. "I have to ask, why didn't you just let me work with you?" *His long lashes are so distracting.* "It was easier to do it together."

My face burned with equal parts attraction and embarrassment. "I wanted to prove I knew what I was doing. At my last job I worked my ass off and was rewarded for that."

He nodded slowly. "Every job and every company is different, though. With new situations, you might need to adapt."

"Maybe, but it could also be my personality. I'm always butting heads with my parents about my life decisions." My voice cracked a little. "What can I say, stubbornness runs in the family."

His grin melted my heart a little. "Does it work? The arguing and standing up to people?"

I shrugged. "I'm a Korean girl working in gaming, against my parents' wishes. And I haven't been fired . . . yet. So I guess?"

"Well, you've taught me something. I should butt heads with people more, especially my uncle and my parents, so I can live my life more the way I want." He placed his elbow on the table and rested his chin on the back of his hand. Then, he leaned toward me, nudged my arm gently with his, sending more electric tingles through my entire body. "You're a good role model."

Tilting his seat as he leaned over more, his cushion toppled to the side, causing him to collapse into me. In one unfluid motion, he elbowed my ribs as he fell to the floor.

He barked out a nervous laugh. "Sorry about that, boss."

Right.

I was his boss.

And all these feelings I had? Wrong, wrong, wrong.

Shoving my laptop in my bag, I barked, "There are some important production meetings I need to attend. Send the files to Ian. He'll be happy because we finished early, so now you can go to the golf tournament with him."

I scooped up all my shit and took off down the hallway. In

the faint distance, I heard Nolan say, "You know, I actually hate golf. With a passion."

Once I got to my desk, I squeezed my eyes shut and took a deep breath. I felt a little bad about my golf comment, but Nolan was a distraction. He and I couldn't be together. Period. I was too busy to date anyway.

Asher was out at an off-site meeting, so I closed the office door and drew the blinds. No more disruptions, interruptions, or diversions. Especially from the intern.

CHAPTER TEN

The fluorescent lights on my side of the floor burned bright the next morning, but the office was eerily silent, like I'd accidentally walked in wearing noise-canceling headphones. I thought I had the place to myself, but Asher sat at his desk, drinking a fucking Starbucks latte. He ignored me, as usual. I couldn't believe he beat me to the office again. Did he sleep here or something?

Well, I could give him the silent treatment, but that would be awkward since we were the only two people on the entire floor and we still needed to work together on this game launch. So, I went with the olive branch approach. "Good morning," I said, with as much exuberance as I could muster at 6:15 in the morning.

He looked up. "Oh, sorry, I didn't see you. Too busy entering hundreds of Jira tickets for your dev team. You know, to build all the hundreds of things you painstakingly listed in your annoying Game Design Document for us to do for your little game?"

Snide jerk. So what if I ran a tight ship when it came to project management, and everyone's deliverables and tasks were focused and clear? I'd been told by numerous people that my documentation was comprehensive and dummy-proof. Everyone, especially me, had been working long hours, but he was acting particularly whiny, more than his usual entitled self. And that petty shit needed to stop. Pronto.

"First of all, it's not *my little game*, it's Seventeen Studios' title. I worked till two thirty in the morning, helping YOU with your Jira backlog. If you have a problem with me, say it to my face. Directly."

His head jerked back as if I'd blown him backward with a gust of wind. His eyes widened and his eyebrows rose so high they almost shot off his forehead. *Good!* I'd surprised the shit out of him. Yeah, this wasn't my first asshole rodeo.

"Whoa, holy PMS!" He laughed at his own sexist joke.

I glared and shook my head. "Well, if we want to throw around sexist terms now, okay. Here you go. Can you grow a fucking pair of balls and stop whining? Do your damn job." This time his eyebrows jumped so high they went up past the brim of his baseball cap. Maybe he'd shut up now and get back to work.

"Whatever. Can you stop assigning stuff so rapid-fire that we have to work through lunch and dinner? Some of us have social lives and like to hang out at work." *Yeah, of course you like people here. They're just like you.*

He snorted and put in his earbuds. I put in mine. No more talking. I tried to log in to my computer to check on all today's tasks, but my laptop wouldn't turn on. The power source, the docking station, and the power button all looked functional, but they weren't. And of course my computer would die way before any of the IT guys I knew came into work. I noticed Asher looking at me with great interest. He disappeared behind his monitor as soon as we made eye contact.

With my laptop tucked under my arm, I walked over to the IT pod. *Please, let someone be there.* My home computer had died recently, and my work computer was all I had left. I relied on it for everything now: music streaming, online bill pay, Amazon Prime purchases. *Please don't die, laptop!*

By some miracle, an IT guy was sitting at his desk, using a screwdriver to open the battery cover of a laptop that looked exactly like mine.

"Hi! I'm Melody. My laptop won't turn on. I'm hoping you can help." I scanned his desk for his nameplate. "Damon." I smiled, hoping a cheery version of myself might make him care more.

Damon was maybe twenty-five years old, superskinny, with blue, slightly bugged eyes. Ghostly pale with gingerish hair. Wearing a size XL Speed Racer shirt on a size S frame.

He shrugged. "Did you submit a helpdesk ticket?"

"No, I didn't. How do I do that?"

"Um, you send an email to helpdesk about your problem." He rolled his eyes and went back to working on the computer battery. He shook his head and softly muttered something under his breath.

"Hmmm . . . my computer won't even power on . . . so not sure how I'd be able to email you." *Don't you shake your head and roll your eyes at me, mister!*

He put down the screwdriver and held out his hand. I passed him my laptop. "I tried to reboot it by holding down the power button, I checked the docking station and the power cord, too. Not sure what happened. I didn't even get the blue screen of death."

He scoffed at the purple, oval "Grrl Powr!" glittery sticker on my laptop cover that Candace had bought me for my first day at Seventeen Studios. He flipped the machine over and tinkered with the battery. Then he took the hard drive out and put it into another machine. "It's your hard drive. I'll need to get you a new computer, but none of the ones here have been reimaged. I can get you set up with a loaner, though. It's a little beat-up."

He opened the laptop he'd been working on and typed a few things on its keyboard. Then he said, "Okay, I'll need you to enter your password."

I typed in the ten-character alphanumeric combo I'd been issued when I arrived. *Note to self, remember to change that.*

When I got a closer look at the keypad, I noticed that the space bar was missing. Damon noticed that I noticed it was missing. "Yeah, the space bar isn't there, and it's not something we can replace."

"But . . . everything I type will be one giant word."

With a halfhearted shrug, he gave me a *not my fucking problem* look. I glanced at the shelf behind his desk. Two new Macs in boxes! "Hey, are those employee computers?"

"Sorry, you aren't authorized to have a Mac. One is for Ian, the other is for one of the designers."

I sighed. "The intern has a Mac."

"Well, he's a special case."

Right. Nepotism. "Okay then. You think my computer will be ready tomorrow?"

He rubbed his head of gingery hair. I fought the urge to smooth it all into one direction. "I'll come by with your new one as soon as it's ready." He opened his mouth, like he wanted to say something else, but then closed it. He went back to his screwdriver and battery, so I took the loaner computer and walked back to my office.

Asher took the earbuds out of his ears and smiled at me coyly with that smug-ass face of his. "In case you were wondering, I didn't sabotage your computer." Actually, I hadn't thought he was involved at all. But now I did. He added, "Good luck with that." He put his earbuds back in and then went back to ignoring me. Ignoring seemed better than strangling each other. The current state of disregarding each other was as harmonious as we could get.

A couple of hours later Damon appeared with a Mac. I raised my eyebrow when he handed it to me.

"Um, one of the designers got fired this morning and I wiped his hard drive. This computer is better than that new one you'd be issued. You should take it."

A MacBook! "Oh, wow, so this one isn't missing any critical keys?" I flipped it open and all the keys were accounted for. Yay! One hundred percent of keys!

He took the loaner from me and clutched it against his chest. "Same login and password on this computer. It has more RAM and more memory, too, and I can get you an external hard drive if you need it."

I swayed in my chair with excitement. "Okay! Hey, thanks, Damon!"

He left briskly and no longer blocked my view of Asher's stupid head. Damon had temporarily eclipsed Asher from my view. It had only been a short-term reprieve, unfortunately.

Asher eyed my laptop like a dieter observing boxes of Girl Scout cookies for sale: with deep desire and hatred. He gritted his teeth and side-eyed me, and I totally knew what he was thinking: *Melody got another "free pass" at this company by getting a coveted MacBook.* But you know what was unfair? Being on a tight deadline and having a shitty computer that died. And then getting issued a loaner computer with a missing space bar. Writing-sentences-with-no-fucking-spaces-for-a-few-hours. That's pretty unfair if you ask me. And it was an older, used Mac, not a new one. Asher could go eff off.

He stood up, slammed his laptop shut, and stormed out of our room. Good riddance.

I logged in to the network and downloaded my email and calendar. Dozens of overdue and upcoming meeting notifications took over my screen. I'd missed a Gartner game industry Outlook presentation an hour ago. Not a big deal. But I was also ten minutes late to a mandatory sexual harassment training in the Orson Scott Card large conference room.

Crap.

I slammed my laptop cover and dashed to the meeting. All eyes fell on me when I opened the door, looking disheveled and panting like I'd just had steamy, mind-blowing sex.

"Sorry," I mumbled and scurried to the closest open seat at the large conference table. While the instructor handed out sheets of paper, I surveyed the room, counting twelve dudes, all but one of them white. Nolan was there, donning his signature J.Crew Outlet look, wearing a hunter-green plaid fitted shirt nearly identical in style and fit to the one he wore when we worked together. I looked away before he made eye contact.

Asher was there, too. He could have told me about this mandatory meeting, but he had been too busy purposefully ignoring me. I would have done the same thing.

"Excuse me, are you Melody?" The grandfatherly instructor, with a faint British accent, asked.

"Um. Yes?"

"Brilliant! We have perfect attendance!" He took a black Sharpie and drew a horizontal line on his pad of paper, presumably crossing off the final name of his participant list. "You just missed our group introductions. I am Charles Sword, your moderator for today's professional training. I was just thanking Nolan here for bringing me in for this session." Nolan ran his fingers through his hair and offered the instructor a sheepish grin. He glanced at me and gave me a tiny wave. Unable to resist, I offered him a lopsided smile. I had to give him some credit, at least he was doing his job.

Charles focused all his attention on me. "I'm thrilled you've arrived. Would you mind reading the lines of the female character in the script in front of you? You came just in time for the role-playing exercise."

Oh, lucky me.

He peered down at his list of participants again. "And . . . Asher? Can you play the male character?"

Lucky me again.

Charles said, "I'll be the narrator because I certainly have the voice for it." The instructor chuckled. "Well, what a serious bunch we have here. All right then, I'll begin." He cleared his throat, not out of necessity, but instead for dramatic effect.

"Jack and Jill work in a relaxed office environment. Jill is typing a memo when Jack enters the room. Go ahead, Asher."

Asher/Jack: Have you met that new chick?

Melody/Jill: You mean Caitlin?

Asher/Jack: Yeah. She has a great rack.

The room busted into laughter. What the fuck was this? An

intense wave of heat moved through my body. The fire in my cheeks burned like I'd doused them in kimchi juice.

Charles the moderator said, "The language Jack uses makes Jill feel uncomfortable. What did you as listeners find problematic about his choice of words?"

Hands shot in the air.

"Yes? You, sir, in the red shirt?"

Red Shirt guy said, "Well, he calls that girl a 'chick' and—"

I cut in. "And you just called Jill a 'girl.' You'd never call Jack a 'boy' in the workplace."

Someone muttered, "Daaaaamn, Jill. That's savage." All the dudes laughed.

Asher said, "I wouldn't have used the word 'rack.'"

Charles nodded. "Right-o! The choice of words was not appropriate for the office environment." *Right-o? Did people really talk like that anymore?*

A guy in a Mariners jersey asked, "Should we use 'chest' instead?"

"You shouldn't be talking about chests at all in the workplace," I muttered. My fierce, crippling stare made him wince and look away.

Asher asked, "How about 'jugs'?" He smirked at me as the room erupted in laughter again. *Damn it!* I wanted to kill him.

The instructor could sense my murderous intentions. He said, "Alrighty. Why don't we move on to the second exercise? In this scenario, Jill is the night manager of the shipping department. One evening Jack approaches her to ask if he can leave early. Jill objects, and Jack offers a massage in exchange for permission to leave and—"

Asher yelled, "No way, I'd die or kill myself before I'd do that to Jill over there." He pointed at me.

I blurted out, "I would taser Jack in the balls."

"You can't say 'balls,'" Red Shirt guy said.

Crossing my arms, I replied, "I'd taser him in the genitals then."

Charles said, "I love the openness of this discussion, and the suggestions of alternative word choices from our training participants. Bravo! But remember, the original problem to solve was 'How should Jill handle Jack's massage proposition?' Accept or decline?"

Asher and I yelled in unison, "DECLINE!"

Our poor instructor. He had no idea how much Jack and Jill mutually despised each other.

"Let's move into scenario three, shall we?" He cleared his throat. "Jill and Jack are hanging out in the break room and overhear a couple of employees picking on a new male employee. They overhear one of the employees call the man a 'homo.' What should they do?"

Mariners guy asked, "But what if he actually is a homo?"

The dude next to him said, "You can't call him 'homo,' you fucking idiot."

Charles barked, "Hey! Let's refrain from name-calling. That is one of the lessons from this exercise." He wiped his forehead with a monogrammed handkerchief and dabbed it above his lip.

Asher asked, "Could they call him something else? Like, 'homosexual'?"

Red Shirt guy said, "We can't say 'fairy' here. Or 'homo,' I guess. They say 'poof' in London, right? So 'homosexual' is the PC thing to say, right?" He looked at Charles, awaiting an answer.

Charles slumped his shoulders and exhaled loudly. "The best answer was to not pick on the employee in the first place, and if they chose to address him, they would do so by name, without mentioning the new employee's sexual orientation."

Red Shirt guy wasn't finished. "Before we move on, can we talk about joking around about illegal stuff at work? Let's say, Rohypnol. Let's say someone hadn't actually roofied anyone or anything but said to a few people that it would be funny to spike the coffee machine with it. Is that sexual harassment?"

Charles shook his head. "No. That's not sexual harassment unless this person planned to drug the coffee for the purpose of sexual advancement in the office. But spiking anything with an illegal substance would definitely be a severe criminal activity. You know that, right?"

"Of course." But the shocked look on Red Shirt guy's face made me think otherwise. He began shaking his right leg, seemingly antsy to get out of training. Perhaps to go pour out the coffee.

"Where were we? Oh, right, the final scenario." Charles skimmed the worksheet and nodded. "Here we are. Jill is nice but has a habit of hugging people when she thinks they are feeling down. Jack appreciates her intentions, but it makes him extremely uncomfortable, because she hugs a little too long. What should Jack do?"

Red Shirt dude elbowed his neighbor. "It depends on whether Jill is hot." They fist-bumped. One of those annoying ones accompanied by sound effects.

Asher looked right at me. "Jill is NOT hot."

Nolan Fucking MacKenzie piped up for the first time. "Hey now, that's not cool to say."

I shot him a piercing look. *I can fight my own battles, intern, thank you very much.*

Mariners guy chimed in. "Well, from where I'm sitting, Jill looks pretty hot to me."

"*Some* people here would definitely feel that way," Asher growled, looking directly at Nolan.

Charles interjected, "Well, everyone, I hate to say it, but it looks like we are out of time!" He had already begun packing up his materials and closed his briefcase, ready to flee in mere seconds. He handed each of us a certificate and a course satisfaction survey.

Certificate of Sexual Harassment Training

Participant's name: Melania Joo

I, *Melania Joo,* acknowledge the completion of Seventeen Studios' sexual harassment training session.

By signing this statement, I acknowledge that I:

Understand the company's policies regarding sexual harassment,

Understand my responsibility as an employee to not engage in behavior that could be perceived as sexual harassment,

If harassed, I understand my right to request the behavior be stopped, and

Understand it is my responsibility to bring sexually offensive behavior to my organization's attention.

Signed,

_____

(Melania Joo)

The course certificate had been printed with my misspelled name on expensive, heavy stock with gold-and-black embossed lettering. I tossed it into the trash along with the survey.

"Hey, Melody, wait up." Nolan huffed and puffed next to me.

Staring straight ahead, I continued marching to my office, pretending I didn't see him in my peripheral view.

"Please? I just wanna talk."

I sped up and he stayed in lockstep with me. By the time I got to my office, we were both panting.

"I just . . ." *Breath*. "Wanted to say . . ." *Breath*. "That those guys were so out of line," he wheezed. "I thought. Training. Would be a good thing. For inclusivity."

I slammed my MacBook on my desk. "You didn't have to say anything in there, you know. I deal with this shit all the time, I can handle myself." Opening my laptop, I checked for damage. I didn't want the IT guy to yell at me.

His eyes widened. "Oh, I didn't mean you couldn't handle yourself. I just meant—" He took another breath. "It's just that, those guys are idiots and I didn't think what happened in there was appropriate."

"Look, you don't need to jump in to save me. *I'm fine!*" I hissed the last two words through gritted teeth and tapped my password so hard on my keyboard that the keys could have broken from the pressure. The intern's like-to-hate ratio had nose-dived to negative since our conference room meeting. Wait, could ratios be negative?

"If you're fine, then okay, I just felt bad is all, since it was one of my inclusivity initiatives and it bombed, at your expense." His shoulders slumped and head hanging low, he shuffled out of the office, passing Asher as he entered. My gut twisted tight as Nolan disappeared from my view. My anger and pride had gotten the best of me. The last thing I wanted was to make enemies with one of the nicer guys here. Especially the CEO's nephew.

"Another lovers' quarrel?" Asher smirked as he sat in his chair.

"Can you do your job, please?" I muttered back.

On Messenger, I found Nolan MacKenzie and sent him a quick message. *I'm sorry I snapped. No sleep and too much going on here, as you witnessed in that meeting. Can I make it up with dinner?*

*My treat. Actually, Ian's treat, cashing in my dining dollars for working
late so many nights.*

In case he got the wrong idea, I added, *Nothing fancy.*

His immediate reply. *Cool. I'm game.*

I smiled and closed the chat window.

THANKS TO MY unplanned computer outage and useless sexual
misconduct training, I stayed at work later than planned. My
Messenger app bleeped around 7:30 P.M.

Nolan: *Ready for dinner yet?*

Oh damn, dinnertime already. Maybe I could take my computer home, assign tasks to our overseas developers in China
and Poland, and then a lot of work could get done overnight
and I'd be on schedule in the morning. I threw my computer
into my black leather satchel. My newly inherited work Mac-
Book weighed more than my other laptop. Those MacBooks
looked slender and light, but I swear those computers were
made out of the same materials as fishing sinkers.

Nolan wasn't at his desk but his computer screen was on,
spreadsheets were up, and of course I had to sneak a look. Using
fancy macros and pivot tables, he was in the middle of building a forecast for the entire company. My mouth gaped when I
skimmed his financial models. I'd never seen anyone work numbers the way he did. He was right, I really should have asked for
his help on those Ian projects.

"Uh, sorry, I had to run to the bathroom. I got so caught

up in work I forgot to go all day." Nolan scooted by me and bent over the desk to save what he was working on, then shut down his computer. His brown curls fell forward, covering his eyes like a sheepdog. I resisted the urge to brush them out of his eyes.

"I'm impressed" was all I could muster. I really was speechless, completely in awe of his expert Excel skills. People always came to me for spreadsheet help. Now I knew who to go to when I got stumped.

"Are you making fun of me?" He raised an eyebrow and cocked his head.

Feigning hurt, I clutched my upper chest. "I'm serious!"

He offered a sad smile. "Well, it's pretty obvious that inclusivity consulting wasn't my forte." Putting his bag strap on his shoulder, he said, "I took on some strategic planning projects with the finance team, which I love, but I've been working late some nights. By the way, where are we headed?"

I held out the Ian-issued gift card options. Johnny Rockets, Red Robin, or P.F. Chang's.

He studied them harder than a normal person would. "P.F. Chang's is close, just over there on Pine, so let's go there."

"I can't. I shouldn't have even included that in the options."

"What do you mean, you *can't*?"

"It's blasphemy, like Taco Bell for Mexican people. My Asian friends and I have an unspoken rule that we aren't supposed to eat at PFC's because it's a fake Asian hodgepodge restaurant concocted by greedy corporate white people."

He barked out a laugh. "I'll bet you twenty dollars that you like the food."

Twenty bucks was incentive enough for me to break trust with my Asian brethren. "You're on."

The rain pelted us from all directions the whole way there, only partially shielded by the giant golf umbrella he held high above us. The entire walk there, Nolan's phone buzzed with texts, which he continually ignored.

"Sounds important," I said as we turned down Pine Street.

He shook his head and frowned. "It's just my parents. Both of them, tag-teaming me with messages. They want me to come visit them during fall break."

"That sounds nice," I murmured. "They want you home." I couldn't remember the last time my parents had begged me to come home to visit them.

"Nah, it's more dubious than that. They want me to move back to North Carolina after grad school."

I swallowed hard and kept quiet. Nothing could happen between us anyway. Not while I was his "boss." Not with Asher ready to get me fired in a moment's notice if I crossed the line.

A booth was ready as soon as we arrived, and the hostess walked us to a table near the window and handed us our menus. My stomach gurgled and made those yeti noises again. I hated to admit it, but each time the waiters passed us with trays of food, my mouth watered. Everything looked and smelled so tasty. We got our drink orders in and pored over the menu tome.

"Mmmm, pot stickers. And egg rolls. And stuffed wontons sound good," I murmured.

He laughed. "That sounds very . . . deep fried. But delicious. Maybe we need some vegetables or salad or something."

"You're right. Vegetable tempura? Just kidding. Let's do edamame. No salad."

He raised an eyebrow. "No salads today, or like, ever?"

"Ever. I hate them, even the ones with fried chicken or bacon bits on top. Lettuce is no one's favorite food. Or tomato. And combining them together to be the staple of any meal is an offensive culinary travesty."

"I see you have strong feelings about this," he joked.

"A salad is a giant, colorful bowl of disappointment. Well, except for taco salad. Taco salad is fake salad because it has cheese and sour cream on it. It's basically nachos with lettuce confetti."

He laughed. "Oh, man, too bad P.F. Chang's doesn't have nachos."

Grinning, I raised a glass as soon as the server placed our drinks on the table. "To nachos." We toasted and I gulped down wine number one pretty quickly. "Okay, time to be serious for a sec. I want to apologize for two things. One, for snapping at you when you were trying to be nice. And second, for assuming you got this job only because of your connections. Clearly you have spreadsheet skills."

His eyes sparkled under the hanging dome light above our table. "And you forgive me for breaking your mug?"

"Nope." I took the wine out of his hand and took a large sip. "Hey, I like yours better."

Nolan leaned back into his booth seat and laughed. When the waiter came by, we ordered our food. "Do you like beer?" he asked me.

"Nah, I hate it."

"A beer for me then." He glanced at me as he talked with the server. "That way she won't steal that drink, too."

The waiter winked. "I do the same thing with my wife. You two are cute together."

My stomach did that fluttery thing again. "We're work friends," I clarified.

He nodded. "Ah, gotcha. But just so you know, my wife and I were work friends, too." He took away our empty wineglasses and walked away humming an unfamiliar tune.

The food came quickly. I handed over my twenty bucks to Nolan while shrimp lo mein dangled from my mouth. I thought about it, but couldn't bear ordering Korean cuisine there, that's where I drew the line. It was already shameful that I sometimes bought kimchi from Safeway. Getting my Korean food fix at P.F. Chang's would make me a full-blown sellout. I'd need a seventy-five-dollar wager to even consider it.

Conversation flowed easily. I even admitted to Nolan that I googled him when he joined the company. "Why do you have so many elitist photos of you online?"

He coughed into his drink. "Elitist? What the hell?"

"You know, photos of you with all those politicians. All those fancy and exotic places you traveled."

He furrowed his brow. "You mean the ones where I was doing a microfinancing project in Lima and Harare for a non-profit?"

I slowed my wine to small sips. "Uh . . . yeah. And how about those photos where you cropped out that girl?"

His eyebrows drew into a deep V. "I *think* I know what photos you're talking about. She's a friend who is good at taking self-ies with fancy filters. You know, you almost sound a little bit jealous."

"Oh yeah, my photo filter game is pathetic," I cut in, hoping to divert attention from his accusation.

We laughed about the weirdos in the office, especially Asher. I told him about my old advertising jobs, and he told me he had finished his first year of business school at UW but wasn't sure he'd go back next semester.

"There are a lot of shark types in my MBA class. I'm not like them." We hit a dialogue lull when he bit his lip and picked the label off his beer bottle. Something big weighed on his mind.

"Okay, you look terrified. Spill it."

He sighed. "My parents are coming to visit soon, and I have to tell them I don't know if I'm going to go back to school. It's just not the thing for me. But I also don't know what I want to do careerwise. Isn't that dumb? I'm twenty-eight and have no clue what I want to do with my life."

I lifted up my wine and toasted him again. It was all about tipsy toasts that night. "Twenty-eight? You're my age! Well, almost my age. I'm twenty-seven. I assumed by now I'd know what I wanted to be when I grew up too. When does the growing-up part of life end? When do we have to make final life decisions?"

He looked at me like I just told him I believed in Santa Claus. "Really? You look like you know what you want in life. You seem like it, anyway."

I coughed some wine out my nose. "Sorry, I'd never heard that before. Ever."

We both laughed. It felt so good to laugh. This all felt so good. *Thank you, wine number two!*

The restaurant became much noisier when a bus let off dozens of European tourists at the bar. He leaned forward so I could hear him. "My parents stress me out. They're cool in some ways. They work hard and want me to make something of myself. And they talk about money all the time. It's all they think about, and it's kind of embarrassing. It's hard to explain."

My parents embarrassed me all the time and were focused on money too. Well, at least my mom was. She tried to manage their cash flow down to the penny. Contrast this to my dad, who stuck to a "looser" fiscal approach. He bought lawnmowers and golf clubs every other month without telling my mother, and they ended up in screaming matches about their month-end budget. His parents could never top mine on the humiliation scale, though. My parents had everyone else beat. Effortlessly.

He exhaled a sad sigh. "They just, really have strong ideas

on how life should play out. And nine times out of ten, it's not what I want."

Part of me wanted to hug him in consolation, the other half wanted to slap him into taking action. As they say in the sexist world I lived in, *Man up, bro.* Also, I knew quite well now, hugging and/or slapping would be an HR violation. "I think you need to think about whether you should fight harder for what you want."

He nodded. "You make it look so easy."

I coughed out a bitter laugh. *Yeah, so easy.*

"I'm serious. You fight for what you think is right, no matter what. It's amazing." He cracked a smile.

"Well, nine times out of ten, it doesn't work in my favor," I scoffed. "Failure ain't pretty."

"You bounce back, though."

"Right. And by that do you mean I don't take a hint and keep trying, or I'm successful at recuperating from failure?"

He looked me in the eyes. "You don't give up. And your life is what you made of it."

"Well, I'm not the type of person who gets things handed to them on a silver platter." I swept my arm and flicked my hand toward him. "I don't usually make friends with guys like you, no offense."

He cocked his head. "You think we're all that different?"

Hahahahaha. Is this guy for real? I leaned forward on my elbows. "Look, I worked hard to get my job, all by myself. None of this silver spoon shit. I don't have any family in high places." I fell back into my booth seat. "That's why I didn't want your help before. I didn't want to be associated with you because people would think I was getting special treatment just by knowing you." A beat passed. "No offense," I added with a wince.

"I don't understand why you care so much about what other people think," he said, thoughtfully drawing out every word. "It shouldn't matter."

I shot forward. "I feel a lot of pressure at work. If I'm too tough on the team when they mess up, they call me a bossy bitch. When I go easy on them, they take advantage of me. Working late means I have no life, even though guys here do the same thing and no one makes fun of them. Can't people just treat me the same as everyone else? Well, the answer seems to be no."

Taking a sip of wine, I continued. "In my old job, I was way more confident . . . and valued . . . and appreciated. They knew I worked hard and I proved myself over time. Here, I feel second-guessed all the time."

Nolan sighed on my behalf. "You're great at your job and the company needs you. I think you should demand a raise. Your game has such visibility, and whether you like it or not, so do you. I bet they'd do it."

It hadn't even crossed my mind to ask for a raise. It was true: the studio needed me. I was a hard worker and the only female producer at the company since Maggie left. "I like your idea. I'm going to *Sheryl Sandberg* the shit out of this and ask for a raise."

He grinned and rolled up the label of his second beer into a thin tube and put it on the table. He shifted in his seat and our knees touched briefly, sending a jolt of tingling warmth through my body. I hoped it would happen again.

When our waiter came by, I handed her the gift card and my credit card tucked underneath it in case we went over the limit.

My phone buzzed and I glanced at the screen with eyes bleary from drunkenness.

Calendar reminder. Call with China. Thirty minutes.

I looked up to find Nolan trying to get a hot sauce stain off his shirt cuff with spit and water, his thick, wavy hair falling forward. He looked up, his eyes crinkling but his mouth frowning a little.

I joked, "Don't worry, you have hundreds of shirts just like that to replace this one." Ones that fit his body perfectly.

He waggled his eyebrows. "Ohhhh, so you notice what I wear?" Lowering his head, he peered at me through his dark eyelashes. "You know, I actually bought more of them because you said you liked the one I was wearing that time."

Oh my god.

The phone bleeped again. I put it away and looked at him. "I have to run."

Our eyes met. He leaned in more, his warm breath reaching my face. "If you need to go, I get it. Maybe we can do a rain check." Weren't rain checks for half- or fully canceled plans? We had finished our meal and drinks. Was he asking me out?

My heartbeat pulsed hard against my ribs. I wanted him to clarify without having to ask.

But . . . I still had so much work to do. And I had to do it drunk. "I . . . I have to go hop on a call now, I'm sorry." The waiter brought the final bill and we headed out the door. My apartment was closeish to the restaurant, he lived the opposite direction in Capitol Hill, so we ordered separate Liftr cars.

"Did you drive to work?" he asked.

"Yeah, I'm leaving my car there, I'll just walk or take a Liftr tomorrow morning. How about you?"

"I take the bus sometimes, but lately since I work so late I've been renting one of those ebikes to get some exercise."

Outside, we were no match for the relentless rain and the freezing temperatures. Because of some facade construction and inconvenient scaffolding, Nolan and I crammed together side by side under a small portion of the restaurant's awning. He briefly opened his golf umbrella, but with the rampant wind, the precipitation seemed to be attacking from down below rather than from the sky.

As more and more people left the restaurant, Nolan and I found ourselves shuffling our positions as people did in crowded elevators. While the rain fell harder, I took a few steps back under the awning to get more coverage, coming flush against Nolan. His chest pressed against my back, and I leaned into him, shivering, convincing myself it was to stay dry and to get relief from the cold, blustering winds.

His breath was warm behind my ear, near the nape of my neck. My skin prickled as he gently stroked both of my arms, shoulders down to fingertips. His body pushed against mine, his heart beat in quick tempo, same as mine.

I lifted my chin up, tilting my head enough so I could look into Nolan's eyes. With a wry smile, he steadily returned my gaze. My entire body felt airy and weightless, just by being so close to him. Losing my inhibition, I licked my lips, ready to make a move.

A blaring honk jolted me with adrenaline as a black Nissan Sentra with a Liftr sticker pulled up right in front of us. "Melody?" the driver asked through the rolled-down window. My phone buzzed soon after. My call with China was starting in fifteen minutes. Asher texted at the same time: *Don't be late.*

I shoved my phone into my coat pocket and stepped out from under the awning. I turned to face Nolan, and with his gaze fixed on mine, he asked, "Hug?," then opened his arms. Hesitantly, I stepped into him, feeling his lean, muscular chest press against me once again, this time from the front. Head to toe, my body flooded with little tingles. But of course, this blissful moment couldn't go on forever. A brief wave of panic hit hard when I thought to myself, *What if someone from work saw us together? What would they think?* We were just two friends having a casual dinner at P.F. Chang's, where we mostly talked about work. If anyone asked, the heat flushing to my face was from all the drinking. It was no big deal.

"I'll see you tomorrow," I murmured as I pulled away from him and got into my car.

He waved as my Nissan Sentra drove off.

AT HOME, I set up my laptop in bed and began adding my work orders into the project queue for the remote developers. It wasn't an easy task for someone who had three glasses of wine. I checked to see if the China and Poland teams were online and the chat status showed Asher was still active. Damn. He worked through my entire dinner.

My phone buzzed with a message from Nolan. Got home safe. You?

Me too ☺

Tonight was fun.

I didn't know how to reply to that. He could have asked to do it again sometime, but he didn't. So I ignored it for the moment and logged in to my work email to see if any of our overseas tasks had been completed on time.

Forty-four new messages. All of them had the same subject line.

Email number one was short.

Subject: Re: "Hey feminazis! Get off my lawn!"
To: Melody Joo <Melody@seventeenstudios.us>
From: Hungggger <hungggggergames@gmail.com>

Hey China Doll

<dickpic.jpg >

The remaining forty-three emails were just as short, equally disturbing, and one was riddled with spelling typos:

Subject: Re: "Hey feminazis! Get off my lawn!"
To: Melody Joo <Melody@seventeenstudios.us>
From: Christof Nugent <christopherrulezzzz@gmail.com>

Go fetch me some coffee, you supid bitch. You feminists have lied so much and none can believe any words you say these days. The campus rape epidemic, the gender wage gap, all lies. Lies lies lies. Fuck you.

What the fuck was happening? I searched online for "Hey feminazis! Get off my lawn!" and found an article that had been posted at 8 P.M. EST by BetaGank, an online gaming magazine and message board for "serious gamers to come together to bash weak scrubs and noobs." That was actually their tag line, not me making a harsh generalization. It was essentially *Gossip Girl* for hard-core gamer dudes. The article named me as a producer at Seventeen Studios and leaked some basic information about me. My greasy appetizers and wine made their way backward through my digestive tract as I read the article.

HEY FEMINAZIS! GET OFF MY LAWN!
By Anonymous

Our inside source at Seventeen Studios has confirmed that a new title, currently named *Ultimate Apocalypse*, will be released in six months, just in time for the holidays. Seasons Greedys!

It is unclear if this is a console game or a mobile one, but given the launch date we are betting it's mobile. Our source "UltimateDDay" has also confirmed that the game will target FEMALE gamers who want to play shooter games. Apparently feministas now need to have their own special snowflake games catering to their feminine whims. Maybe they'll have in-game clothes to buy and mascara in hidden treasure boxes. Head of production and game creator Melody Joo (pictured here) is a total newcomer to gaming, so we'll see if this game actually launches on time, and if it will suck. We're betting no, and yes. Click here to contact Melody.

I skimmed all my new emails. Thanks to an anonymous informant at Seventeen Studios, freaks and creeps flooded my inbox with lewd comments (including not-suitable-for-work images) and sexist diatribes. Who were they? Where was all this anger coming from? And why go after ME?

I texted Asher to let him know I couldn't make the call.

Not knowing what to do next, I texted the one person who had to be awake.

How would you reply to people if they sent you, hypothetically speaking, dick pictures?

Nolan called me immediately. "Wait, what? Someone is sending you dick pics? Why?"

"Don't worry. Never mind. I figured it out." He stayed on the line with me while I downloaded an app that added googly eyes to any picture. With a few clicks and swipes, Hungggger's dick photo had metamorphosed into a googly-eyed penis masterpiece. I emailed it back to Hungggger with the comment, "China Doll has a sexxxy pic for you." I attached a return receipt and went to the next email to respond.

Proud of myself for coming up with a creative solution while drunk, I told Nolan exactly what I did. "Mel, what the hell are you doing? You shouldn't respond to any kind of harassment. I'm serious! Ignore it all for now, and if it gets bad, we should talk to the police, depending on how fucked up this situation is."

My inbox jumped to fifty emails. After picking a handful of more dick pic ones, I googly-eyeified them and sent them back. Dozens more emails appeared with each inbox refresh, and I couldn't keep up with the volume. Hungggger had responded to my googly-eyed masterwork, venting his discontent with my mockery of his heroic cock. If every time I responded to any of the harassing emails it would turn into a heated escalation, this would quickly become an uncontrollable situation. Plus, HR wouldn't like me sending googly-eyed dick pics from our company email server. I rubbed my temples, trying to think of what to do.

"Mel, I know this will be hard for you, but I think you should get off email and go to sleep. You can deal with this stuff in the morning. The last thing you should do is drunk-email people. You are smart enough not to do that."

He was right. Emailing while drunk was a terrible idea, and my one inebriated decision to googly-eyeify penis pics already turned into an escalation. I could (and should) deal with my work backlog and email harassment in the morning, with a clearer head.

The wine, compounded with weeks of sleep deprivation, helped me fall asleep fast, but I didn't have a restful slumber: I dreamt that all my post office mail had been compromised and flooded with dick pic first class and bulk mail. Restoration Hardware catalogs, Valpak coupon mailers, and voter registration notices, all plastered with penii. Waking up to pee in the middle of the night helped put a stop to my stupid dick pic nightmare. But as the night wore on and I sobered up, it hit me that nothing prevented these terrorizers from just showing up on my doorstep. How bad had this situation become?

CHAPTER ELEVEN

A night of off-and-on dozing and a newly formed hangover didn't put me in the best state of mind to think through what I needed to do next. Who had been leaking proprietary information from inside the company? Who were these assholes who immediately jumped on the hate bandwagon without giving me the benefit of the doubt? And who would go as far as emailing me grotesque porn images, coupled with ignorant commentary disparaging women?

I glanced at the clock on my nightstand. *Crap!* I needed to be in a status meeting in thirty minutes.

As I untangled myself from my bedsheets, my mom texted. *MELODY CALL BACK VERY IMPORTANT1!!!*

Three missed calls from her, and two from my dad. My hands shook as I returned their call. "What's going on? Are you guys all right?" *Please, god, let my mom and dad be okay.*

My mom shouted, "What is happen with you? Someone call our house in the middle of night and asking for you. He say he is secret admirer or something blah blah and want to talk to you. I told him he has wrong house because no way my Melody have any secret admiring boys. He get very angry and curse at me and then hang up."

Those trolling assholes had moved on to harassing my parents. "Mom, are you and Dad okay? If you get any more calls like that, please call the police."

"We be okay. No one usually bother us, so we call you right away. We hope you not ever dating him. That's why we want you to marry nice Korean boy."

Deep breath in, and exhale. "Could you guys just turn your ringer down and let the calls go to voice mail? It's a long story, but a bad person posted some information about me online, and now it's really blowing up." I put the call on speakerphone and logged in to my work email.

My dad jumped on the other line. "Melody? Are you famous now?"

I skimmed my emails quickly on my laptop. Three hundred forty-two messages. "Am I famous? Not really. But I am getting a lot of hate mail and fan mail, so I guess I'm more famous than I was just twenty-four hours ago."

"Okay, call our cellular phone later. We going to IHOP now. They have senior citizen early lunch special. Goodbye!"

I jumped into the shower, lathered and rinsed my hair, loofahed my entire body in ten seconds, and hopped back out, all in under a minute. After patting on powdered foundation and twisting my drippy hair into a clipped bun, I threw on a random assortment of clothing and ran out the door with my laptop bag.

My fifteen-minute meeting alert popped onto my phone screen as I called my Liftr car. I barely had time to think about work with all the shit going on thanks to the BetaGank article.

I got to the office and had only two minutes to spare. Except, there *was* no meeting, because it had been canceled. Ian, the head of Human Resources, and the publicity director all stood in my office, along with a stuffy corporate guy carrying a briefcase. That's when I knew this had all officially turned into a nuclear shitstorm.

IAN CLOSED MY door and motioned for me to sit down, even though everyone else remained standing. I put my bag down on my chair and continued to stand along with the others. This wasn't going to turn into some weird power play where Ian and his cronies would look down at me, literally. No thanks.

Sue, the head of HR, got straight to it. "We have a huge heaping pile of shit on our hands. The PR team got hundreds of negative social media alerts about the *Ultimate Apocalypse* game this morning. What the fuck happened?"

When a bunch of sexist, racist trolls flame your company on a grandiose scale, the head of HR has permission to stop the PC talk behind closed doors.

Joe, former college varsity baseball captain and now publicity director, looked at us pleadingly. "I've never dealt with anything like this before. I used to do social media communications here before I got this job. This is way beyond posting cute memes and aspirational quotes from famous dead people online. It's a real shit-ton of crazy fucking shit and, honestly, I'm way out of my league here."

Everyone looked at Ian, the only executive left to speak. "Well, don't look at me. Yeah, people hate me, sure, but I'm a white dude with serious gaming street cred. They're trying to bring her down, not me." He pointed straight at my face, making it clear he was referring to me.

The briefcase guy said, "Ian, these trolls are trying to bring this whole place down, not just Melody. And you are the leader of this company. As your outside counsel, from my perspective you have two options." He pulled down the knot on his tie to loosen the choke hold. "You can replace Melody with a new producer, but if you picked someone from within this company, the person would likely be male, and you'd see major backlash for that. Or you can keep Melody on the project and stay the course."

What? That was like saying, *You have two choices. You can do the wrong thing, or the logical, right thing.* What the fuck kind of options were these?

"Both options have their risks." He smiled at me reassuringly. "Honestly, I've heard from a few people that she's doing a good job, so pulling her now could be detrimental to the business."

Sue asked, "Do we know who leaked the game info?"

Ian barked, "Sue, it's much more important to deal with this online backlash first. We're in triage mode here."

We heard a knock at the door, and another stodgy corporate guy carrying an old-school briefcase waltzed in. Great, now we had two briefcase guys. "I'm Brian Wallace, a crisis PR consultant. I've been called in by the board to assist with your communications." He shook hands with all the executives.

Crisis-prevention Brian said to me, "Melody, I recommend that you refrain from engaging with any of the comments, accusations, and threats against your company, and at you. To minimize personal harm and unnecessary stress, please also deactivate your personal social media accounts. One wrong move or one misconstrued social post and this could lead to a bigger PR nightmare. Or they might try to hack you. As they say in this business, don't feed the trolls." He repeated, "This bears repeating. Do NOT feed the trolls, no matter what. I'll work with Ian and Joe on issuing a formal company statement that the game will not be canceled. But you all need to decide soon whether we remove Melody or not."

Ian didn't even hesitate. "Let's replace her with someone like Asher. That wouldn't be a problem."

My heart pounded so hard it hurt to breathe. Replace me with Asher, just like that? Was HE the mole? He knew everything about the game launch. He also had motive. That cocky, backstabbing motherfucker.

And where was Asher? I looked over at his desk and saw a half-eaten muffin. He was probably holed up in a conference room, leaking more game info.

Sue chimed in. "Actually, if you remove Melody it would

look really, really bad for our company. No woman would dare apply here and we'd be seen as sexist. The long-term repercussions of this within the industry would be unsurmountable. For months now we've strived to add diversity to our studio community. This would set us back tremendously."

Joe grimaced and paced the room. "PR-wise, I agree, it would be a bad move. Social media is sixty percent women, and women form virtual communities. As soon as word got out about this, you'd be looking at an angry mob of estrogen maniacs who rally for nationwide boycotts of our games and organize large-scale protests outside of our office. It would be a huge nightmare." He threw his hands open wide. "And this might turn superpolitical real fast, with equal opportunity, fair wages, and all that other women stuff."

His dismissive comments couldn't go unchallenged. I couldn't help myself. Executive Joe needed to be called out. "Estrogen maniacs? Women stuff? A mature use of words, Joe."

I scanned Ian's and Joe's faces, trying to detect any humanity. "I'd like to stay on the project and see it to completion. I've met every internal milestone deadline and earned the trust of the team. I respectfully ask that you keep me on as production lead. Also, if you don't, I agree with Joe that this could turn into a media nightmare, making you look like an antifemale company." I didn't say, *Oh, and by the way I would totally sue your asses*, which was what I was thinking.

"Fine." Ian glanced down at his watch. "Joe, we need to send a press statement out ASAP. I'm having a conference call with the board of directors to let them know we're working on defusing this situation. Oh, and Melody? I asked the IT guys to help you sort your inbox so you don't see all the garbage and hate mail. We don't want you to get distracted by all that during crunch time. It'll get forwarded straight to legal for them to deal with legally and criminally."

He looked at his watch again. "Since we're on a tight schedule, we want you to be productive and not spend a single minute sorting through pictures of torsos and hairy balls. Plus, as you said, it would look bad if we replaced you. The risk of crazy female activists beating down our door is a more real threat than some loser teenage asshole trolling you and blowing off steam on some message boards." Damon, the IT guy, appeared at my office doorway and set up email folders on my computer while the discussions continued. Thank goodness the legal team was handling all these emails.

AN HOUR LATER, the PR team released the Official Statement of Seventeen Studios on our website and emailed it to our entire company:

> To our friends in the gaming community:
> Unfortunately, a small group of people have been saying awful things online about our company and our games, games we will continue to release because we won't be bullied into canceling them. They have been

harassing one of our female employees, and they have been tarnishing our reputation as gamers with their unacceptable behavior.

Gaming should be a fun experience, both positive and uplifting for everyone, whether you're a gaming newbie or a veteran. We aren't trying to quash freedom of speech. We just ask that everyone try to be respectful.

Remember, there is another person on the receiving end of your communications. They're part of your community.

(And next is where Ian must've veered off-script . . .)

You don't shit where you eat.
Seventeen Studios stands against hate and harassment.
Thank you,
Ian MacKenzie and Melanie Joo

Damn it. He didn't even get my name right.

Within minutes of sending out the press release, email responses poured in from female employees at our company, nearly twenty total, letting me know they stood by me in solidarity. Knowing I had allies at work supporting me lifted my spirits and helped keep me focused on my work. I wasn't in this alone.

Because my launch date didn't magically get pushed out due

to the BetaGank incident, I still needed to get a ton of work done that day. I messaged one of the lead developers, who was also one of Asher's buddies, to see why Asher hadn't shown up at work yet. He wrote back, *Out sick brah, says he's gonna work from home.* Right. He's "sick." More like he was too terrified to come into work and deal with the spiraling vortex of racist and sexist shit he'd instigated with his BetaGank leak.

Against Ian's wishes, I peeked into the "DO NOT READ: HARASSMENT" temporary folder Damon had created in my inbox. The messages directed to this folder would auto-send to legal after five minutes. There were sixty-two new messages in the five-minute harassment repository.

> @nastymasta82 *Us REAL gamers are sick and tired of you stupid feminists ruining everything. Not everything is sexist. Attention whore*

> @BigSky22 *Feminism has taken over our society and people like you want to punish men for just being men. You want more girls in games? More games should have neh-kid girls characters*

> @fellasquad *It's pretty clear to me that this Melody person got special treatment just for having a vagina. Affirmative action at its worst. Dumb bitches*

> @GoBackToIndia *Go back to China. Never mind. Just die*

Some idiots had sent pictures of other random Asian women (named Melody Joong, Melody Jung, and Melody Joon), mistaking them for me. Yeah, I wasn't supposed to read those messages during work hours, but shit, I couldn't help it. That got me worked up, with people calling me a bitch, making fun of my ethnicity, and calling me an attention whore. Me? Had they ever met Jane? They called me stupid, too, which really struck a nerve. Those assholes knew nothing about me. And no one who knew me would ever call me stupid. You know who was stupid? Someone who would blindly pass judgment on another person they didn't know at all. I was not stupid. I could out-calculus any one of those troll motherfuckers. Was I clumsy? Yes. Awkward? Absolutely. Did I do stupid things sometimes? Um, yeah. But that didn't make me stupid.

Messages had also escalated in severity: I saw death and sexual assault threats, and hundreds of requests for nude pictures and graphic sexual propositions. My stomach knotted as I read these vile words. How could people make snap judgments about me based on tidbits of information they gleaned from the internet? It was like racial profiling with uninformed stereotyping and armchair psychoanalyzing. This practice always led to misinformed conclusions, and potentially dangerous results.

I wished this was all just a bad dream, but it was very real. My full-body numbness prevented me from ugly crying in my office.

Wild-eyed, jittery publicist Joe slammed my door open just as I finished my email skimming. Sue trailed a few steps behind him. Since that morning he looked like he'd walked into the eye of a tornado and aged five years.

"Hi. Sue and I need you to look over these new rules of engagement as soon as possible, drafted by Ian, our lawyer, and a few members of the board." He paced around while I read.

Per these new rules, I was not allowed to talk to the media about the *Ultimate Apocalypse* game ("hereby in this document referred to also as 'UA'"—ugh) or about the company itself. This included but was not limited to: information about the people, the culture, and the male-female ratio. I couldn't respond to any of the email or social media harassment; this was being handled by our legal and PR team. Playing any online games was prohibited, in case someone figured out my gamertag. And last, I needed to refrain from any public discussion about these ongoing developments. There was a chance we may need to file criminal charges if this ballooned even bigger, and the fewer people involved, the better.

Joe said, "I am so sorry about everything. We're trying to figure out how to handle this on the fly. This is uncharted territory. And all these restrictions, the dos and don'ts, are overwhelming. It's like drinking from a fire hose, I'm sure."

Not quite accurate. It was more like I was trying to drink from a fire hose that was actually on fire, while spraying out fire.

And then, just as I hit an ultimate low point in my life, Jane texted me.

I booked a wedding dress appointment at six bridal boutiques this Sat. I'll need you to tell me if I look amazing or not. Then we need to look at shoes. Btw I'm going to start on the Whole 30 diet thing tomorrow. Maybe you should too?

I was, without a doubt now, so clearly and utterly fucked.

And to make my utterly fucked state even more fucked, Nolan, Mr. Worst Timing Ever, stopped by my office just before I was leaving for the day. Today he had on a brown-and-black-checked shirt, not my favorite on him, but still hugged his body nicely. "You doing okay?"

I nodded. Barely okay.

"Um, do you want the bad news, or even worse news?"

Sighing hard, I melted into a blob in my chair. "I don't care. You pick."

"Ian imported the graphs you sent him and accidentally broke all the formulas."

Okay, that was bad, but that wasn't horrible.

"He also changed some of our retail pricing for the holidays, so some of our assumptions need to be updated and accounted for in the new graphs."

I nodded slowly. "You mean, the graphs with the broken formulas."

"Yeah."

Fuck fuck fuck fuck fuck.

I pointed at Asher's empty chair and beckoned Nolan to bring it over. He sat and wheeled over to me. Here we were again, right next to each other, me breathing in his intoxicating Nolan scent, faintly woodsy with a top note of fancy hotel soap. He leaned over my laptop to pull up Ian's files from the hard drives, his muscular arms distracting me from all that had happened in the last twenty-four hours. Instead of staring at the line graphs, my gaze traveled down his body, craving for him to touch me again.

A sense of unease swept through me as I remembered Asher, sitting over at his desk, reciting excerpts from that stupid handbook. How smug he looked when he thumbed through the pages, spouting off all the reasons why I couldn't be thinking about Nolan this way. And Asher had been right: I was a supervisor, and Nolan was an intern.

Jumping to my feet, I paced back and forth. This was getting dangerously close to overstepping boundaries. Companies turned a blind eye to some people breaking the rules, but I wasn't one of them.

"You keep doing that and you'll wear a path through that carpet," Nolan joked. He continued to input numbers into the spreadsheet while I paced to and fro in the background. After a half hour passed, Nolan squinted at the monitor and said nonchalantly, "I think I'm finished. Want to grab a bite to eat?" He saved the file and uploaded it to the shared drive.

Worst-case scenario, this was one of those misconduct simulation scenarios in the making. No thanks, I couldn't afford

CHAPTER TWELVE

For the first time ever, I got the prime parking spot directly in front of my apartment garage elevator, which opened immediately as soon as I pressed the button. Could the universe be signaling to me that my life wasn't all gloom and doom? I unlocked my door and exhaled quietly, comforted by my messy, lived-in apartment, with its familiar smell of Bounce dryer sheets and old coffee grounds. Home at last.

Firing up my laptop before dinnertime turned out to be a terrible idea. Out of morbid curiosity I searched my name online and HOLY HELL. My appetite disappeared, boom, just like that.

I found hundreds, maybe even thousands of disparaging messages and comments about me. A chunk of them were about the shittiness of the *Ultimate Apocalypse* game concept, and the widespread hatred of it, but most of the posts and comments were just personal attacks on me. The "fucking feminazi." The "stuck-up asshat ho." And my favorite, from @alfredfem: "cunty fuckign slut." @alfredfem needed to spellcheck that shit before he put it online. Also, was 'cunty' even a word? And, me . . . a slut? That word was so contemptuous, and if any of these people actually knew me, they'd get why that was so fucking ridiculous to say. I had NO sexual game. Those fucking ignorant, vocal assholes.

Chewing my nails was a nasty habit I had stopped in high school and resurrected again during my current life crisis. My life derailed overnight, without any warning, and I couldn't manage to get it back on track. It had already really taken a toll on my mental health and my body. Skipping lunch that afternoon, I needed more nourishment than a bowl of cereal from breakfast. I poured myself a wine, grabbed some baby carrots from the fridge, and nuked a Trader Joe's corn dog. It felt like a corn-dog kind of day. Quite possibly a two-or-three-corn-dog kind of day. All these racist, sexist, homophobic messages and comments hit me where it tore at my soul and I needed some hot-dog-wrapped-in-cornbread sustenance to shoulder this torment.

While settling into my meal, Ian sent an email to Joe, Sue, and me at 8:53 P.M. "Joe, please draft a response to the online petition calling for action to fire Melody and boycott of Seventeen Studios. Let's meet 6 A.M. tomorrow to discuss.—I.M."

What online petition? I searched for "Melody Joo petition" online and fucking hell, a crowdsourced document with hundreds of signatures was the first search result, demanding my removal from *Ultimate Apocalypse*, as my involvement in game production caused "tangible detriment to the entire gaming industry." The consequences according to the ranting petition, if the request was not met, would be a worldwide boycott of my game when it launched.

Anti-Melody online discussions were everywhere and I couldn't stop reading all the angry and bitter commentary surrounding my femaleness. These misogynists were all over the globe, spewing vulgarities toward me at all hours of the day. Some cloaked their hate with anti-left-wing feminist arguments, hearkening back to the good old days when games were all about men, for men. This seemed to be about the categorical hatred of women by certain men, and these jerks finding an outlet to vocalize their opinion. I group-messaged with Candace and Jane, to vent.

Jane: *WTF is wrong with everyone? Why all the hate?*

Candace: *Yeah, WTF???*

Jane: *Seriously! I took tons of art history classes in college (4.0 GPA!) and studied Western classic art, and men used to CELEBRATE women in their artwork. Even ugly women. Remember Leonardo's Mona Lisa? She was like a four out of ten on a bombshell meter.*

Me: *That's a funny way to describe the Mona Lisa.*

Candace: *Raphael's Sistine Madonna, also celebrated. She was pretty though.*

Jane: *I did a sr. thesis on Monet. Women in the Garden.*
Very pro female. And Matisse's Woman w/a Hat. The
Dance. All pro XX chromosomes!

Me: *If angry trolls got to rename these masterpieces:*
Bitches in the Garden. Feminazi with Hat. Nekked
Hos Dancing.

Jane's point was on point, though. Women used to be depicted positively in art. Centuries ago, women in distinguished works of art had been portrayed with reverence and tastefulness, even those presenting nude female subjects. Well, except for Picasso. He created some pretty jacked-up, abstract paintings featuring women. But Picasso didn't create portraits of women with glistening DDD breasts and raunchy attire, à la the game industry.

After venting to Jane and Candace for a few more minutes, I got back to revising production timelines and taking notes from one of the game production books Kat had lent me.

A buzz from Candace's text shook me awake. *Maybe you should quit. I want you to be safe. It's gotten really bad.* I'd fallen asleep on my new laptop keyboard. I felt the side of my face: my fingers traced the key imprints across my left cheek. Thank god my pool of drool on the keyboard didn't short out my computer.

It was the safest way out of this, quitting. The controversy would die down if I threw up my hands and yelled "You win!"

But then, well, the bad guys would win. And bad guys should never win.

I wrote back. *This game might bomb, but I'm not quitting. I'm staying and fighting these bullies. And my game is going to launch on time, damn it. And it will be profitable. I'm going to make this happen because I'm not standing down!*

I'd invested so much time already into it. I couldn't back out now.

Candace wrote back. *100% here for it . . . I have no doubt.*

I wished I could say the same.

At 6:00 a.m. sharp, I met the others in Ian's office. Everyone looked so haggard, including me. More nights with troubled sleep, tossing and turning with worry. I tried to add some early-morning humor. "What, no catered breakfast?" Joe and Sue looked up at me with dead eyes. *Note to self: no breakfast jokes to add levity at 6 a.m.*

Ian, on the other hand, snorted. "If you can get us out of this mess, I'll pay for your catered breakfasts for a whole year." A pretty tempting offer. Too bad I had no idea how to make this problem go away.

A shadow moved outside of Ian's office, triggering all the automatic lights in the executive hallway. Asher, in the office at 6:10 a.m. with a goddamned Starbucks again. I'd need to confront him later about his role in this whole fucking fiasco. But now I needed to focus on the crisis at hand: the online petition.

Joe said, "Ian and I consulted our legal team. We could go out with another official statement against the petition, but sending another one out so soon after the previous one would look incompetent from a PR standpoint. I think we could post a statement on our website, but not necessarily blast it out in any of the gaming outlets."

Ian furrowed his brow. "That seems sensible." He added, "This type of controversy has never happened to me before. I never thought the gaming community would come after me like this. The game community loves me."

Sue chimed in. "Well, to be frank, it's because you're a man that you've never dealt with this before. How many other female production leads did you have at your last company?"

He struck *The Thinker* statue pose. "None. So let's suppose you're right and it's all about bashing women. Isn't this game launch a no-win situation? Aren't we going to fail because no one will buy this game?"

BANG! BANG! BANG! BANG!

The loud, rapid-fire knocking made my heart stop. Kat threw the door open and almost knocked Joe's coffee mug out of his hand. "Sorry I'm late. My kid projectile vomited Cheerios all over the kitchen and I had to get an emergency babysitter." She met my stunned stare and waved at me. I wasn't expecting Kat to be here. What a relief. A familiar, trustworthy face.

Joe said, "I asked Kat to join us for three reasons. One, she is a core team member of the *Ultimate Apocalypse* project and is integral to its success. Second, there's a leak at this company so I want to keep our circle of trust to just us. Kat knows a lot of people here and might be able to help HR home in on the culprit. And third, she's a chick. I mean . . . a woman. Er . . . female? And she's been in the gaming industry for a long time. We could use her advice and street cred to aid in digging us out of our hole." I scanned the room for any dissent. Nope. None. Even Ian nodded in agreement. If I went down in flames, it wasn't just my career that would be destroyed. Seventeen Studios and Ian MacKenzie would go down too. Ian's life and mine were intricately intertwined. He had all the incentive in the world to make this situation better.

Ian cleared his throat. "Okay, can we focus here and get back to my question? Isn't this game inevitably going to fail, with all this bad press?"

This was my chance to jump in. "Well, I worked in advertising for a few years, and what I do know is that this game has gotten a ton of buzz in a short period of time. It's gone viral. There have been over five thousand mentions of the *Ultimate Apocalypse* game in the last week, most within the past two days. I say we take advantage of this."

Everyone asked me in unison, "How?"

"I don't have a ton of ideas right now, but with a proper brainstorm, I bet we could get more. The first thing we need to do is to collect newsletter sign-ups on our company website and create a game website to allow people to sign up for a newsletter there, too. We can send exclusive updates, announcements, and insider scoops to all the subscribers. Even if people hate the game, and they hate me, they might subscribe just to share the intel, so they seem 'in the know,' and they'll still buy the game just to play it and complain about it."

Kat raised her eyebrows. "Hmm, this is something we've never done before. It's a good idea. Remember, there are also a ton of nonhater people who will want to buy the game to support women in gaming too."

I chimed in. "Yeah, this morning on my drive in I was trying to think of ways to turn this situation around. Make lemonade out of lemons. Polish a turd. You know."

All eyes swooped over to Ian, who had gotten up to stride in a loop around his office. I had nothing more to add. Neither did Kat. We waited for his verdict on the newsletter idea.

Ian stared at me, and then at Joe. "The marketing team's pretty stretched as it is. But hold on."

He picked up the phone receiver and punched a four-digit extension. "Can you come by my office?" A beat. "Now, please."

Within seconds, Nolan burst through the doorway, panting heavily. Trying to smooth out the untucked gray-checked shirt he wore the other day, he asked Ian, "What's so urgent?"

"Nolan, I need you to set up a marketing newsletter, and get a game website spun up this week. Drop everything you're doing."

My face fell instantly at Ian's suggestion, just as Nolan sent me an excited look. There was no way he misinterpreted my deep frown of disappointment. But I had good reason: Nolan had zero marketing experience outside of his MBA coursework.

Damn it, why'd they assign my marketing idea to an intern? I steadied my breathing, pushing down the anger rising within my chest.

Nolan glanced away from me and met Ian's authoritarian stare. "But you asked me to clean up all the PowerPoint slides for the board presentation."

Ian let out a huge exasperated sigh, one that could fill up an entire balloon in one blow. "I'm asking you to pivot."

"Pivot?" Nolan repeated. "But isn't the board presentation really important?"

"Yes, but shift gears." Ian looked at Joe. "Try to reschedule the board meeting. It's probably too late but there's too much negative shit happening and I can't get ahead of it." His gaze swept the room like a searchlight. "You guys can all go. Let's meet again tomorrow, same time." He clapped and rubbed his hands together. "Oh, wait, before all of you leave, I had a cool idea for you guys this morning! I was thinking, maybe we should change the game completely, kind of a rebranding? Like, instead of strippers ridding the world of apocalyptic threats, maybe we make this a first-person shooter game that's called *Zombies or Hobos?* The player would have to determine if it's a hobo or a zombie before they shoot. It adds some strategy to the game. What do you think? It's a little left field, I know."

When no one responded other than offering him looks of surprise and horror, he asked, "Bad idea?"

Joe the PR guy, Kat, and I shouted in unison, *"Bad idea!"*

Ian looked at Nolan, who nodded silently.

"You'd have a lot of homeless advocacy groups go after you with pitchforks," Kat explained. "And that's the last thing you need right now. Oh, and in general it's a pretty fucked-up idea. Shooting humans. Some of those guys are vets, you know."

Ian nodded. "I suppose you're right."

Nolan trailed Ian out the door, hanging back to talk to me before exiting. "Way to have my back in there, Mel," he said, with resentment seeping into his voice.

I crossed my arms. "Well, look at it from my perspective. You don't have any marketing experience, and you're now leading two big marketing initiatives."

He shook his head. "You dismissed me because you thought I couldn't do something just because I've never done it before. Isn't that what you're always complaining about? People second-guessing you?" His accusation hit me like a wallop to the face.

Before I could explain myself, he was already gone.

Later, I found Nolan in the kitchen, pouring himself a coffee. "Don't worry, I brought this mug from home. I didn't steal it from anyone."

Ouch.

I was terrible at apologies, but now was the time to try to get better at them. "I'm a hypocrite. You were right. I shouldn't have dismissed you like that. You're smart and you're good at everything I've seen you do here. I'm sorry." For some reason, I couldn't just leave it at that. A simple, straightforward mea culpa. "But don't fuck up the marketing stuff, please." I meant it as a joke, but his face read *not funny* loud and clear.

He shrugged. "Fine."

I expected him to say more. When he shoved his hands into his pockets and said nothing else, it was his signal we were done. The tightness remained in my chest, and the apology I offered him didn't relieve any of that pressure. And it was all my fault.

Across the hall, Kat motioned for me to come over to her office. "For a gaming noob, you've managed to cause quite an epic shitstorm. You've even made that poor intern work overtime."

"I know, I know." I sighed. "What a mess. I didn't want any of this to happen."

She laughed. "People who cause epic shitstorms never, ever do."

The truest words I'd ever heard.

CHAPTER THIRTEEN

Asher's greenish-yellowish skin pallor scared me into examining the light fixtures in our shared office. Either the overhead fluorescents were so jacked up that they cast a pukey hue only on Asher's side of the office or the lights were in working order and he looked like total vomitus shit.

"Asher? Do you still need another sick day? I'd rather you go home than breathe in your contaminated oxygen."

He lifted his eyes from his laptop screen. If they narrowed any farther, they'd be closed. "I took a sick day yesterday. I don't have any more PTO time, so I need to be here today, otherwise I'd need to take unpaid leave. But thanks for your concern."

I booked a conference room for the day to get away from Asher's germy air, because really, could I afford to get sick during this crisis, during this production crunch time? My essentials for a full day of conference room camping included a laptop, notebook, pen, cell phone, and water bottle.

Asher glanced up again, and this time I detected a half-relieved and half-smug look on his face. Before I left for the day we needed to talk about a few important things.

"So, Asher, I'm leaving now, but before I go I need to ask you something. Forgive my bluntness, but did you leak that game info to BetaGank?"

"Me?" He looked neither surprised nor guilty. He just looked feverishly sick. Goddamn pukey poker face, masking all emotions.

"Yes, you." I needed to know if he leaked the news of my game to BetaGank and left me out to hang.

"You want the truth?" He took his hands off his keyboard and put them in his lap. "I was glad to see that info get leaked. Because I didn't think you deserved that job. I'd been here way longer than you and they didn't even consider me for the lead production position. And you waltzed in here and got to work on a big title. Fuck the board of directors. Yeah, the fact that BetaGank called you out made me happy. But don't look at me when you're looking for someone to blame. It wasn't me."

His voice softened a little. "Honestly, I didn't expect such a fucking shitstorm to come of it, though. It's all pretty fucked up right now."

He propped his elbows on his desk and placed his chin on his interlocked fingers, like a pedestal. His open body language made me believe he was telling the truth. But I couldn't read him. Could I trust Asher? If he was being truthful and he didn't leak the insider information, then who did?

I chose my next words carefully. "Thanks for being so candid. I'm sorry you felt that way about my involvement in production. I was the creator of the game, though, remember that? I'm taking my idea to completion, it's as simple as that. There wasn't any plan to steal a lead production job from underneath you, just so you know. It just sorta . . . happened. But I'm a quick learner and a damn good project manager." He stayed in his pedestal position, so I went on. "I know we got off on the wrong foot. And by that, I mean we just hate each other. I'll go ahead and say it."

He sniggered. "Yeah, I guess the feeling is mutual."

"Well, the good news is we definitely have something in common. Our mutual dislike." He and I laughed. "I need your help, though, Asher. We need this game to be a success. The company does for sure, and Kat and I have a lot at stake here. Can I please count on you?"

Could flat-out asking for his support backfire on me? With zero leverage, I couldn't even give him a freebie sick day. This all hinged on whether he would be okay with doing the right thing for the sake of doing the right thing. I'd be willing to set aside our differences if we could work this out.

He snorted out his nose. Was that a sarcastic snort? Goddamn Asher poker face.

Then, he sighed deeply. "Look, I get it. And as much as we can't stand each other, I don't want this game to fail because a bunch of misogynistic assholes brought it down for the wrong reasons. I have twin sisters who are seniors in high school, and well, all that loathing these fuckers are spewing out online for the entire world to see isn't okay. So count me in on your crusade. But with some conditions. I want to be the game spokesperson and handle the media interviews. I think you'd be bad at that."

He was right. The second I flubbed up an interview, the trolls would skewer me for it. And if Asher could take that responsibility from me, no problem.

He added, "AND . . . you need to convince Jane and Sean not to make us dance together at their wedding. Because I hate dancing, and it would just be weird, us twirling around with fake smiles on our faces when we can barely stand each other."

Yes. He was right about that, too. Another good idea.

"I'll do my best. I'll even give you a sort-of sick day today. Just work from home, and if anyone looks for you, I'll tell them you looked like you were dying. Sound good?"

He gave me a weak smile, and his puke-colored face lit up as much as it could. He took only a nanosecond to undock his laptop, shove it into his backpack, and rush out the door. His chair spun for a solid ten seconds after he ran out the door. I went to the conference room anyway so I wouldn't inhale more of his germs.

I'd just made a deal with a demi-devil. *You're welcome, bro.*

As I plowed through my email backlog, a new email alert from Nolan came through. Instead of a friendly hello, it was an email about the newsletter and website.

Hello Melody,

I've attached the rollout plans for the e-newsletter
and *Ultimate Apocalypse* game website. Please let me
know if you have any questions or concerns.

Regards,

Nolan

Ouch. Each formal and distant word, hard punches in the gut.

I opened the attachment. There were timelines with deliverables and dates, as well as a few gorgeous design comps. I'd never
seen a preliminary project plan like this before, so organized and
logical. What a fool I was to think he couldn't do it.

I replied back via email. "Nolan, this is absolutely perfect.
Thank you." I looked up at the ceiling. *Please, Nolan, I've been
an idiot for second-guessing you. Forgive me.*

THE NEXT DAY just before lunchtime, Kat popped her head into
my office. "Oh, good, you're here. We need to go to the lunchroom. We're already late."

"What are you talking about?"

"The email this morning from HR. Today is Gaming
Women Appreciation Day."

Dang it. An email I hadn't gotten to yet.

She continued. "It seems kinda bullshitty to me, honestly.
It's a new industry annual thing now, where the women who

work in gaming are given appreciation for . . . being women? That sounds weird now that I said that out loud. But they have free food downstairs, so let's go check it out."

The building's ground-floor event space had been converted into a fashion runway, with loud dance music playing from a tablet hooked up to some subwoofer speakers in the corner of the room. The lights dimmed, the music lowered, and then Ian appeared on the stage with a microphone. I scanned the room for Nolan but couldn't find him. I pulled out my phone and texted him. *You're missing your women inclusivity lunch.*

Instantly, he replied.

> *Oh God, that's all Ian, not me. I'm done with being inclusive.*
> *Err, I mean, done being an inclusivity intern.*
> *Chained to my desk, more forecasts due tomorrow for the finance team ☹ Was here till midnight and back in the office early. Enjoy your womanhood!*

A wide smile spread across my face. Maybe I'd stop by his desk later to say hi.

"Ladies of Seventeen Studios, thank you so much for everything you do. We hope you enjoy the women-in-gaming performance, plus the free food and fem-friendly festivities!"

The music cranked back up as Ian hopped off the platform. Then the "show" started.

A parade of women dressed as female characters from all different game franchises sauntered down the runway. Male employees hooted and hollered as the performance went on, drowning the music out. The Lara Croft model looked exactly like the character in the game but had a slightly rounder face and a slighter build. Then, after Lara's appearance, the show basically went from PG-13 to rated R, and possibly X. The procession of heroines went from suggestively clad, to partially clad, to so nearly nude I had to peek at them through my fingers. They posed onstage, bending over and arching their backs, making Victoria's Secret catalogs look rated G.

A chain mail bikini-clad woman with spiked heel boots and a gun holster belt ended the fashion show with a meek announcement. "Please visit the activity stations behind the stage. Thank you, fellow female warriors, for everything you do!"

Kat rolled her eyes. "I have nothing in common with that woman. Let's grab some free lunch and get the hell out of here."

Taking food and fleeing back to my desk would have been the right thing to do. Instead, I walked over to the activity zones and was then accosted by Bridget, the studio's HR internal communications assistant. She sent out companywide emails about "Food Truck Wednesdays," benefit changes, and parking garage tow notices.

"Hiiiiiiiii!" She pronounced it *hah-eeeeeeeeee*. "We're doing a company blog post about this event. Can you tell me what's the best part about being a woman in gaming?"

She had her notebook and pen ready to take notes.

"Hmmm, what an interesting question. What did everyone else say?"

"You're the first person I'm interviewing." *Lucky me.* Bridget looked at me with her giant anime-like eyes. "And you're the only one I could find who didn't grab food and run." Awww, poor Bridget. I threw her a bone by answering some of her questions.

"Well, the best thing about working at Seventeen Studios for me is that because there are so few women, the ladies' restrooms are always empty." She wrote this down, so I continued down the restroom theme. "Related to this, the bathroom stalls are never out of order because there isn't a lot of toilet usage compared to the men's restroom, which always seems to have Out of Order signs posted on the door. Oh! There's also always toilet paper and toilet seat covers. Same reason. Less throughput."

"Any other good things about being a female in gaming?"

There had to be something else besides empty bathroom stalls. "Dudes don't really drink tea. At least not in our office. So there's plenty of tea supply in the kitchen."

"Anything else?" She didn't write the tea thing down.

"When there are parties, no one drinks the rosé or sparkling wine except for me. So those extra bottles usually come home with me afterward. I have, like, three bottles of bubbly in my fridge at all times."

She waited for me to say more. I shrugged.

"Okeeee, thank you so much, Melody. Byeeeeeeee!" *Baheeeeeeeee, Bridge!*

As I passed the fem-friendly cooking station, a friendly Martha Stewart clone with an apron called out to me, "Sweetie, would you like to learn how to make a low-carb, high-protein, gluten-free casserole?"

Um no.

Not ever.

I moved past the jam-packed "Edible Flower Arrangements 101" area and ended up at the fem-powering sewing corner, where attendees could learn how to make a throw pillow. I saw Ian with a plate of food, being interviewed by Bridget. I about-faced and hoped he didn't see me.

"Hold on a sec," Ian said. "Melody, come over here!"

Goddamnit.

"Oh, hey there. Happy Women's Appreciation Day, Ian." I raised up my hand and gave him a little wave. And a little forced smile.

Ian lifted his glass to cheers me. "Times are changing, ladies! I want you to know from this point forward, I'm your double X chromosome advocate, you got that?"

I nodded. "Does this mean you'll be restocking the bathrooms with tampon machines that don't charge a quarter?"

Bridget giggled.

Ian lowered his drink. "Melody, I want you to know I hear you, and your female perspective is always appreciated at this company." But then he shook his head no.

Glancing over at another group of executives nearby, he

pointed at them and walked away from Bridget and me without saying goodbye, essentially telling us to our faces that he was ghosting us. I said goodbye to Bridget, too, and pushed through the slow-moving crowd.

Near the exit, I stopped at the airbrush T-shirt area. I chose my light pink plain tee (the only color available) and carefully stenciled and airbrushed PIES B4 GUYS, a parody of the novelty shirt that Asher sometimes wore under his plaid button-down that read = RIGHTS FOR BROS AND HOS. I added cherry pie kawaii art to my shirt to complete the look.

Kat walked over with a plate full of assorted sandwiches. "This whole pro-female event had to have been planned by a guy, right? What woman in her right mind would have put something like this together?" She lowered her voice. "I hope it wasn't Mr. Intern."

My cheeks burned hot. "Nah, he's doing finance stuff now."

She rolled her eyes so far back I thought they'd get stuck in a perma-roll position. She continued her rant. "Sponsored by the morale committee that has Booze Day Tuesday, and then Thirsty Thursdays and Beer Pong Fridays back to back, and the company that has all its conference rooms named after white male science-fiction and fantasy guys."

"All hail the unescapable bro culture at Seventeen Studios!" I took a roast beef sandwich off her plate, saluted her with it, and took a bite.

Ian came up behind me and clamped his hand firmly on

my shoulder, making me flinch. "Enjoy your day, Melody. Kat. This is something that no other game company has done. We're showing how much we appreciate women here."

I motioned that I had food in my mouth, faking excessive chewing just to get out of speaking with him. He nodded and moved on to appreciating the next female victim.

Kat frowned. "You know, there are almost as many female gamers as guy gamers now. I really wish more women worked here."

I sighed heavily, and we walked out the door together.

The actress in the string chain mail bikini handed me a stack of free games and said, "Thank you from Seventeen Studios for being a woman in gaming." She shouted "Nice shirt!" as I made my way back to my desk, wearing my oversize airbrushed pie tee over my work clothes.

The stack of games she handed me featured all the women they'd showcased onstage. And the game on the very top of the pile?

Kaizen Five.

AFTER A QUICK stop in the kitchen for coffee, I walked by Nolan's desk to find him pacing around in his tiny work space while bellowing on the phone. He had on a short-sleeved, collared black shirt. What the heck?

"You said a couple of weeks!"

Pause.

"No, Mom, I heard you right. I even put it in my calendar the day you told me."

Pause.

"Yes, it's problematic because I work. And I took the wrong week off. And I'll be in New York then, because I THOUGHT YOU WERE COMING IN TWO WEEKS." He noticed me standing there and I saluted him with my "World's Best Grandma" mug. He smiled weakly.

"Well, don't worry about that now. I'll cancel my trip, or maybe you can just get a hotel and borrow my car or something if I can't get a refund."

He muted his phone. "My parents are coming soon. Sorry. I'm just annoyed because I might not be in town while they're here!" He closed his eyes and a sigh escaped him. "Did you read my email? I'll stop by later."

"Yeah, sure."

He held a finger up. "No, please don't fly to New York to meet me there, I'm going to a bachelor party." He whispered to me, "I'll catch you later."

Turned out that Nolan's crazy relationship with his parents rivaled mine. Watching his situation spiral reminded me to call my parents when I got back to my office. It had been a while. Mom answered on the second ring.

"Hi, Mom."

"Melody? Where are you?" I really hated it when she asked that. Did it really matter where I was?

I sighed. "I'm at work."

"Why you call?" Her raised voice made me even wonder why I bothered to call, ever.

"I wanted to check in and see how things were going. Were you busy or something? And why do I sound echoey?"

"You on speakerphone. I am making kimchi and my hand have hot pepper and garlic and shrimp paste. We have church picnic next week and I making kimchi for everybody."

"Wow, are you making it in the sink? Where do you have enough room for all that cabbage?"

"I make it in bathtub."

"You're marinating the kimchi in your bathtub?"

"No, *michyeosseo*!" She let out an exasperated sigh.

Michyeosseo. "Foolish." She was making kimchi in a bathtub, and I was somehow the crazy one.

She explained, "I making kimchi in baby bathtub."

What?! "You bought a baby bathtub for this?"

Another sigh. "You need to try listen! I find your old baby bathtub in closet and I clean and wash it. It is perfect size for making kimchi."

I didn't want to continue this discussion about making kimchi in a makeshift basin that I most certainly had pooped in as an infant twenty-six years ago. Who was the foolish one now?

"Anyway, I called to check in and make sure you weren't getting any more weird calls from online stalkers."

My dad shouted, "We are fine, no problem."

I sighed with relief. "Oh, that's good to hear!"

"You don't sound good. Like you have froggy voice. You okay?" my mom asked.

I hesitated. "I'm okay."

"You sound bad," Mom said.

A hushed Korean conversation took place between my parents. They'd gotten better at putting their hand over the phone receiver. My dad shouted into the phone, "Okay, Melody, we decide we coming to visit. You sounding terrible."

Oh, hell no. "It's okay, Dad. You don't have to come. I'm so busy with work. If you come another time, maybe after my game launches, I'll have more time for a visit."

My dad huffed, "No, we go there to make sure you eating."

Mom added, "But not too much or you get too fat."

A meeting reminder chimed on my computer. "Don't worry about it, I'm eating. I need to go now. Important meeting. But glad to know that you guys aren't still getting harassed."

"No one call us anymore for you. Don't worry for us," Dad assured me.

"Good. Don't worry about me, either."

THE BOARD MEETING recap was excruciatingly dull. Ian had advised us to not multitask just in case some board members would be videoconferencing in, and he didn't want anyone looking disengaged. Yawning, I tried to keep my eyes open while the finance team flipped through dozens of pie charts and line graphs.

Ding!

Five minutes later. *Ding!*

I snuck my phone out of my pocket and read the messages.

> *We hold plane ticket for trip to Seattle, we want to buy.*
> *Nashville to Seattle nonstop!*

> *Okay we not hear from you so we go ahead and buy. No*
> *refund ticket. Can you find us hotel if you can't fit us?*

Shit. Mom and Dad were coming to visit.

I glanced up and saw Nolan looking straight at me from across the aisle. He turned beet red but didn't break his stare. He mouthed, *What's wrong?*

Shaking my head, I mouthed back, *My parents*, and made a choking gesture on my neck.

He laughed.

"Are those our slides up there?" I whispered, pointing at the presentation.

He nodded. Then made the choking gesture.

Stifling a giggle, I tucked my hair behind my ears and went back to watching the presentation, staring intently at the financial projections, wondering if Nolan had a girlfriend here or back home.

"I have to ask, why are you wearing that shirt?" I whispered.

He leaned toward me. "You like it?"

I shrugged. It was a nice, black button-down. It fit him. But it wasn't very Nolan. I'd grown fond of his signature workwear. The shirts that he bought because he thought I liked them.

"I wore black because if something went wrong today, it would be my funeral. And I was mad at you so I picked a shirt I knew you'd hate," he said with a sly grin.

A mic squawk interrupted us. "If I could take a moment of your time, I'd like to thank Nolan for making sure the A/V worked and the slides in the presentation looked good." A smattering of clapping filled the room. Ian scanned the crowd and gestured for Nolan to stand. "He's been working hard, and this guy is going places. He's got the MBA brains and, of course, the MacKenzie genetics." He pointed to the back of the room. "There are leftover croissants and cookies from the morning's board meeting. Help yourselves."

Dozens of dudes streamed to the back of the room to snag some free food. I noticed most of the executive team walk over to Nolan, thanking him for his prep work on the board meeting. All these higher-ups, fawning over an intern. The CEO's nephew. And Nolan looking so comfortable with all of it. Shaking hands. Smiling. Joking around. Bitterness washed over me as this breed of people whom I felt so different from carried on like they were some exclusive club I had no business being part of.

Rage flared inside me as I stormed out of the room. Was I angry that they were like this? Or was I angry at myself for wishing I was part of it?

Maybe both.

CHAPTER FOURTEEN

Can you help me button this?" Jane padded out of the fitting room and beelined over to the three-way mirror. Candace and I exchanged looks. We played rock, paper, scissors while Jane checked her teeth for lipstick smudges.

One, two, three, rock.

Candace was paper.

Damn it.

I stood up from the bench and Candace, seated right next to me, went down with a thud thanks to the unstable furniture. *Sit down gently, Melody, lest you catapult your pregnant best friend into the ceiling fan.*

Jane lifted her hair so I could fasten the buttons, and there were approximately fifty of them. *Fuck.* Each loop fit tightly over its corresponding satin button, which meant it took about a minute to button five of them. The skin on my fingertips chafed as I carefully pushed each button through its delicate ivory satin loop counterpart. *Please, God, don't let me misalign them!*

As I started working on fastening button number six, Jane glanced at her reflection and said, "I don't like this dress. Get me out of this ugly thing." And so the unbuttoning process began, and it took just as long to undo.

She held up a stark white dress with long-sleeved lace and double the number of buttons in the back. It also had a train the length of a football field.

"That one won't show off your yoga arms," I said. Candace looked up from her phone and nodded.

Jane had already gotten in the gown and had almost pulled it up to her chest. She paused for a second and nodded at me. The dress fell back to the floor and she kicked it away.

The next dress was a simple halter, with a bunch of shiny, sparkly shit on the top half of the bodice. But don't get me wrong, I loved shiny, sparkly shit. This gown was old Hollywood glamorous, in the way that the Miss Universe pageant dresses were gorgeous. The diamondlike crystal sequins on the top looked even better when Jane put the dress on. Oh my, we had a winner.

This dress had 90 percent fewer buttons down the back than that other one, and the bustle in the back unhooked easily so the train was easy to maneuver. *This* was the dress. After three weekends of bridal gown browsing, this *had* to be the dress. Jane looked at herself from the front, back, and turned side to side so she could see herself from all angles.

"Jane, you look stunning from all three-hundred-sixty degrees," said Candace, smiling. Jane slowly turned around so Candace and I could ooh and ahh.

She had chosen the dress. Or maybe the dress chose her?

Jane took a few steps back from the mirror. She pivoted to her right, and then left, like an oscillating fan. Then, cocking her head like a little bird, she asked, "So you don't think this makes my arms look big?"

"NO!" Candace and I yelled simultaneously. I shook my head. Jane really made my blood boil sometimes.

The sales assistant came over and whistled softly. "Wow, that dress is beautiful on you! It's a one-of-a-kind couture creation that we just got in this week. It is so hard to pull off because you basically need a perfect body because it's silk, not satin. And then the top bustier draws attention to the bosom, which is an area where you are also blessed. You look stunning."

Jane beamed. Yes, this was the dress.

I asked, "How much is it?," and Candace whacked me in the arm. *A tacky question, I guess? Oops.*

The sales assistant replied, "I need to look it up in the computer. We didn't put a tag on this dress because the fabric is so delicate."

I leaned into Candace. "They didn't include the price tag because it costs the same as a car." She whacked me again. *Geez!*

The assistant clickety-clacked on the keyboard awhile and looked back over with a gleaming smile. "The entire dress was hand-sewn, and you can tell how high quality it is by the fine-quality silk, plus the stitching and beading." This was an exquisite dress, no doubt. But even Jane caught on that she didn't disclose the price.

"How much?" Jane asked.

That smile remained plastered on her face. "Without tax, it's twenty thousand dollars." How did she manage to say "twenty thousand dollars" with that cheery grin?

Candace let out a squeak. Or maybe that was me.

"Shit, you can pay for a small wedding for that amount!" Oops. That was me. No filter. But really, she could buy a car for that price. This was probably what Cinderella felt like when all those other bitches went to the fancy ball and she was left in rags.

Jane sighed. "Can you help unbutton this?" Candace and I both frantically worked at getting her out of the gown.

The clerk didn't want to lose this sale. "Were there any other dresses you want to try on?"

Jane shook her head. She headed back to the dressing room.

The saleswoman followed her in and knocked on her stall. "Would you mind disclosing your budget?"

"Ten thousand. Maybe twelve. That's the max." *Well, shit, that could still buy a used car.*

Candace and I shifted our stares from Jane's stall to the sales clerk. *Your move.*

"I'll be right back." She ran back to her computer, clickety-clacked some more, and then grabbed the store phone and dialed. She kept looking over at us, and then back at her computer screen while she spoke. She nodded a few times and hung up. The verdict was in.

The gleaming smile spread across her face again. "I just got off the phone with the designer of the dress, Yun-Hee Lee. She's a lovely person and I explained how in love you were with her gown. She agreed to drop the price to eleven grand, but it's conditional. She wants to style you, and outfit your bridesmaids in her signature dresses, too—at a discount, of course—if she can do a photo shoot of you in her dress for her marketing materials. Would that work for you?"

Yun-Hee Lee dressed A-list movie stars and country music celebrities. Her tasteful wedding dresses were popular among the Microsoft and Amazon nouveau riche in the Pacific Northwest. And now Jane would be famous by association. Jane asked, "Does Yun-Hee do maternity bridesmaid dresses? This one is preggo." She swept her hand in the direction of Candace.

"She can absolutely accommodate her, she's so tiny!" the sales clerk chirped.

Candace beamed. "I won't be tiny for long. My baby's the size of a small baked potato." I always thought it was weird that people compared their baby size to food. But cooked food seemed even more disturbing.

Jane looked at Candace and me and said, "You swear to god this dress doesn't make my arms look huge?"

"NO!" we shouted again.

I whispered to Candace, "We're lucky. You know why? We're

done with wedding dress shopping!" She giggled and covered her mouth.

"Hey, could one of you help me out of this dress?"

One, two, three, scissors.

Candace was rock.

Damn it.

CHAPTER FIFTEEN

With his noise-canceling headphones on, Asher couldn't hear me cursing at the email on my laptop screen.

"Melody, please work with Kat and the rest of your team to make a prerendered trailer for *Ultimate Apocalypse*, and a demo build. Someone dropped out of GameCon Northwest and we got a screaming deal on a show booth. We're going to GameCon Northwest with your game reveal at the end of the month!!! —Ian"

GameCon Northwest? Where Xbox and Nintendo first announced product release dates? I needed to talk sense into Ian. This deadline was impossible.

My stomping shook the floor as I stormed over to Ian's office. He was hunched over his desk, swaying to Debussy with his eyes partially closed while drinking a French press coffee that he brewed on his desk. *Could he be any more pretentious?*

Before I uttered a word, and without even looking up, he said, "I see you got my email."

"Yes. I did. And I have some questions."

He gestured for me to sit on his couch while he pressed more coffee. "Would you like some?"

His craft brew smelled amazing. But screw him.

"No thanks."

He poured himself a cup. Then he poured a second cup and placed it on the glass table in front of me. He looked me in the eyes, ready to talk. God damn that tantalizing coffee aroma.

Leaning back on his stuffed leather chair, he took a small sip. "For several early mornings and late evenings, Joe and I have talked through some PR ideas that could save this company from imminent doom. As you know, we're still going to launch your game with you at the helm. We haven't found another lead female producer yet, even with all our recruiters working on it, so you'll be the one to take this to the finish line. You need to get used to unplanned marketing and PR opportunities popping up here and there before the launch. We need to take the ones that are worth the time. It's something a producer needs to handle when these situations come up."

I took a teeny sip. Heavenly.

He continued. "We already have over a thousand names on our newsletter list, thanks to the collection of email addresses on the site. And we finally caught a break when I snagged a canceled booth at GameCon Northwest! That booth was originally for the new *WarMaster* game by a new Korean studio, but the company's president died while playing it. Isn't that fucked up? Imagine *that* PR nightmare! Anyway, we're going to have an amazing booth, and all we need is Asher and you to be on the floor, talking to the press, promoting the game. Sound good?"

That was a ton of information to sift through, and I wasn't ready to speak just yet. So instead I sipped the delicious coffee some more. Mmmm. It didn't even need sugar or milk.

"So you need a demo and a trailer from me. In like three weeks?"

He nodded.

"With no concept or storyboard?"

He nodded again.

We only had a few scenes from the game we could use, and we had no art assets to make a full video. We were so screwed.

He poured himself another cup. "Well, Kat and you can figure it out. You can hire whoever you need, as long as they fit reasonably within our budget." Thanks to my advertising background, these types of video projects were right in my wheelhouse. I had some friends who could help me get them done, but we would be cutting it close.

"Oh, one more thing. We need to hire some cosplay actors. To walk around and pull people into the booth."

Cosplay was something I was familiar with from my comic book fandom days in high school. Tons of GameCon attendees would be dressed up as game characters. "So you want actors that look like the characters from our game?"

Ian's phone rang. Before he picked it up he said, "Your main characters are male strippers, so go hire some strippers. I need to take this call. Feel free to take the coffee with you."

I shut the door behind me and headed back to my desk with my drink. He really wanted real strippers in the booth? Maybe I could add this new job duty to my résumé. Production responsibilities include: establishing long-term feature schedules, communicating project milestones and deadlines, and recruiting male strippers.

I texted Jane and Candace about the stripper casting call.

Jane: *BEST NEWS OF THE WEEK. COUNT ME IN!*

Candace: *Can we go recruiting later tonight?*

I had the best friends ever.

AFTER A JAM-PACKED day of meetings with production, legal, PR, and marketing, I had dinner with Candace and Jane to talk about weddings, babies, and strippers.

"Okay, you go first, Candace. What's going on with you?" I asked with my mouth stuffed full of fried calamari. It was rude, but I had worked through lunch and had enough food in front of me to feed two Melodys.

She squealed and threw her arms up in excitement. "Ahhh! We got a marriage courthouse date! If you can come, we're getting hitched this week, at 11 A.M. on Friday; I know, it's a workday. If you can't make it, don't worry about it."

I checked my calendar. "I have that day off because my parents are arriving that morning. I planned to meet them at Sea-Tac and take them straight to brunch. But they can get a taxi or Liftr, it's not a big deal."

"Don't worry about it. It's so last minute on my part. If their plane comes in late, maybe you can come. Other than the wedding news, the baby seems healthy. He or she is the size of a small head of cauliflower now." I tried to picture what that looked like. I stabbed a fried zucchini stick with my fork and held it up to see how big that baby would be in zucchini stick units. About six, maybe seven.

Jane blurted out, "My wedding planning is going great!" *Okay, I guess it was Jane's turn.* "We put a deposit on a gorgeous hotel near Alki Beach, secured a caterer, and because Sean's friend knows the son of the conductor of the Seattle Philharmonic, they'll be playing at our wedding, too. And your bridesmaid dresses came in. They are gorgeous!" She scrolled for photos on her phone. "Here, take a look."

Candace and I peered over Jane's shoulder to see the couture gowns. I pinched the screen and made the picture bigger, to make sure I had the full visual experience before commenting.

Candace beat me to it. "They look like . . . Grecian togas."

She nailed it. They looked like motherfucking TOGAS. Like ancient Grecian garb, but what a dude would wear, not a lady. Sure, the designer added some small adornments to make it look slightly more contemporary, like using airy fabric and a feminine sea-green color, which was the hue of Crest toothpaste. A color that I never wore because pastel colors like that looked terrible on me. Any cool palette against my skin made me looked jaundiced.

Jane shrugged. "Togas are Roman, not Grecian."

She missed the point entirely. Roman, or Grecian, whatever. Togas were hideous.

I asked, "Can we ask the designer to scale back on some of the fabric? It looks like it would be heavy and hot. I definitely couldn't dance in that." This might be a good way to get out of dancing with Asher at the wedding. Maybe I found an out!

Jane smirked. "Oh, that's the beauty of the dress! The over-the-shoulder fabric can be let out in the back. It forms a long flowy train. And that train is also removable. That's why I love Yun-Hee Lee's designs. She always has clever, versatile pieces!"

Damn it, this meant I'd need to find another way to propose a best-man-plus-maid-of-honor dance boycott. She showed us pictures of the unraveled toga. Without the over-the-shoulder fabric, the dress looked a million times better than the full-on toga dress. The color was still problematic, but honestly, the fact that Jane settled on dresses that she liked made me want to high-five everyone in the restaurant.

"Do you want us to wear Grecian sandals, too?" I joked. There was no way in hell Jane would want us to wear flat, manly sandals to her wedding.

"No fucking way," she answered. "Here are pics of the shoes

that'll go with the dress. Yun-Hee also designed them." Again, I pinched the photo to enlarge it. She picked peep toe heels. Six inches high.

I wasn't a heel person. My go-to fancy shoes were geriatric, comfy pumps, which weren't great for adding height. There was no shame in that shoe game. I couldn't walk in real heels, and I'd surely fall on my face when walking down the aisle, shattering my elbows from a fraught attempt to protect my makeup and hair. And then an ambulance would haul me away and I would have to get emergency surgery in an ugly fucking toga. Nobody wanted that.

Candace said, "Jane, these shoes are beautiful . . . but by the time the wedding comes around I'll be as big as a horse. I won't be able to wear heels at all." Thank god Candace got knocked up.

Jane made a face. "Fine, we can ask the salesperson for flat shoes. I want you two to match."

Just when I was ready to celebrate this shoe triumph, Candace said, "Mel, it's your turn. What's going on with you these days?" She sipped her nonalcoholic mint lemonade as I let out a heavy sigh.

"Where do I start?" I told them about my parents unexpectedly coming to town, the ongoing troll warfare, and the Game-Con Northwest conference. I expected them to be bored when I rattled off my life events, but they leaned in, wide-eyed and nodding along.

"And there's this guy at work—"

They leaned closer. Jane asked, "Ooooh, are you hooking up with someone at the office?"

My entire body flushed with heat. "Oh god, no, he's the CEO's nephew. And he's an intern."

"Huh, I never figured you as the robbing-the-cradle type, but I'm impressed. What is he, like twenty?" Jane asked.

"He's an *MBA* intern, and I was just going to say that his parents are crazy, too, so it's nice that someone else has to deal with that, not just me. He's the guy Asher was calling my 'boy toy' at your engagement dinner, but we're *just friends*. Can we change the subject, please?" I took a sip of my ice water to cool down my flushed face. "Maybe we can talk about the fact that I'm still getting death threats at work on a minute-by-minute basis?"

"Still? Do you need an employment lawyer, by the way?" Jane asked. "Based on everything I've read about other women victimized in the tech or gaming fields, they got pushed out or fired from their positions. They blamed the women, not the pervasive sexist culture around them."

Candace frowned. "Melody didn't do anything to cause this, other than being a woman, and being Asian. It's so unfair. She needs a bodyguard, not a lawyer. How bad are the harassing comments now?"

"Bad. They'd almost be comically bad, with all the over-the-top shit that people write, hiding behind fake social media accounts and bogus usernames—if it weren't happening to a real person, it'd almost seem like a parody of trolling."

Candace put her hand on my arm. "Mel, why don't you quit?

You say you're fine, but I know you. In some cases, maybe even this case, quitting is different than giving up. You need to take care of yourself, there's no shame in that."

I'd thought about finding a new job and hoping all the trolling craziness would go away. But I was doing great at work now and managing all the timelines and juggling things well as they came up. I'd earned the respect of people just by sticking with what I started. And in the past few months I'd met so many female gamers who played games like mine, who aced any shooter game that came their way. More women were gaming than ever before, in casual games, but also in role-playing games and first-person shooters, too. This growing group of women needed more game variety to hold their interest. They needed more games like mine. Well, not *exactly* like mine (because how may games with male strippers fighting for survival could the market realistically bear?).

"I want to stay, to show all those assholes I can do it, holding it all together when the entire world thinks I'll fall apart. I want to make a difference."

Candace held up her lemonade. "Okay then. To making a difference!"

We clinked glasses, and I gulped down the rest of my vodka soda and scooted my chair back. "Who wants to come with me to go recruit some strippers? Ian actually gave me petty cash to go to some strip clubs to 'scout talent,' no joke."

Candace and Jane stood up in a hurry, almost knocking down their seats.

"We volunteer! Jane, the baby, and me!" Candace giggled and locked her arm in mine. Jane looked up the best strip clubs in the area on her phone and was ready to roll. I loved that Candace and Jane stood by my side as I fought my uphill battles. And yeah, I understood the irony of going to a strip club to fight for my dream.

JANE CALLED A car, and we pulled up to the Stallions Club in a gleaming white Cadillac. A bouncer/valet/footman came to our passenger door and opened it for us. Under his black shirt and black pants, you could tell this guy had major muscles. I mean, he had deep indentations where the in-between muscle parts were. This guy was a stripper, too, right? He had to be.

"Welcome to the Stallions. My name is Carlos." He rolled his *R* a long time, which made his name sound both sexy and comical. A weird combo, but I liked it.

Jane and I tugged Candace out of the back seat. Now that she was further along in her pregnancy, little things like pulling herself out of a bucket seat were no longer trivial.

"Thanks for the assistance!" Candace smoothed out the back of her skirt. We all entered the venue exuding a direct representation of our personalities. Jane walked in like she owned the fucking place. I looked around guiltily, like a teenager who sneaked out of the bedroom window to go see a strip show with a fake ID, and Candace, well, she just giggled at everything. The cheesy dance music, the steamy hot hosts, and S&M-themed

decor caused her to erupt into hyperventilating giggles. Was enough oxygen getting to the baby?

This was my first strip club outing and I had no idea what was supposed to happen. Jane whispered something to the host, and he smiled. "Yes, please come this way to the VIP room."

"Don't worry, it's on me," Jane said coolly.

I asked, "Why do you look so at ease here?"

She laughed and tossed her hair back. "All the guys I work with go to strip clubs. Sometimes I need to go, too, because we're entertaining clients, or someone gets promoted and the team's congratulatory outing is at a strip joint. At first it felt icky and uncomfortable, but now I'm desensitized to all this. Think of it as a show, and these guys here are all actors."

"Really hot, muscular, sexy actors," Candace squeaked. *Pipe down, horny preggo girl!*

"Speaking of actors, remember, the goal for tonight is to hire some of these guys to be cosplayers. We're not here to . . . engage."

Jane said, "Right. Hire strippers to play strippers at your nerdy trade show. Got it. Let's hurry up and go to the VIP room! They'll have the hotter guys there who know what they are doing. They put the more inexperienced guys on the main floor."

My purse vibrated. A new text alert from Nolan. *You at work? Order dinner?*

I replied immediately. *Nope, long story, will explain later. I'm at a strip club. Please don't ask.*

Jane looked over my shoulder and then smacked my arm. Hard. "Who's thaaaaat?"

I shook my head. "Just a coworker. You need to focus. I need to recruit people for the show, remember?"

Candace nodded. "And in case your coworker is maybe more than just a coworker, you don't want to look desperate by being so available."

"Like a hooker with no clients," Jane added, raising her drink. *Thanks, Jane.*

"You both are reading too much into this," I said, shaking my head.

The host bypassed the central area by taking us down a lengthy hallway. Dark red velvet walls lined the corridor, giving this place a sensual, almost carnal vibe. It looked a little bit too much like traveling down someone's birth canal.

I shouted above the music, "Remember to look for friendly, approachable types."

The VIP room looked smaller than what I had imagined. The decor was minimalistic, like a fancy IKEA modern living room, but with black couches and red walls. The music didn't make the walls vibrate in here, but I still had to yell over it at times.

A six-foot, blond, European waiter with zero percent body fat walked in, wearing only a red thong.

"Oh wow," Candace yelped. *Oh wow, indeed.*

"Where do you guys put your name tags?" I asked.

He winked at me. "I'm Marco. Don't worry, you will not forget my name."

Jane, Candace, and I exchanged looks and burst out into laughter. If I wasn't such a fish out of water here, like if this was a regular dance club, I could actually see myself drinking with my girls and having a good time. But it wasn't a regular ol' club. How had I conceived a game centered around characters like Marco, someone I was so utterly awkward around?

Jane asked, "Mel, you're looking for someone friendly and approachable, right?" She grabbed a black VIP menu off the side table.

"Are you ordering drinks? I need a ginger ale." Candace yawned. She was fading quickly. We needed to move things along fast.

"Not yet." She waved Marco over. "We want one classic cocktail, maybe an Old-Fashioned. Clean. And maybe to spice things up, one dirty, DIRTY martini."

"Hey, you didn't order my ginger ale!" Candace whimpered.

Jane focused on the door. "I'll order that in a minute," she answered distractedly as she looked down at her watch. She muttered to herself, "We'll see if they're as hot as Marco."

Marco reappeared, with two strapping men right behind him. Hottie number one, dressed as a (hot!) cowboy, had an all-American, clean-cut yummy type of look to him. He had a lasso, too. Hottie number two was dressed in a modified tuxedo. He was hot in a Miami sensual summer sort of way. He oozed dirty sex. They came over and introduced themselves.

"I'm Dan." Cowboy tipped his hat. *Oooh, it suddenly got a little steamy in here.*

Dirty Sex said, "My name is Paul." He grabbed Candace's hand and kissed it. She blushed so hard I thought her water might break right there on the floor of the VIP room.

I looked at Jane. "These guys are perfect. How did you . . ."

She waved the menu in my face. "I ordered them."

"You WHAT?" I looked over at Candace, to shoot her a look of *can you believe her?* but she was too busy flirting with Paul. Paul was a much better stimulant than ginger ale. Who would have expected to see a woman carrying a cauliflower-head-size baby flirt so hard with a stripper? I needed a drink. Desperately.

Jane tossed her hair back. "Well, at the fancy strip clubs we go to for work, they have these menus where you can use innuendo to request a type of stripper to come to you. Usually they're drink menus, so you might order a tall White Russian if you want, well, a tall White Russian. One time I went to a dessert-themed strip club and they likened types of women to ice cream flavors. So fucking weird, right?"

This whole thing was weird. But I couldn't help wondering what kind of "order" I would give for Nolan. A bourbon, neat? A Gold Rush? Maybe Whiskey Smash?

Melody, stop thinking about Nolan and smashing. Stop it.

No one in my entourage seemed to remember why we were there, including me, so I took charge and handed Paul and Dan my business card. "Gentlemen, no stripping required today. I have a well-paying job for you two, and it will be fun and worth your time, I promise. Call me tomorrow."

Paul eyed Candace up and down and said, "Count me in."

Dan tipped his hat in agreement, and Paul followed him out of the room. Candace giggled and bit her lip. "Where do you think they put their business cards?"

Jane sat back into the couch. "Well, you got your cosplayers, and I got some killer ideas for my bachelorette party." She ordered the overdue ginger ale and handed Marco a hundred-dollar bill, which he rolled up and put in his thong. The lack of pockets didn't stop Marco from collecting cash in his crotch bank. Maybe he had a hidden slot for business cards, too. As we left the club, I wondered what Marco did with spare change.

CHAPTER SIXTEEN

My friend Nick Cabot was the first person I called to help with the game trailer. He had just moved back to Seattle after working at an ad agency in London for two years and had some time to take on this freelance video project. Hooray!

Ziiiiiip. Nick talked to me while opening boxes with an X-Acto knife. "Mel, darling, the only games you and I REALLY enjoy playing are those junky time wasters on our phones." *Ziiiiiip.* "Are you still playing *Candy Casino*? And that ridiculous one where you fling rubbish at the British aristocracy?" Nick had been my boss and mentor at my previous job, and he had started a new ad agency in the SoDo district. They had a few local clients, but their main source of revenue came from creating trailers for independent films.

"No, I'm not addicted to those anymore, thank you very much. Anyway, I really think your video experience making gorgeous film trailers will be perfect for this assignment." His design aesthetic and promotional sensibilities would work well for this game trailer. I proceeded to tell him about *Ultimate Apocalypse*.

He laughed before I could finish. "I love how ridiculous the premise is. And it sounds so fun. Okay, so the goal is to create buzz around the game? Well, I know we can do that. I can do the storyboards and trailer rough cuts and edits, but can you help with writing copy? We're a little short-staffed in that area. I also need to know what high-res game images and video assets you have available." We spent another thirty minutes talking about budgets and the three-week turnaround. I also mentioned he would have real-life male strippers to use for green screen filming at his disposal.

"It's a tight timeline, I'm not gonna lie. But I'm excited! I've never been briefed on such an absurd project in my entire life," Nick said, laughing so hard he actually choked.

With Nick working on the game trailer, and Asher and Kat putting together the game demos, things were back on track. We had three weeks until the trade show, so there was no room for error. Somehow, we'd managed to hit every production milestone despite the addition of GameCon deliverables to our demanding schedule.

Asher came into the office later than usual, with two coffees and two bagels in hand. Was he being nice for once? Nah, turns out they were both for him. He alternated bites between the two bagels ("Oh my god, Melody, the new bagel shop near my house just opened this morning and the bagels are perfect. So chewy and soft. You should go there sometime") and drinking the two coffees with lots of slurping bravado. The last few days I had brought in doughnuts, pastries, and muffins from the bakery around the corner, which had a LINE every morning, and fed all the producers, developers, and artists working on my project. And yet Asher couldn't even think to get me a stupid bagel. Or add a third coffee to his greedy order. Bastard.

Ian walked by my office and backtracked to the door. "Melody, aren't you coming to the meeting?"

"What meeting?" I checked my calendar. Nope, no meeting.

"Oh, I thought I'd invited you." He looked on his phone. "Here, I'll add you to the meeting invitation. You should come to it." The meeting he invited me to, called "Meeting," would start in one minute. I saw no agenda listed.

I grabbed my laptop and trailed behind Ian to head to "Meeting." The only thing I knew about it was that the selfish double-coffee and bagel-eating monster Asher wasn't invited.

Around the executive conference room sat ten other people evenly spaced around the table. A few Indian and Chinese developers, our black receptionist, and Kat and me. And Ian. And some cheeseball dude with a loud fake laugh and gray moussed hair, wearing a shiny oxford shirt with damp armpit marks, standing in front of the whiteboard.

"Welcome! Please take a seat, we were just about to get started." I looked around for some clue on what this meeting was about. Kat sat on the other side of the room, so I couldn't ask her. "I'm Rafael. I've been brought in by Ian to facilitate diversity sensitivity discussions. We asked for you to join this meeting because you represent a minority group here at Seventeen Studios, and we want to hear from you."

My stomach dropped, like I'd just plunged down a roller-coaster hill.

Ian said, "HR thought we should do this because of the recent controversy around our newest game launch." He shot me an exasperated look. I averted his glance by looking down at my notebook and writing "Diversity Discussion" in bubble letters.

Rafael read from a sheet of paper. "According to our roster, we have a wide range of representation in this room. We have foreign nationals from India and China," he said, glancing at the developers. "We have Asians and Blacks"—he nodded to the receptionist and me—"and we also have LGBTQ." He looked at Kat.

"I'm not LGBTQ, I'm straight." Kat scrunched her brow and leaned forward, like a cat about to pounce. Did they think she was a lesbian just because she had short hair and drove a Subaru? Almost everyone in Seattle drove a Subaru.

Rafael didn't know what to do. He looked at Ian. "Oh. Should we cut her loose?"

Ian thought for a moment. "I really thought she was L. But she's still a woman. We could use that input." He scanned the room. "But maybe someone else in here is L, though." His eyes fixed on mine like a predator spotting prey. "Melody?"

My mouth dropped open. "I-I-I'm not a lesbian."

And with me saying this, you'd think we were done. But no.

Ian asked, "Not even . . . B?"

I shot a pleading look at Rafael the moderator. Rather than moderate this cringeworthy dialogue, he looked at me in earnest. He, too, wanted to know if I was bisexual.

Kat jumped to her feet and flung her chair back. "Oh hell no, I'm way too busy for this fake diversity rah-rah bullshit. We have a game to launch and a trade show coming up soon. If you need me, I'll be at my desk." She stormed out, mumbling, "Why do I fucking work here?" She slammed the door hard enough to make the walls and table shake.

I leaped up too. "Kat and I have the same deadlines. And . . . I'm not bi."

Ian shrugged, and Rafael handed me a diversity questionnaire to fill out and mail to him by the end of the week.

I clomped back to my desk in a hurry and skimmed the three questions.

Do you feel singled out for being a minority at Seventeen Studios?
(Yes. Please refer to the bisexual discussion.)

Do you agree with this statement: "Gaming is for guys."
(No.)

Please explain.
(I shouldn't have to.)

Is there anything Seventeen can do to help you feel more comfortable and welcome at this company?

(Yes. Put Ian and the rest of you executive idiots through diversity and sensitivity training.)

What a joke.

I crumpled up the paper and threw it in the trash. Walking back to my desk, Kat's last words played back over and over through my head. Why *did* I fucking work here?

Honestly, I couldn't think of an answer anymore.

CHAPTER SEVENTEEN

My parents weren't paying attention when I pulled up to the arrivals area at Sea-Tac airport. They were arguing about something. Without even saying hello, they continued their bickering in Korean while I opened the trunk and put their luggage in. My mom sat in the back and Dad got in the front.

"How was your trip?"

My dad made a *harrumph* sound as he pulled the seat belt across his chest. "You ask your mom!" He crossed his arms and stared straight ahead.

"Um, okay. Mom, what happened?"

"He mad because he say I forgot to buy his heart medicine. And now we have almost empty bottle. We need to refill here."

My dad had a pretty serious heart attack a few years ago, but he recovered like a champ. Since then, though, he had to take daily medication, a blood thinner, to make sure it wouldn't happen again.

"Dad, why didn't you refill it yourself? Mom isn't the only one who knows how to do that at a drugstore."

My mom yelled, "Yes! I'm not his maid!" while my dad shouted, "I am older. She need to help me."

Yet another one of their pointless fights where they ping-ponged angry words and then refused to speak to each other.

They needed to cut this shit out. "I think it's good for you two to discuss this with each other. About why Dad expects you to fill his meds, Mom. And, Dad, why you depend on Mom to do this for you. But you can do this at your hotel room, and not with me in public. I'll drive you to the hotel and you can check in early. We can eat around there and skip brunch. Too bad, it was going to be at an all-you-can-eat crab place, your favorite kind of restaurant."

Mom and Dad looked at each other and came to a quick nonverbal peace treaty. "We want to eat crab." My dad gave me a sad puppy-dog look, upset that I could so easily yank away this privilege from them. I wasn't going to reward their bad behavior.

Mom chimed in. "We not angry anymore, Melody." She reached into the front seat, grabbed my dad's hand, and then she swung their arms a little bit. "See? We are friends. Drive us to crab brunch."

I picked out this seafood brunch buffet because of the number of high reviews, and because my parents couldn't get good seafood where they lived in the South. They could eat hundreds of dollars' worth of Alaskan crab legs in one sitting, so foodwise they'd be in heaven. Whenever my parents went to any buffet, they went straight for the seafood section. They never had salad. Or rolls. Sometimes my dad would have clam chowder. "Salad is waste money," he'd say, as he cracked open crab shells with his steel-trap-strength teeth, ripping out the juicy flesh with surgical precision.

The table was ready when we arrived, and the hostess seated us near a bay window overlooking Puget Sound. The hanging fog obscured our view, but at least it wasn't pouring rain.

"Waaaaaa!" Mom and Dad oohed and ahhed over the scenery. Seagulls swooped down and around the water, mesmerizing my parents into silence.

A man's southern voice boomed a few feet away. "Well, son, this certainly is a treat. What a spectacular view!" I looked up from the menu to see a ginger-haired, ruddy, giant man in a light blue oxford shirt and pleated khakis walking to the table next to us. Behind him was a lovely older woman, maybe sixties, with a blunt brown bob and perfectly applied red lipstick. And behind her?

Nolan MacKenzie.

Nolan, with his neatly pressed, tucked blue shirt, perfectly centered silk blue-and-gray-checkered tie, khaki-colored cords, and brown laced Oxfords. He looked like a different person entirely with his preppy, evenly combed hair. While his parents got seated, he walked over to say hello.

"Hello, Mr. Joo, Mrs. Joo. So nice to meet you. Melody talks about you so much at work."

My parents exchanged looks. Mom spoke first. "You work with Melody?"

He laughed. "Yes, she works hard."

My dad tipped his chin up and smiled proudly. "She take after us."

"Melody, I'd love for you to meet my parents."

I stood up and walked over to their table. Next to me, Nolan whispered, "Should we make a run for it?"

I looked at him beaming at me and giggled.

Nolan's dad took his napkin off his lap and stood to greet me with a knuckle-crushing handshake. His mother remained seated.

Nolan said, "Mom and Dad, this is Melody." His father's firm handshake still lingered on my hand. His mother's hands felt baby soft and delicate, like she'd never done a day's work in her life.

My mom shouted to their table, "Melody-ya! Why we not push two table together? Then we all talk together."

Before I could protest, Nolan's dad said, "Well, what a wonderful idea!"

My mom and dad jumped into action, pushing our table over to theirs, first with little shoves and then one big heave-ho. *SC-SC-SC-SC-SCRREEEEECH!*

My parents carried over some chairs and plopped back down, content and exhausted. I sat across from Nolan and bumped his knee. He didn't flinch.

Mrs. MacKenzie gave me a once-over. "My, my, Melody, you are very pretty." A compliment I didn't hear very often.

"Melody?" My mom snorted. "She look like monkey when she born. So much fur. But she look much better now. Much more pretty." That was my mom's version of praise.

Nolan gently knocked his knee into mine and gave me a smirk.

His mom added, "She's as pretty as a China doll!"

Nolan's face fell instantly, and I forced a thin smile. She had meant that as a compliment. My whole life I'd heard things like this. Racial gaffes that had "come out the wrong way." This time Nolan got a small peek into what it was like to be me. Being nonwhite. Sometimes it outright sucked.

My mom threw her shoulders back and grumbled, "We are Korean, not Chinese." Nolan's mom smiled and appeared unfazed, like she had simply mixed up Keira Knightley and Natalie Portman.

I introduced my parents. "Mr. and Mrs. MacKenzie, these are my parents. My mom, Hyun Joo, and my dad, Sang Jin." After a round of enthusiastic hand shaking, Nolan said, "This is my mom, Joanna Jean, and my dad, Nolan Senior. He's Nolan too." Pleasant laughter filled the air. We were back to a great start.

"Would anyone like a popover roll?" Nolan Junior held up the bread basket. Bless his heart for trying to keep the conversation going strong.

My dad said, "Roll is cheap. They try to fill you up with cheap thing." He ate one anyway. My mom took one, too.

"I'd love a roll, thank you, sweetheart." Joanna Jean had such a thick southern accent. She inspected the bread assortment and picked one. "I am so tuckered out from that flight. But we're so happy to have made it. Where are y'all stayin'?"

My dad said, "Holiday Inn in downtown. We stay there before. We like it because they have free continental breakfast. And *USA Today* every morning is no charge!"

Joanna Jean smiled and cut a tiny sliver of butter and spread it on the top of her crusty roll. "We're staying pretty close to here actually. At the Fremont Vista Inn." The Fremont was a *Condé Nast Traveler* Top 100 Hotel in the World. Sure, it was like number 98 on the list, but still. That place was fancy, like $500-a-night kind of fancy. Luckily my parents didn't know this. They were really weird about money, and if they figured out that Nolan's parents booked themselves at a luxury hotel, they'd flip out.

Joanna Jean patted her husband's hand. "We had to fly six hours to get here. From North Carolina. I'm so glad that flight is over! Now we can relax on our vacation. I simply cannot wait to sightsee around here and go shopping. We already bought Nolan this tie from our hotel lobby."

She lifted his tie, twisting it back and forth so we could see the exquisite shimmery material, pulling it at just the right angle for me to see the Hermès label.

My mom skimmed the menu. "Waaaa! This place too fancy.

You can buy two Red Lobster senior citizen dinner for this meal price."

"Well, hopefully no one will order the Dom Pérignon." Nolan Senior chuckled and wiped his eyes.

My parents, on the other hand, didn't laugh. My mom asked, "What is that? Is that the fancy steak that taste bad because there is no fat?"

"No, Mom, that's filet mignon. He's talking about a champagne."

All this time I assumed my parents were clueless (and a tiny bit endearing) on bourgeoisie things because they had lived in the outskirts of a major metropolis in the South for a long time, but apparently that wasn't the case. Joanna Jean and Nolan Senior lived in the suburbs in the South, too, and they sure seemed to know a lot about fancy champagne and first-class hotels, even though they lived in an even more rural area than my parents.

"Nolan, before we forget, thanks so much for letting us use your frequent-flier miles to upgrade to first class. They gave us lunch and provided the cutest bottles of ketchup." Joanna Jean brought her Louis Vuitton shoulder bag to her lap. This leather masterpiece from their new spring collection had to have set Nolan's mom back at least four grand. It was the same one Jane had. Joanna Jean pulled out a tiny bottle of Heinz ketchup that she had swiped from the plane. A truly adorable little bottle.

My mom snorted. "We take stuff all the time from restaurant and hotel. Melody, remember when we take the basket of cheese biscuit at Red Lobster?" I winced, mortified by her outburst. It was totally true, though. A few years ago, they delivered a whole basket of fresh bread to our table just as we paid our check and we didn't want to see it go to waste. So my mom jerry-rigged a bunch of napkins together to make a giant sack for the biscuits. We ate them all week. It was shameful, but not wasteful, and so delicious.

With her mouth full of sourdough roll, my mom semicoherently sputtered, "Is that real LV bag or fake?"

Joanna Jean ran her fingers through her blunt brown bob and placed her neatly manicured hands over her mouth in surprise. She coughed on the mimosa she carried in her other hand.

"Heavens me, that's quite a surprising question. It's real."

My mom scooted up to the table, stood up, then leaned over to get a good look at the handbag in Joanna Jean's lap. She sat back down and nodded. "If that is fake, the stitching very good." My dad nodded, as if he, too, was an expert in counterfeit designer goods.

Social protocol–wise, what are you supposed to do if your mother sort of accuses your work friend's mom of carrying a fake handbag? It was probably best to move the conversation along in a different direction. Nolan's parents and mine weren't going to end up best friends and go on cruises together. If this meal ended immediately, both parties would probably be relieved.

I clapped my hands together. "I think it's time to hit the buffet. I'll stay here with Nolan while the parents go up first."

My parents, as predicted, went straight for the crab legs. His parents went toward the soup and salad.

I whispered to Nolan, "Could this be any more painful?"

He looked around to make sure his parents weren't on their way back. "Sorry about them saying all that stuff about the hotel and champagne."

This was my chance to bring it up. "Yeah, so, what's the deal? Are you guys loaded or something?" I laughed nervously.

"Um, my dad exports tobacco." He winced. "I know, it's terrible, so I don't ever talk about it. But yeah, our family has been in the tobacco business for many generations. My dad's trying to grow other crops, too, now, but it hasn't been easy. They live . . . um, comfortably. Uncle Ian didn't want any part of it."

I hadn't really asked him much about his family's financial situation but never once had taken him as the tobacco empire type.

"What does living comfortably mean?"

"Um, I dunno. They don't worry about money."

I said the first thing I could think of that could determine a household's wealth because asking for his family's net worth would be tacky. "How many toilets do you have in your house?"

"What? Like, how many bathrooms?"

"Yeah, how many bathrooms do your parents have in their home?"

He furrowed his brow and went silent for a few seconds, counting.

What the fuck?

"Nine."

"You have NINE fucking bathrooms?"

"Well, there are seven in the main house, and two in the guesthouse."

He had a guesthouse? Like a maid's quarters?

"They're coming back. Thanks for never telling me that you were a tobacco czar," I complained. His degree of wealth was so hugely different from my family's financial situation, it was hard to even comprehend its immensity. Nine bathrooms. Even Jane's well-to-do family had only five.

My mom and dad each carried two plates. Mom had piled her plates high with crab legs and claws. My dad's extra plate showcased a precarious tower of mussels. They jutted out their chests, as if they'd caught the seafood themselves.

Nolan's parents came back with small salad plates and kid-size soup bowls. My mom made the *tsk tsk tsk* sound. "We paying forty-five dollar each person. You eating rabbit food. That's bad decision. You should eat crab, or mussel, or shrimp." My parents dug right in, skipping their usual prayer before meals. They were so enticed by the buffet that they forgot to thank God for his blessings. Like the blessing of seafood buffets with unlimited crab legs.

Nolan and I had our turn at the buffet, with the goal of leaving the parents minimal time to interact without our supervision. We divided and conquered: he attained the meat and seafood plate, and I got the veggies, fruit, and dessert. We did it silently, with Nolan looking over at me. I wasn't in a talkative mood, not even chatty about all the breadth of desserts on display, which included a chocolate fountain. We were both seated again in less than forty-five seconds.

The table went quiet, with everyone digging into their food, no one knowing what to say next. Nolan Senior broke the silence. "So, Melody, I hear you make and play games for a living. I'd love to get paid for that!" He guffawed at his joke, which was a pretty good one, by parent standards. I grinned and nodded.

"It's definitely different from your farming business," I said with a shallow laugh.

He asked, "So what game are you working on now?"

Hmmm, how could I explain to Nolan's tobacco-heir parents that my game involved male strippers who tried to save the world from ultimate destruction? Everyone waited for me to speak. Even my parents leaned forward, pausing their crab cracking, eager to hear about my job. And I didn't know what to say.

And then, Nolan jumped in. "Her game is top secret. They don't want any leaks. It's like Apple and how they make everyone sign nondisclosures and stuff."

I smiled politely. *Thank you, Nolan.*

Nolan's dad winked at me. "Well, we can't wait to see it when it launches. Maybe Jo and I can download the game on our phones." I tried to picture Nolan's mom and dad playing a stripper shooter game in cooperative game mode. Two sixtysomething-year-olds with stripper avatars taking on the world's survival, blasting zombies and aliens with machine guns and grenade launchers. Oh my god, that would be amazing.

My parents ate two plates of seafood each, and then had some kind of cream pie that they shared with each other. Their culinary preferences were quite different from the spread the MacKenzies had eaten. They had ended their meal with fresh fruit, cottage cheese, and black coffee.

My dad wiped his mouth with his napkin. "So you are farmers."

"We don't need to talk about work, Dad." I needed to intervene before things got awkward with the money stuff.

Chest puffed, Nolan's dad boomed, "Oh, we don't mind. We're hoping our boy will come home soon to take over the family business when he gets his business degree."

Nolan Junior and I exchanged looks. Is that why he didn't want to graduate?

"The family's been farming tobacco since the late 1800s," Nolan Senior added, sitting up straighter, proud of the family heritage.

My dad wrinkled his forehead when he said "tobacco." Then his eyes grew wide. "Did you own any slave?"

Oh shit.

The MacKenzies all exchanged glances. His dad chuckled and wiped a single bead of sweat from his forehead with a handkerchief. "We don't get asked that question a lot. From what I know about our family's deeds, our ancestors bought the farmland after the Civil War ended."

My parents went back to eating the cream pie and didn't have any additional farm/slave questions.

When the check came, all the parents clawed for the bill. In the end, Mr. MacKenzie Senior grabbed it the quickest. He was also the tallest, so playing keep-away with the check by holding it far above and behind his head was easy for him. He waved down the waiter and handed him a black Centurion American Express card, the same one Jane had. That had a $10K annual fee or some wild shit like that. Were all tobacco farmers like this?

My parents thanked the MacKenzies for paying for lunch. As we all walked out of the restaurant, my mom said, "You should come over tomorrow morning for our continental breakfast. It free. They have croissant, cream cheese pastry, and slice bagel. We will be there just two day." She leaned in and whispered, "They won't check for room key." Mr. and Mrs. MacKenzie smiled civilly and graciously declined. It bothered me that my parents didn't invite ME for free breakfast. I was always down for free food.

My dad said to the MacKenzie elders, "Very nice meeting you." He and Nolan Senior shook hands. Then Dad turned to Nolan and patted his back. "We give our blessing if you want to marry Melody someday."

My jaw dropped, and Nolan's did too. I glanced at the

MacKenzie elders, and both of them looked like someone had jumped out of a bush and yelled, *BOO! Here's your new daughter-in-law!* My parents ducked into my car and slammed the doors while I stood there quietly with all three MacKenzies, pulse racing, trying to process what had happened. Before I could apologize on my parents' behalf, my dad leaned over from the passenger seat and beeped my horn four times.

Ready.

To.

Go.

Now.

If this were a play, this is where I would yell, "And . . . end scene!" for comic relief. But, unfortunately, this was not a play. And there seemed to be no end to this insanity.

I'm so sorry, I mouthed to Nolan. I jumped into my car and drove the Joo family away at breakneck speed. Too bad we didn't wager on who had the most embarrassing parents. I would have gotten my $20 back.

CANDACE TEXTED ME while I was unloading my parents' luggage at Holiday Inn. Her court marriage appointment had been delayed a couple of hours, but it was back on again.

After circling the courthouse and coming to terms with the fact that no street parking was available in the vicinity, I drove under the building where every full hour of parking was $5.

The judge, Candace, and Wil hovered together, each with a

pen in hand, just as I entered the courtroom. When Candace saw me walk into the courtroom, she squealed, "Oh my god, Melody! You made it! You get to witness us getting married! I'm still single right now for a few more seconds!"

The judge chuckled and waved me forward. The court-appointed witnesses had just picked up pens to sign the papers, but the judge allowed me to sign the document as witness number one. I scanned the room for Jane.

Wil noticed. "Jane? She was here a few minutes but had to leave once our appointment got bumped."

After putting my name to paper, I took a photo with the happy couple. Candace, in a gorgeous sleeveless silk dress looked stunning. Wil looked pretty good, too, wearing a classic black tuxedo with a silver bow tie. Candace's bouquet was an assortment of wildflowers tied together in a thick ribbon that matched her dress.

The judge smiled and declared Candace and Wil, Mr. and Mrs. Fung, husband and wife. Candace and Wil kissed for my photo and then continued to kiss about fifty times. I'd never attended a wedding so short.

The photographer tapped his foot. "We need to get to the museum for the photo shoot before it gets too dark. A storm is coming, and I don't want it to ruin your photos." Translation: get out of their way and let them do their planned photo thing. I waved to Candace and Wil as they drove away in their Jeep, with cans tied with strings clattering along as they turned out of the courthouse parking lot. As their car grew smaller in the distance and eventually disappeared, I thought about how happy they looked during their ceremony. I wanted what they had: to be with a partner who was caring, down-to-earth, and accepted me the way I was.

I'd only parked there a total of twenty-five minutes. According to the signs, parking was free for thirty minutes or less. Woooo, free parking! The parking attendant waved me through and I headed home with a gigantic smile plastered on my face. At least something went amazingly right that day.

CHAPTER EIGHTEEN

For three straight weeks, it was just work, work, work. No play, play, play. And no distractions. I tuned Asher out, skipped out on any employee trainings and workshops, and ignored all Nolan's impromptu social visits and playful messages. I was just too embarrassed by my dad's marriage approval comment and hadn't worked through my feelings about Nolan's immense wealth. After a while, he got the hint. It probably helped that I just flat out said, "Sorry, I'm busy," anytime he tried to interact with me.

Nick, my mentor and career savior, called me at 7:30 A.M. the day of GameCon Northwest. "Good news! The game trailer is rendering now and will be ready within the hour." He and I had pulled an all-nighter to get the video finished.

I groaned and said, "GameCon floor opens at nine, we're barely going to make it." The late delivery of the trailer wasn't Nick's fault. Ian insisted that we include some of the latest game clips that had just been finished the previous night. Nick didn't complain, though, my company paid a hefty fee for the redo. The video looked amazing, even with the last-minute touches.

"Yes, but we ARE going to make it, Melody," Nick reassured me. "Have I ever missed a deadline?"

The demo build had come along nicely too.

GameCon NW was one of the largest gaming conventions on the West Coast and was also the fastest growing. Both inside and outside of the venue, Stormtroopers, Sailor Moons, superheroes, and mutant cosplayers milled around, studying the show floor maps and taking selfies. Luigi from *Mario Brothers* gave me a high five at the main entrance.

I had come to the convention the day before to make sure we had no problems with the video monitors, Wi-Fi, or the electricity. Setting up our booth twenty-four hours in advance paid off because our display only needed minor final touches the morning of the show. The last thing on my to-do list was to pick up my preordered cosplay warrior costumes, fake machetes, and hunting knives from the nearby costume rental shop.

Ian came by the booth while Asher and I put our mics on. He whistled when he saw the booth. "Wow, Melody. I am so glad we came to this convention. Aren't you glad I got us in?"

"Well, it's the hard work from the team that makes this look so fantastic." The Seventeen Studios events team scurried past him, carrying boxes of swag and stacks of controllers. "Our A/V guys just uploaded our demos. They're amazing." One of them waved a hello with his screwdriver and continued securing the video monitor to the booth backboard.

"Right. Great job, everyone." Ian pulled his hands through his hair. "Did you get my email this morning about the show talent being unapproved by finance? They said we couldn't risk having strippers on the payroll because it might flag an ethics violation."

I frowned. "Wait, what email? I didn't get anything from you."

He scrolled through his email and said, "Oops, looks like it's still in my email drafts. Let me forward it to you now."

My phone buzzed. The content of Ian's email was a repeat of what he just told me, which left out the fact that the finance team had already reached out to Dan and Paul this week to let them know their services wouldn't be needed at the convention. No one told me.

Being cautious, I pulled Ian aside to have this discussion out of earshot of my team. "Ian, you authorized them. They were the big splashy draw to our booth. No one else has male strippers."

He held up his *hold that thought* index finger to my face and picked up his buzzing phone. After a few seconds, he put his hand over the speaker. "Well, you have a few minutes to think of a plan B." He removed his hand and said, "Yes, I'd be happy to give you an exclusive interview today. Let me come meet you now." He shuffled away, leaving me standing there with plastic machetes in my hands.

Asher walked up to me. "I eavesdropped, sorry. What are we supposed to do now, boss?" He wrinkled his brow and awaited my response. The team needed me to look coolheaded and collected, not panicked and vomity.

Think, Melody, think.

Shit! Shit! Shit!

Fuck fuck fuck!

Wait.

I had an idea! A terrible one, though. But at least it was a feasible one. Ugh, a truly terrible, feasible one. And it meant I'd have to do something I never, ever wanted to do. I bit my lip and weighed my options before requesting a group video chat with Candace's husband, Wil, and Nolan.

"Hey, Mel, what's up?" Wil was at the gym, in the weights area.

Nolan picked up, too. "Uh, hi, Melody?" He came into view with the shower behind him, tucking in his towel around his waist. I hadn't talked to him since the humiliating parent brunch.

"Wil? Nolan? Um, hi there! Wil, meet Nolan, he works at my company. Nolan, this is Wil, he's my best friend's husband. Sorry about the group video but I'm crunched for time. I need a huge favor from you both, and I might get fired if you don't help me, but no pressure. And I'd owe you both big. Like many-years-of-future-babysitting-for-Wil and a-year-supply-of-P.F.-Chang's-dinners-for-Nolan kind of big." I took a deep breath in and out.

Wil asked in a whisper, "Oh wow. Is it illegal?"

"Of course it's not illegal!"

Nolan asked with a giant smirk, "So what exactly is happening here? Is Melody Joo actually asking for . . . help?"

I pursed my lips together and hesitated. "I . . . I am. I'm asking for your help. Please."

"If it's shady or embarrassing, can I wear a disguise?" He tilted his chin up, pondering the situation.

I tapped my finger on my bottom lip. "Hmmm, yes, you can. I know you are both busy on weekends, but I need you to dress in costume as characters in my game. Like, in an hour. I thought of you two because, without sounding too weird or pervy, you guys have physiques that women should flock to, and the male stripper talent I'd recruited fell through. The only thing you'll need to do is stand in the booth with me, and be all friendly and smiley with people, with your shirts off. Could you do that?"

"Oh . . . so you've checked out my physique?" Nolan teased.

"But we'd have pants?" Wil asked in a panicked tone.

I laughed. "Yes, Nolan, no shame in admitting this given my current predicament. And yes, Wil. I picked out tasteful long cargo shorts, don't worry. They have more coverage than what you'd wear to the beach. We'll give you sunglasses and give you different hairstyles, too, if you want. PLEASE, can you guys help?" *Please say yes. Please say yes.*

If it hadn't been for their stunned blinking, I would have assumed my phone had frozen. Honestly, I had no idea how they'd respond. How would I react if either of them asked me to show up to a trade event in less than an hour, dressed like a stripper? It would've taken at least thirty minutes for me to stop laughing hysterically. And then the remaining thirty to go through a wide range of feelings about what I should do, simply because someone I trusted and respected had just asked me to parade around at a convention in stripper garb.

Nolan finally broke the silence. "I'll do it, but you have to cosplay too."

Wil quickly added, "Yeah, I'll do it if you cosplay. In three months I'll be busy changing diapers, so this is probably my last chance to do something exciting like this! Let's make it count!"

I'd planned on wearing a black fitted Seventeen Studios T-shirt to match the rest of my team. If they wanted me in costume, too, then I'd need to find an outfit like one of my female characters, to be true to the game. The women in the game wore more clothes than the dudes.

My heart soared as I agreed to their demands. "Okay, I'll dress up too! It's a deal then? Can you two get to the Seattle Convention Center in less than fifty minutes? We can expense your transportation. And you get free lunch!"

Wil nodded. "I need to hop in the shower first, and I'll head straight there."

"Well, I'm already showered." Nolan accidentally dropped his towel but then pulled his phone up just in time. My heartbeat sped up as I imagined what was under that navy-blue terry cloth.

C'mon, brain, focus on the job!

"See you soon." I flapped my hands, fanning myself, and then sat a moment, letting it sink in that with my resourcefulness I'd just avoided a train wreck.

I found strippers! And to fill my end of the bargain, finding a costume was top priority. There was a scene in *Ultimate Apocalypse* where a woman in full-on army combat gear wearing camouflage face paint comes storming out of the woods, offering advice about the dangers of the wilderness that gets them farther along in their journey. She would be my character. An army-navy surplus store within walking distance of the convention center opened at 9 A.M. I told Asher I had a new plan and left the costumes for Nolan and Wil with him.

As SOON AS the store unlocked its doors I rushed to women's combat gear and brought every item in that section to the checkout counter.

I asked the checkout clerk, "Does anyone here do face-paint camouflage designs?"

He yelled to the back of the store. "Uncle Gerry! Come to the front!" A bald, tattooed Uncle Gerry appeared, wearing a T-shirt that read GOD BLESS 'MERICA.

I asked Uncle Gerry if he could help me, and he answered in a gravelly voice, "I learned the face-painting trade by studying pictures of soldiers' faces in Desert Storm." I took that to mean yes.

He sat me down on the swivel chair behind the counter and got to work. Ten minutes later, I took a look at the finished creation in the mirror. A transformed Melody Joo stared back at me, with a green splotchy face, looking like a sickly Hulk.

But I had no time for any artistic suggestions. I handed over a five-dollar tip, changed into the war gear in the bathroom, and charged out the door like a crazed apocalyptic fanatic.

The main doors to the event were still closed when I arrived. A few hundred game enthusiasts waited outside, ready to storm the show floor. Film crews from all over the world, teenage YouTubers doing selfie videos, and hard-core cosplayers lined up, anticipating the grand opening to the all-weekend event. Straggling food truck vendors pulled up to the front of the venue, offering quick-grab breakfast options while they prepared for the future lunch rush. I flashed my vendor badge and the security crew allowed me to enter the premises while two onlookers complained, "Awww, why does she get to go in? Is it 'cause she's a chick?" and "Maybe I should flash my boobs, too."

I turned around and gave them the finger.

Because our booth was located in the very back of the conference hall, I took in all the rock music, flashing lights, and nonstop game-related videos as any attendee would along the way. It was like someone brought Las Vegas, Dave & Buster's, and Times Square all into one place, balled them all up, threw them into the air, and blew that shit up with a glitter-spraying frag cannon. The convention patrons paid good money for this blingy, flashy, epileptic-seizure-inducing experience. Exhibitors shouted their product pitches at me and shoved free T-shirts, rolled posters, and food truck coupons into my arms as I looked for my team.

Asher stood in the booth with Damon, the IT guy, who had

taken the A/V guy's place while he went on break. They were trying to load Nick's game trailer onto two of the monitors, while Wil and Nolan, both shirtless and wearing cargo shorts, waited for my arrival. My gaze traveled down Nolan's defined chest over to his lean, muscular arms, a look I preferred far more than his daily checkeredness. My throat went dry as I handed them each a pair of aviators from the surplus store and camouflage-printed bandannas.

Nolan folded his and tied it around his forehead. "How do I look?" His eyes searched my face as he strode closer to me. Army-green face paint covered my blushing cheeks, concealing my attraction to him. My whole body flushed with intense heat at the prospect of him being around me all day. Close to his freshly showered body. His tall, muscular, and lean body. Shirtless. Body.

My mind drew a blank. "Wh-what was the question again?"

He breathed every word. "How. Do. I. Look?"

I swallowed hard. How did he look? Was "mouthwatering" a way to describe a person?

Before I could answer, Asher said, "I'd do you, bro."

Nolan coughed as I barked out an uncomfortable laugh.

Wil put his bandanna around his neck, going for the cowboy look. I handed them both ammunition belts and gun holsters, which they put on gleefully. Wow, they were ENJOYING this. Meanwhile, as they transformed into sexified hotties, I looked like a fucking doomsday loon. But if the talent was happy, that made me happy.

Wil asked, "So what exactly are we supposed to do again?"

Nolan chimed in. "Besides look hot and studly?"

"Yes, besides that," Wil snorted.

"I need you two to scan the badges of anyone who even looks remotely interested in our game. Or anyone you manage to speak with. We need to collect names for our launch newsletter."

Asher tapped me on the shoulder. "Boss, we have a problem. Our internet isn't working so we can't get the trailers to display on the monitors." I looked over at Damon, our IT guru, who sat there texting and avoiding eye contact. Not really the problem-solving, roll-up-your-sleeves type.

Asher added, "Damon said he tried everything and claims it's the TV monitor, not the connection. But the monitors worked in the office when we tested them last night."

Nolan came over. "We had these same monitors the last place I worked. Let me fiddle with them." There was nothing more distracting than watching a brainy stripper fix my mechanical problems.

Wil joined him and after a few minutes of troubleshooting together, they came back over to me with a solution. Nolan asked, "Does anyone have a spare Ethernet cable? The Wi-Fi adapter isn't working right, but the monitor has an Ethernet port, and that might do it."

I walkie-talkied Asher, who had gone MIA for a short while, and asked him to see if the show's equipment vendors had an Ethernet cord we could rent. He came back shortly with a thirty-foot cord. Wil flicked on the monitor and the trailer appeared on the screen, perfectly clear. We all hugged and high-fived one another, like they did in all those NASA movies when they successfully land a space shuttle after a major equipment malfunction.

"Thank you," I managed to say to Nolan.

He placed his hand on my shoulder and squeezed. "All's forgiven in the coffee mug war, right?"

Electricity from his touch rippled down my shoulder and through my arm. "You're debt-free. And now I owe YOU," I said with a smirk.

"Great." He grinned and rubbed his hands together, his prickling warmth still imprinted on my shoulder.

"Oh shit. Here they come." Wil's eyes widened.

I looked behind me to see what spooked him. A tidal wave of gamer geeks headed our way, flowing in the direction toward our booth.

"Ready?" I asked Asher.

"Yup."

The first wave of gaming enthusiasts appeared and immediately clamored for demos. Wil and Nolan soon became the crowd favorite of college girls who took selfies with them and posted the pictures on social media. I mean, it made sense. Who wouldn't want a picture with two cosplaying strippers? That was the whole point of having them there.

After a short while, pitching our game wasn't even necessary. Barraged with an unending flow of questions from members of the press and general admission game enthusiasts, our frontline team kept the answers rolling.

"Is this the game that people wanted to cancel?"

"Didn't they get enough signatures on the petition to fire you?"

"Can I get an autograph and a picture?"

"What swag do you have?"

And of course, the most popular question, "Where's the nearest bathroom?"

As we scanned badges, gave out branded Nerf guns, and took swigs of water from talking so much, the crowds just kept coming. As it neared lunchtime, though, the flow finally began to die down as the showgoers left the building to get food truck fare.

Asher said, "Hey, I really need to go take a piss. Sorry, I mean go to the bathroom. Wow, it's already been a long day, and it's only noon. I'll tap out our dynamic stripper duo to take their bio break when I get back."

Wil and Nolan were still killing it on the floor, even with the lunchtime intermission. Anyone who walked by, both men and women, young and old, looked on with curiosity. Somehow, at some point, both of them ended up with body glitter all over their chests. Their pecs glistened in the indoor light as they spoke to various gaming constituents about the merits of the game.

While I took a water break, I glanced over a few times at Nolan. At one point he caught me staring and grinned at me. I smiled and hastily walked a loop around the booth, mortified that I'd been looking at him so long that he witnessed it.

Stay focused on work, Melody. No distractions.

When I came back around, a group of white, young male vid bloggers walked up to Wil and asked, "What do you do?"

He answered, "You mean, what does the character do? Or like, in real life, what job do I have?"

The goatee guy rolled his eyes. "Like, what's your signature thing in your game? Like, roundhouse kicking? Nunchucks? Samurai swords?"

Wil smiled but replied tersely, "Well, in the game I'd use a crossbow, my weapon of choice. In real life, I do boxing. Given my mood, I could probably pummel a few heads into a bloody pulp."

Goatee guy sidekicked the air and yelled, "Ha-yah!" and then karate-chopped his friend. The group laughed and walked away with some of our swag bags.

Cringing, Nolan asked, "What kind of racist shit was that?"

I rolled my eyes. "Yeah, welcome to our world. I get those racist remarks plus the sexist ones. Pretend those same guys had stared at your chest the whole time while saying those horrible things and then walked away mumbling explicit remarks."

Wil's and Nolan's mouths fell open. Nolan stammered, "Oh, that's just . . . I . . . I'm sorry."

A curious onlooker walked up to me with a small spiral notepad full of notes. "I've never seen a game like this. Male strippers as protagonists? Women wearing combat gear instead of fishnets with a bulletproof camo bikini? This is all so curious and odd." I'd seen him circling the booth a few minutes, waiting for the right time to engage. This fiftyish-year-old man wasn't anywhere near my target demographic, as *UA* skewed twenties and female, but maybe he was someone's dad or something. He continued firing off questions about the origins of the game and asked for one of our mobile devices so he could play the first level. He had mad skills: he cleared the level faster than I'd seen anyone do that day.

He grabbed some branded swag and asked, "Did you know that your game has already gotten over a hundred reviews on IGN?"

I searched IGN on my phone and found an *Ultimate Apocalypse* game overview link, along with the average rating of 1.5 stars out of 5. These sham reviewers were undoubtedly the same trolls who had nothing better to do than write bogus reviews or trash me on various message boards. Skimming the one-star reviews, these insightful gamers really demonstrated their knowledge and expertise with thoughtful comments such as "I like your tits," "I'm gonna beat you down with my giant cock," "I'd rather play *Mass Effect: Andromeda* than this game garbage," and my favorite, "I would rather eat my own big butt than buy this game" (um, WTF).

Blinking back hot tears, I blew out a slow exhale and tried to think of ways to handle this disaster. Because of the restrictions placed on me by my company's legal team, I couldn't go on the counterattack. But also, it wouldn't make a difference. These trolls were everywhere I looked, like disgusting cicadas during their hatching season, or a never-ending game of whack-a-mole.

As I fought back tears, my mind wandered in despair. Quitting my job, curling up in front of the television, and crying into my bowl of ice cream was an easy way out, and oh so tempting. I could go back to my old job, bored to tears, feeling unaccomplished and unsatisfied. I had known breaking into the game industry would be challenging, and here I was, living what I thought was my dream. How would I know if it was really my dream if I didn't see this to the end?

No way was I going to give up now. I'd made a promise to myself that I would get this game launched, no matter what it took. I thought about my team and how far we'd come. These asshole bullies wouldn't defeat Melody Joo. Fuck them, and their big butts, right?

A food vendor came by with a display of sandwiches, chips, and bottles of water, and I bought lunch for everyone. We all wolfed down our food in silence: talking nonstop and standing for several hours had wiped us all out. Wil and Nolan finished their food first. "Back to the grind!" Wil said as he pulled Nolan up off the floor. They jumped back into stripper cosplay mode just as the wave of postlunch traffic hit our booth. By 3 P.M. the booth crowds began to die down again, so the stripper duo walked the floor with the badge scanners, asking for newsletter sign-ups. By late afternoon we had real-time results on how many email addresses they had gotten for us. Four thousand new email addresses! Go, strippers, go!

Ian came by the booth again, letting us know that the social media alerts from our show presence made us the media darling of the convention. The biggest PR boost was a write-up from BetaGank, yes, the same gaming media outlet who had leaked the news about our game in the first place. The blurb was written by senior correspondent Gavin McGrath, who had uploaded pictures and real-time updates from GameCon. I enlarged his bio photo. Holy shit, Gavin turned out to be the guy I thought was someone's dad! Thank goodness he took a bag of our best giveaways.

Cautiously optimistic, I read his review:

The Seventeen Studios booth was certainly one of the plainest displays at the show, with your typical booming music, typical game demos, and no-frills booth design. The thirty-second game trailer for *Ultimate Apocalypse* impressed me, though, as it wasn't the typical twenty-nine seconds of explosions and one second of game logos. The writers focused on a clear story arc here (strippers unite to save the world!), and the team at Seventeen whittled the trailer down to a solid half minute of stunning cinematographic and intriguing game play. In addition to the allure of having two fantastically gorgeous male models walking the floor with gleaming (heavenly?) smiles and chests, the game creator and lead producer, Melody, hung out on the floor, too, fielding my annoying questions. She was sharp, passionate, and approachable as she described her game with so much enthusiasm it made me want to download it on the spot. Unfortunately, it's not available yet.

I'm not part of the gaming illuminati, or in the target market for this mobile masterpiece, but I do think this title is worth a second look, for all the naysayers who dismissed it without really seeing it first. Shame on you for the one-star reviews, by the way. The game looks entertaining, fresh, snarky, and there's plenty of both male and female eye candy, even though the characters are more overtly covered than expected. I'm going to download the game when it releases in a few months. Good job, Gamer Girl, Melody Joo.

In a rare moment of completely losing my shit, I galloped around the booth squealing, "Oh my god! Oh my god! Oh my GAWD!" This Gavin guy, a senior writer at BetaGank, *was* the illuminati of gaming, and he just endorsed my game on a highly trafficked website. *Holy. Fucking. Shit.* "Guys! This is HUGE!" I laughed and then hugged my coworkers and some conventiongoers standing close by. Luckily, no one called security on me. Or HR.

WITH A HUGE smile plastered on my face, I hummed and whistled while packing away our main equipment in boxes for safekeeping. The next weekend shift would be setting up again the following morning, sans stripper talent.

I'd tried to send Wil and Nolan home, but because they were still so pumped with adrenaline, they went to one of the show's exclusive after-parties. They had somehow become GameCon demi-idols: in just one day they had been in hundreds of uploaded selfies and gotten thousands of likes in social media. Each of them received invitations to host upcoming gaming esports events and bachelorette parties, and both had even been invited to work at another game studio's launch party (Nolan said, "No thank you, we are exclusive to Seventeen Studios," and declined politely).

Thanks to Asher, Nolan, and Wil, we'd catapulted *Ultimate Apocalypse* into the spotlight, despite all the negative baggage we had to overcome to do so. A miracle had been pulled off, and this was easily my biggest career accomplishment to date.

As I responded to texts and social posts congratulating me for not fucking up, Ian pulled Asher aside to speak with him. Ian flapped his hands around and continually shifted his stance. Left. Right. Left. Right. Repeat. Asher stood next to Ian unsmiling, yet nodding. Did someone in Asher's family die?

Then Ian said rather loudly, "I'm expecting big things from you," and friendly-slapped Asher in the back, nudging him back to the booth. Asher frowned and shot me a pained look. I couldn't help myself. I had to ask.

"Hey, Ash, what was that dudes-only pep talk about?"

Asher didn't answer right away. He chewed his bottom lip

before speaking. "Uh, he told me not to say anything but I feel like I should tell you—"

Ian reappeared in a flash, like one of those bad guys in a horror movie who just can't leave the protagonist alone. Surprise! "Melody, on the heels of that amazing BetaGank review, I wanted to let you know that we're launching a new flagship game. Asher pitched it to me a few months ago. It's called *Girls of War*, or *G-O-W* for short. *Ultimate Apocalypse* is just too risky to be our flagship title, and Asher's father suggested we mitigate the risk by adding a new title to the portfolio." Asher fiddled with his zipper on his fleece jacket, avoiding eye contact. "His dad is investing ten percent in the company and is one of our key stakeholders. Now Asher's game is priority number one, so we'll be changing your status from flagship to back burner."

His words were so astoundingly brutal that breathing and blinking became instantly taxing. I steadied myself on a table covered in controllers that hadn't been packed away yet.

To my dismay, he continued bombarding me with bad news. "We'll be redeploying some of your staff to Asher's team. Oh, and of course that means Asher will be off your team now. We need some of your developers, too, and a portion of your earmarked marketing budget will go to Asher's project. You can maybe keep Kat for now and a small incubator team to get this game done."

"Could I get Nolan to help, too?" I asked in a whisper.

Ian cocked his head. "Nolan? My nephew? No, you can't. His internship's over soon."

"What?" A tight knot formed in my stomach. Why didn't Nolan tell me he was leaving?

"I'm surprised he didn't tell you." Ian slapped Asher on the back a second time. "Melody, I know this takes the wind from your sails, but for the company, this is great! We're a force to be reckoned with, thanks to *UA* being in the news!" He nodded at me. A nod of thanks for guaranteeing him an end-of-year performance bonus.

A hard lump formed in my throat, and swallowing didn't make it go away. My voice caught as soon as I tried to speak, so I kept quiet. This was a blessing of sorts, because words would be followed by a tidal wave of tears, and I could not allow that to happen. Not after everything I'd already accomplished.

I couldn't reveal what lurked inside me.

On the outside, with every ounce of my willpower, I tried to display strength, confidence, and flexibility. Inside, I was a cyclone of anxiety, vulnerability, and demoralization. Spinning out of control.

The day's peak was the best day of my career. Then Ian and Asher pulled the rug out from under me, and I fell down flat with the wind knocked out of my chest. Then Nolan Fucking MacKenzie shattered my heart.

That selfish jerk, why didn't he just tell me?

After all those blows, I couldn't breathe and didn't know if I could get back up again. Or if I even wanted to.

CHAPTER NINETEEN

After my big GameCon day I lay in bed through the next afternoon. In the dark, under my covers, I could cry without witnesses. The hateful online posts, the threatening emails and calls, working till 11 P.M. most nights and weekends had all collapsed on top of me at once.

Nolan texted me dozens of times. He was worried about me. Blah blah fucking blah.

He finally sent a message that almost got my attention. *Heard about Asher's Girls of War game.* ☹ *Would doughnuts help?*

Not even doughnuts could make me feel better. Not this time. Not even the chocolate old-fashioned ones from Top Pot. Instead, I sobbed into my pillow, waterlogging the down feather stuffing with my pool of tears.

Nolan called and I let it go to voice mail. He called again. And then again. I tried to turn it on "do not disturb" mode but my phone kept crashing. Exasperated, I picked up the next time he rang. "Hello?" I croaked.

"Hey, you didn't reply to my doughnut text. You have me worried. Do you want to talk about it?"

I gave him the play-by-play of Ian and Asher's betrayal and left out the part about his internship. "Now I have to get everything done with only half the team and a basically nonexistent marketing budget."

"You'll find a way. You're resourceful. You always get yourself out of messes."

"Gee, thanks," I said drily.

"You know I mean that in the sweetest way possible."

Feeling a smidge better, I smiled a teeny bit.

"If you want me to say it, fine, I'll say it. You're the strongest, smartest, coolest, most stubborn woman I know."

The hurt I felt inside didn't allow me to appreciate his flattering, heartfelt words. "Don't forget abandoned."

"Uhhh . . . what do you mean?"

I said flatly, "Ian told me your internship was ending."

He let out a sputtering exhale. "Oh. Oh no. I'm so sorry. I . . . I was going to tell you, I swear. To be eligible for an internship, you need to be enrolled in school, and I just withdrew enrollment from business school a couple of days ago. My parents aren't talking to me right now, because I explained to them that I just didn't see myself taking over the family business, and now I desperately need a job to pay off school debt since they fully cut me off. I did try to stop by at work to talk about it, but you kept saying you were so busy, and I could see you were stressed about GameCon. And honestly, I didn't know what to say. That I'll be an unemployed loser, an MBA dropout, and have no direction in life?"

New tears brimmed in my eyes. All this was happening when I was laser focused on work. "I wish you had told me," I said, letting out a sad sigh. "I wish I had *let* you tell me."

"If it makes you feel better, I'm trying not to leave. I've applied to some internal full-time positions at Seventeen and Uncle Ian said I have a good shot at them. So there's a chance I'll still be working there, just not as a lowly intern. I also applied to some other jobs at local gaming companies and ones in California, since a lot of the big game companies are there. My goal though is to stay in gaming and live in Seattle. I like it here. And . . . I'm happy I met you."

"Really?" I brushed the tears rolling down my cheeks with my pajama sleeve. His words briefly cheered me up, but hearing that he might move to another state brought me right back down again.

"Really. I don't dress up like a fake stripper on a moment's notice for anyone, you know," he said.

"Thanks for that, by the way." I laughed. Nolan MacKenzie really knew how to win a gal over. With stripper talk.

"It had always been a fantasy of mine, and you made my dream come true yesterday. If you ever need me for more stripper work, I'm your guy."

I could feel him grinning through the phone. Could he feel the same?

"Mel, you'll find a way to get your game launched on time.

I'll be in and out of the office for interviews the next few weeks, but I can help out as much as I can before I go, just ask."

I don't know why asking for help was so damn hard for me all the time. Doing everything all by myself wasn't sustainable, and it wasn't smart. Long-term success meant having to say no sometimes, just to get the job done. Setting limits, sticking to them, and getting help from teammates when necessary was key to doing well at Seventeen Studios, and I needed to work on all that.

Swallowing hard, I asked, "Would you please help me until you leave? I'm gonna need all the help I can get."

"Yeah, no problem. I have interviews on Monday and Tuesday, but I'll pitch in to help when I get back."

"Thank you. For everything. And good luck with interviews."

When we hung up, my brain synapses fired like never before. He had always been right; I couldn't manage all this by myself and I needed to ask for help. My own pride got in the way of my success. But I knew just the person at work to give me advice. Someone to confide in and trust. Someone who could help me get this done.

Kat.

I jumped out of bed and grabbed my phone from my messenger bag. *Hey! I know you're not working weekends but I need your guidance. Would you please help me? Ian is taking all resources away but not moving the go live date. Will set up meetings with you first thing Monday morning. I'll bring coffee.*

Within ten seconds she replied. *Caramel macchiato. And get some rest or you'll get sick.*

I could do this. I felt better. Not great, but better.

Like I-could-eat-a-couple-of-glazed-doughnuts better.

"I DIDN'T KNOW if you wanted an iced caramel macchiato or a hot one, so I got both." I'd stopped at one of Seattle's iconic bikini drive-through coffee kiosks on the way to work, where barely dressed baristas greeted me at 6:30 A.M. with giant, perky . . . smiles. "Princess" had taken my order, and as she leaned over to grab my twenty-dollar bill, I wondered if I was helping or hurting the world by supporting this local business.

Kat smiled greedily and grabbed both from my hands. "I can't choose between hot and cold, either. That's like asking if I like my son or daughter more." She leaned in and whispered, "My son makes me toast every morning, though."

I laughed and then told her about all the shit that went down at GameCon.

She whistled and leaned back in her chair. She lightly tapped her pen on her desk, to an adagio metronome beat.

She stopped tapping and frowned. "This sucks. I'm not gonna lie."

"I know. I'm hoping you might have some ideas on how we can get this game launched with half the team. And no marketing money."

She scrunched her brow and nose at the same time. "Well, you're the one with the marketing background, so I'll leave that part up to you. But the design and development stuff, I might have a thought or two." She took a sip of the iced drink and then tried the hot one. "The hot one's better." Her face lit up and she clasped her hands together. "Okay, so you may hate these suggestions, but I'll tell you what I think. We have two programmer interns, both still in college, both Chinese citizens with visas. If they do coding on the evenings and weekends, in exchange for, say, help with English assignments and essays and such, you might have a workable solution."

"I'm not good at writing essays, though."

She swatted her hand at me playfully. "Look, I'm just telling you where I see opportunities for mutually beneficial opportunities. Got it?"

I covered my head and winced. "Yes, ma'am, I'll shut up. Keep going."

"Production-wise, I actually think you're doing great. Asher leaving will hurt us but he loaded all the remaining Jira tickets and all the projects into our shared tracking system. The receptionist Kedra isn't too busy, she's hyperorganized, and she's been dying to break into game production. She's smart, too. I think she could be a good coordinator. Your intern friend can assist her." She nodded, like she'd just realized something. "I'll make sure you get the design resources you need. Those guys will listen to me over Asher because they like me better. I'm glad you came to me, by the way. It's better to rally with a team than to be a lone avenger. If you tried to do it all, you'd for sure fail. No offense. And to tell you the truth, I'm really enjoying the break from *Zooful Nation*."

If Kat's ideas panned out, I could have three new people on the team by the end of the week. With the energy and enthusiasm of fresh new teammates, and me putting in more hours, *Ultimate Apocalypse* could get back on track.

"Thank you, Kat. I'll set up some meetings this week with the developers, Kedra, and Nolan and bring them up to speed on everything. You've been so helpful. I owe you so much." I tapped one of the bobbleheads on her desk as I stood up from her guest chair. Its head projectile-launched off the spring, slammed the wall, and fell to the floor.

"Oh god, I am so sorry about that."

She scratched her brow. "Don't worry about it. It was broken and I hated that one anyway." She pointed to her coffee cups. "If you bring in coffee again, I'd love the hot one." She took a sip of the iced one again. "Yeah, the hot one. Oh! They just opened up a trendy coffee shop down the street, you should check it out. It's gotten great reviews."

DURING MY LUNCH break, I stopped by the new neighborhood coffee place Kat had raved about to get her an afternoon macchiato. What she had omitted from her narrative was that this new coffee hot spot was a kitten café. Seattle had so many coffee shops downtown, and new shop owners tried to find new ways to differentiate, such as having feline animals on the premises to cuddle and pet while drinking coffee and/or reading the morning paper. What I didn't disclose to Kat, because she didn't tell me about the live kitten motif, was that I had a severe allergy of cats. Kittens, no matter how snuggly and adorable, could shut my body down.

Opening the Critter Café door triggered a cheery meowing tune, signaling a newcomer's arrival. I tried to remember what venue had been there before it turned into yet another coffee place. Was it a furniture store? A boutique? Oh, wait . . . Seattle's oldest tattoo parlor. The now-defunct badass tattoo parlor had been replaced by an animal-themed café with cartoon paw prints on the window and signage written in comic sans.

The aroma of slightly charred coffee grounds wafted in the air. In the corner of the room the furry blurs of kittens caught my eye. I took in the entire room—the randomly placed scratching posts, giant catnip plants, and fishing-rod-type toys with dangly cat lures on strings on various tables—and my heartbeat quickened. My breathing turned to panting. My arms and face prickled. I had to get out immediately.

I ordered a drip coffee for myself and Kat's caramel macchiato and threw down a twenty-dollar bill. I'd taken my allergy meds earlier that morning, but that wasn't extra strength enough. The hives and itchiness came first. The sides of my neck and chest grew hotter and I tried to scratch it through my scarf. Then, the wheezing struck.

While squeezing the caramel drizzle, the cheery barista said,

"You know, research shows that animals can be therapeutic and calming. Would you like to hold one of our kittens?" Her tie-dye headscarf had cat faces on it. "I made this bandanna myself," she said proudly, noticing my stare.

She slid the two coffees my way. One of the coffees sloshed out of the sipper top and burned my hand. I didn't even feel it.

I grabbed the drinks and flew out of there like a bat out of kitty allergen hell.

Clomp. Clomp. Clomp. Clomp. My heels echoed down the street. Water splash marks covered the calves and ankles of my jeans. When I got to Kat's office, I handed her the macchiato and told her about the adorable kitties triggering my full-blown allergy attack.

She took a sip. "This is amazing. The coffee shop sounded so cute, with all those little furballs running around. I hoped that place would help you relax. It's weird your allergies flared up because all the breeds of cats they have there don't shed and are all hypoallergenic." She took another sip. "Thanks for the coffee! It'll help fuel my late-afternoon push."

Was that a panic attack then? A side effect from massive sleep deprivation? Maybe a psychosomatic episode? This had never happened before. Could I really harm my own body so brutally? I walked back to my desk, with less clomping and more of a light meandering step, contemplating what had happened to me at the café.

Maybe these harassers, haters, one-star reviewers, trolls, whatever you called those assholes, not only messed with my head, but they now made me susceptible to physical harm, too. They'd tried to wear me down for months. And damn it, it was finally working.

THAT EVENING, CANDACE and I accompanied Jane to a wedding cake tasting appointment. Normally this would be something the bride and groom did together, but her fiancé had recently diagnosed himself with a gluten intolerance, so she asked her bridesmaids to fill in. And who was I to say no to free cake?

Miraculously on time for once, Candace came out of the bathroom, pulling back her long brown locks with a hair tie. "I'm almost ready," she said.

"This isn't one of those hot dog or pie eating competitions, where pulling your hair back might be an advantage," I joked, elbowing her lightly in the arm.

She giggled. "I know; it's more that I want to be able to see everything. Pregnancy has made my hair grow faster and thicker."

We took our seats at the restaurant holding the tasting, flanking Jane from both sides. Just as we pulled our napkins onto our laps, a petite, older Asian woman with a kimono and perfect hair bun brought in bento boxes with three compartments of cake samples.

She said only three words. "Yuzu. Lavender. Chamomile."

For cake? Gross. Yuck. Ugh.

Jane read my mind. "I know this isn't chocolate, but give it a try," she whispered from behind her napkin.

So try I did. A small bite of all three of them.

Jane asked, "What do you think?"

Truthfully? "They're okay," I answered with a wince.

"Be honest," Jane begged.

"Honestly, they taste like spa lotion." Her face fell a little, so I added, "But really fancy spa lotion. Maybe you go in this direction but also get a crowd-pleaser dessert, too?"

Candace jumped in. "Can I have yours then?" I looked over and she had polished off all three of her minicakes. She swapped boxes with me and finished mine, too. "Final trimester," she muttered with a mouth full of whipped icing.

A tiny elderly woman dressed in head-to-toe black swooped away our bento boxes. Our cake hostess pulled open the curtain from the kitchen and brought us three more cake samples. Rosewater Honeycomb, Orange Blossom Twist, and Coconut Cream Chiffon. Great, more spa lotion. And the coconut one smelled like sunscreen.

My phone buzzed twice in a row and I looked at Jane for permission to check it. She nodded.

Two messages from Nolan. One saying, *Here are final versions of the newsletter and website, for your records. I'm pushing the website developer to do two versions that we can A/B test.* The next message was images of all the things Nolan had been working on.

Jane leaned over to read my screen. "Wow, those look really good." Looking up at my face, she added, "I haven't seen your face light up like this in a long time, and I don't think it's just the photos. You'd think I'd invited you to a Baskin-Robbins ice cream cake tasting instead."

I didn't hide too much from my girlfriends, but there were things I kept tight to my chest, like my dream job of being a radio DJ. My inexplicable love of Crocs clogs. And my desire for a relationship with an MBA intern that was not destined to be.

Jane continued. "You're blushing, lady." She looked over at Candace. "Maybe she's going to be walking down the aisle next!"

With a hard shove, I pushed my bento box halfway across the table. "He's just a friend. Nothing's going to happen between us. Plus, he's looking for a job, in case you have any leads."

Candace pulled my bento over to her and finished all my untouched samples. "That's too bad," she said with cake-filled chipmunk cheeks.

Jane pensively tapped her lower lip with her index finger. "We have a strategic analyst position opening up at my company. If you don't have any feelings for him"—she paused to take a quick drink of water—"then I can email you the job description that you can pass on to him. But the job is in New York, so he'd have to relocate."

My stomach sank as soon as she said the words "New York." This job was perfect for Nolan, but it was over two thousand miles away.

Before I could ask any more questions about the open position, the hostess reentered the room with one more sample. "Chef's special, custom-made for you, dear." Hibiscus-cardamom sponge cake with lychee puree on the side.

Jane took an eager first bite. "This is it." I hadn't even tasted it, but it's not like Jane and I saw eye to eye on any of this anyway. I passed my small plate over to Candace, which she gladly accepted.

The bride-to-be announced to the hostess, "Yes, we'll take this one, and I'd like to add a Belgian chocolate accompanying cake, too, for my guests who want something more"—she searched for the right word—"familiar." She smiled at me and squeezed my hand. For the first time ever, I'd convinced Jane to change her mind about something. Life achievement unlocked.

CHAPTER TWENTY

Asher moved to a different floor so he could be closer to his development team. *Au revoir, bro!* I didn't hold my breath, though, because I knew that any day I might have to share the office with someone else, or something else, like those stupid *Kaizen Five* life-size cutouts again. But I appreciated the temporary reprieve.

Thanks to the team putting in extra hours in the evenings and on weekends, with just two months left before the big launch, we were still on track for our release. My tight-knit incubator team had found our stride after a bumpy start. Processes became more streamlined, the designers worked well with the engineers, and Kedra the receptionist (moonlighting as our production coordinator with Nolan's assistance) had done a great job with keeping our tasks organized and on schedule.

Every morning I brought doughnuts to our daily team meeting. The engineers usually dove in first, taking the chocolate glazed with custard filling, our designers went for the seasonal flavors, so after a few days of collecting doughnut data I could predict the crowd's favorites. No one would have to consume second-tier doughnut calories. Not under my watch!

Kedra hooked up her laptop to the overhead projector. Even the people closest to the front of the room squinted at the hundreds of tasks listed in our production schedule. She zoomed in and we could see all the to-dos on the horizon.

I dunked my doughnut into my coffee. "We still need to make sure this game can run on all operating systems on all common phones." *Mmmmm, coffee doughnut.*

Kat said, "We just started testing on different devices, and to get the constant frame rate throughout the game experience, we need to sacrifice some visual effects." She saw me eating the sugar glaze I'd picked off my napkin. "Hey, don't eat too many doughnuts, Melody. You don't want diabetes someday. Sorry, being overprotective mama bear."

I laughed. "Okay, no more doughnuts for me. At least not today. If I needed to justify to the press why the stripper characters were say, shirtless ninety percent of the time, could I say that we had to limit our clothing options to improve performance? It would reduce texture memory and polygon count, right?"

Xin, the engineer intern, nodded furiously. "Yes! Yes!" That's all he said, but that was enough for me.

I walked up to the screen and pointed out the upcoming milestones, trying to avoid the blinding light of the projector beam. "Once we get the game running with a consistent frame rate, we'll have the alpha version ready for the team to tinker with. Wait . . . do we actually have any testers for our game, or did Ian steal those, too?"

Kat shrugged. "I have friends in that department. We'll find someone. They like doughnuts too."

The other developer intern, also named Xin (maybe our technical recruiter liked people named Xin?), asked, "Can you approve which size you want?"

"Which size? What do you mean?"

He pointed to his laptop and toggled between three screens. Each had the same female lead character, with different boob sizes.

Xin number two said, "You want small, medium, or large? I can also make . . . bigger."

On screen three he typed in some commands and the character's breasts inflated from B cups to DDD.

My mouth fell open and I gasped. "Please stop!" The breasts were now so big they covered her face.

Xin number two turned to look at Xin number one. "This is too big. She cannot breathe."

Death by boob suffocation. "Let's go with medium," I said definitively.

With the help of our talented artists, Kat's game characters looked so lifelike, a far departure from her zoo games, where the romping animals were doe-eyed and cartoony. Not that I'd seen a ton of strippers and apocalyptic female warriors in real life, but the character depictions looked amazingly realistic. The men looked heroic. The women looked athletic, but not like she-beasts.

"Everything you touch is magic," I said to Kat. "Your work is stunning."

"This was all possible because of you." She smiled, which wasn't something that happened often. "You had one hell of a steep learning curve, but honestly, you're the best producer I've ever worked with at this company."

Everyone around the table nodded and smiled. The Xins held up their doughnuts and saluted me.

"And I have the best team," I said, choking up. It was true, I'd never had the pleasure of working with such passionate and creative people in my life. Even though my job had a lot of ups and downs, seeing the impact I had on my team (and they had on me) made me want to stick around to finish what I started.

While we chattered about the good work we'd been doing, my phone vibrated a few times with several text messages from unknown senders.

> *How do I say this in the most non-misogynistic way possible? Fuck you, bitch!*

> Slut bitch whore slut slut slut sluttttttt

And then this one: *You dumb cronut. I hope you die.*
Quickly followed by: *Cunt. Autocorrect.*

I shot a panicked look across the room. How did this loser, or group of losers, find me? I googled my ten-digit number and discovered that UltimateDDay had fucking *doxed* me: my cell number, apartment building address, and work location had been posted online for the world to see. He'd even added a link to a Google Maps location of the office.

I scrolled through more posts and came across a friend of UltimateDDay who declared he'd be visiting me later that night, through my window. He posted a street-view picture of my apartment building. Another troll suggested that someone get me "swatted" (which I had to look up because I had no idea what that was), and it turned out he tried to get someone to call the police to send a SWAT team to my apartment building.

What the holy fuck.

There were pages and pages of sickening posts from the last few hours. My chest constricted, like a larger, stronger person had bear-hugged me and refused to let go. With each inhale it became harder and harder to take in oxygen.

My sobs caught me off guard, like I was having an out-of-body experience. Why would someone target me like this? Why did I even matter to anyone? Kat jumped out of her chair and grabbed my shoulders. She looked me in the eyes. "Okay, Melody. Just breathe slowly. Inhale. Exhale."

I did as she instructed and showed her my phone. "My god, Melody, we're leaving and going to the police. **NOW.**"

Before we left the building she wrapped my scarf around my head and made me wear some neon-pink promotional sunglasses I'd picked up from GameCon. If the goal was to not draw attention to myself, we had failed.

We sped through the workstation maze. "Keep your head

down, Melody. We don't know who the mole is." Kat guided me past the kitchen, copy room, and mailroom. We went down seven flights of stairs and ended up at the parking garage. I had no idea that back stairwell existed.

She started the ignition to her Subaru. "That used to be my escape route when I needed to make pediatrician appointments, or pump in my car. You'll understand one day if you have kids."

As we hightailed it to the police station, Jane messaged me. *I'm freaking the fuck out. My wedding planner just quit! She said I stressed her out. I can't believe she'd say that to me. It's my wedding! Of course I'm stressed! Can you meet today, I need to vent. I can stop by your office if you're around. And just emailed you what I'd like you to do for my bachelorette party.*

And one from my mom: *You dating anyone yet? Your umma and appa are old. We want grandchilds.*

And another from Jane, ten minutes later: *Hey, I just stopped by your office. The receptionist (Kendra?) said you went to the PO-LICE?! Holy shit, this must be bad! Don't worry about the bachelorette party email, but just note that we should be RSVPing places by this weekend <3*

Kat dropped me off in front of the precinct while she found parking. I walked in through the door and didn't expect to see a modern-looking, IKEA-esque office interior. Maybe I'd watched too many crime shows on television, but I sort of envisioned a front desk behind bulletproof glass, and then jail cells somewhere in the back, with a bunch of imprisoned people clamoring for their lawyers or their one phone call. This place didn't look like that. Instead, this police station looked like it might have a legit Starbucks coffee machine.

The officer sitting in the front barely looked up at me. "Um, hi? I wanted to speak to someone about a harassment complaint."

"Name?" she asked with a yawn not politely covered by her hand. I stared at her badge. Officer Greeley.

"Sure, it's Melody Jae-Eun Joo."

Officer Greeley's downturned mouth accentuated her frown lines. "Melanie Choo? C-H-O-O?"

I sighed. "Melody J-O-O."

She henpecked the keys with her two index fingers. "It says here that someone has already filed a harassment complaint on your behalf. A lawyer from Seventeen Studios. This investigation opened a few weeks ago. If you show me your ID I can print this out for you."

She printed out over fifty pages and handed me the stack. Kat came up to me, panting hard. "I had to park a long way down. And I thought it would be a good idea to run back here. I'm sweaty. Sorry."

She looked over my shoulder and we skimmed the police report document together. A few sections stood out to me:

BlueBaller42 interview: Traced IP address. BB42 admitted he sent threatening emails to the work email address listed on BetaGank website but he does not actually own a sawed-off shotgun. Jamie Frazier (alias BlueBaller42) understood it was a federal crime to send messages like these and will never do it again.

SamuraiStud: Active tweeterer (sp?). Made death threats from his grandma's IP address. Just turned 18, and out of our local jurisdiction.

NoHmburgrH8rs: Heard about victim on BetaGank and 4chan. Could not recall specific comment he made about killing anyone named "Melody" but believed his comments were jokes. The post has since been deleted.

Dozens of these threat investigations were declared dead ends, inconclusive, or ended with a light slap on the wrist. None had moved forward as prosecutable due to a lack of concrete evidence. Numb and light-headed, I sat down and squeezed my eyes shut. The Seattle Police brought in the WBIS (Washington Bureau of Investigation Services) to investigate some of the more large-scale threats (like multiple bomb threats targeting Seventeen Studios, which employees didn't know about), but the WBIS dismissed them as hoaxes, and no serious effort went into hunting down and punishing the culprits.

With eyes still closed, I said calmly, "This report only covers a handful of the threats I received. What about the hundreds of others?"

Officer Greeley answered, "Miss, we don't have a large team

here. It's still an ongoing investigation." My eyes shot open and my steady breaths quickened.

Kat raised her voice. "Look, you've only researched a dozen of these and it took over two months. At this rate she'll be retired by the time you finish this investigation."

I exploded. "Or I'll be blown to smithereens tomorrow by someone who actually has a sawed-off shotgun at his disposal and knows how to use it!"

Officer Greeley continued to look at us with an uninterested gaze, as if we had offered her a ho-hum Salisbury steak microwave dinner and weren't talking about saving my goddamned life. She'd been with the department for twenty-three years, according to the framed certificate above her head. She had several pictures of her family on her wall and appeared to have grown children. She didn't seem the type to know anything about gaming or have a clue what an IP address was.

I pleaded, "If you look through these threats, you'll see that this could happen to anyone." I glanced again at her picture frames. "You have daughters. Granddaughters. Please help me."

Candace texted while I stood by Officer Greeley's desk. *Jane told me what's going on. I know people who can help.*

Kat whispered, "Let's go." I clenched the police report to my chest and followed Kat out the door.

Once we were outside, she turned to me. "I didn't realize how unhelpful the police would be at handling your situation. I'm so sorry."

Driving back to the office with Kat, I noticed Candace called a few times and left voice mails. Worried that something was wrong with the baby, I called her back immediately. She picked up on the first ring. "Oh good, it's you. I have a group of . . . um . . . friends . . . that have agreed to help you."

My whole body tensed. "What kind of friends are we talking about?"

"Well, you know in my early PR days I worked at a firm who handled celebrity clients. I met some interesting people along the way. These friends of mine are a group of um . . . female renegade investigators. They're wanted by the government because they're straight-up hackers. Well, they are more like social justice avengers really. They've been called hacktivists in the media and they like that term. Their sole mission is to right the world of unjust things, and, well, this problem of yours is exactly the kind of thing they take an interest in."

I wasn't politically inclined, so maybe these fem-hackers wouldn't take my case. I voted, most of the time, in presidential elections. But that was it. Being a die-by-the-sword social justice warrior wasn't my thing. I was more the "social justice worrier" type.

"How do I get in touch with these friends of yours?"

She cleared her throat. "I'll go ahead and send them your email and phone number now. They'll reach out to you soon and send you a link that will activate an encrypted video chat right away. They'll probably grill you with questions, but remember, their intentions are noble, and their goal is to help you and they'll explain how. It's a motley crew of women:

security consultants, computer programmers, there's even a stay-at-home hacker mom of twin toddlers."

"Okay, at this point I'm desperate. Thanks, Candace."

"No problem. Let's chat later."

Kat and I pulled into our work garage. "Thanks, Kat, for everything. And about what you just heard—"

She opened her door. "I didn't hear anything."

"I need some quiet time, so I'm going to sit in my car a few minutes. I'll be back up soon." She hugged me and headed up the elevator. Ian had parked his Porsche next to me and gave me so little room that I dinged his car when half opening my door. Oops.

Brrrrrrring!

A new message notification popped on my screen. Amazing that my phone worked so well in the garage. "Please click on video chat link sent to your email from WheedWackerPony." The creativity with some of these bizarre online names astounded me.

The link on my phone opened up on my browser, cycling through a series of redirected URLs. This happened a dozen times before I landed on a screen with a static picture of a My Little Pony. The rainbow one, Rainbow Dash? She had swirly black-and-white eyes, like she was being hypnotized. Very dizzying, yet calming. I shut my eyes, in case this was a weird plan to put me under a hypnotic spell and steal my bank account number.

The screen switched from Rainbow Dash to a gender-ambiguous silhouette. A voice that sounded like Morgan Freeman boomed from my speakerphone.

"Melody Joo! We have a question for you. What justice do you seek?"

Could anyone bring justice for what had happened to me? An online troll mob was out for my blood. Justice would be for all these monsters to quit hiding behind the cloak of anonymity and show their faces, and then get locked away forever by the police or FBI. But that wasn't ever going to happen.

"Um, I'm new to all this. What sort of justice are you able to get me?"

Morgan Freeman answered, "We at the Justice Brigade believe in . . . well, getting justice. You have been viciously attacked online, and you have restrained yourself from responding or going on the counterattack. We respect your restraint."

Interrupting Morgan Freeman to mention the company's gag order didn't feel appropriate. I'd bring that up another time, maybe.

The baritone voice continued. "We can help you. We want to help you. Many of your attackers have been problematic before, and we now have the resources and tools to figure out who these persons are behind the pseudonyms and avatars. We can trace IPs, hack into the gaming message boards, and dox these assholes right back, too." It was weird to hear Morgan Freeman say those words.

I looked down and caught myself wringing my hands. "This is all so impressive and I appreciate your willingness to help. But I'm extremely risk averse." In fact, so risk averse that I drove the speed limit exactly and always paid parking tickets and taxes months in advance. *What the hell am I doing with these rulebreakers?* "Is everything you're doing within the confines of the law?"

She laughed hard. "Melody, you are very funny. You don't worry. We'll get you justice. We can figure out the identities of these assholes and we'll take full credit for bringing them down. You don't even have to take part in anything."

"So that's basically a no then."

This whole idea of fighting evil with more evil didn't seem to be the best way to handle this. Like drinking black coffee on an empty stomach, an acidic uneasiness in the pit of my gut presented itself physically. A wave of nausea hit. "Um, Miss WheedWacker, before you publish anything, could you let me know what you find first? Then maybe we, I mean you, can decide what to do with that information. I want to see who we're dealing with, like if it's an eighty-year-old granny from Kansas, or a twelve-year-old schoolgirl from Osaka, I'd be less excited about retaliation on those types of people."

She paused before answering. "Yes. That is an acceptable arrangement. We'll bring the info to you as it comes in, as you requested," said Morgan Freeman. "We've actually already tracked down a few IP addresses since we've been on the phone with you. We should have some verified identities revealed in the next few hours."

"Wow! Thank you so much. I mean it." Although this path we were taking felt a little uncertain, it was nice to have people rallying around me. Even if they were hackers flying under the radar of the authorities. "Also, since you're investigating, could you find out who leaked the original info to BetaGank in the first place? The person who started the shit tsunami?"

"It might be difficult, but we will try. You're a friend of Candace, so you're a friend of ours." The call ended, and I headed back upstairs, feeling more optimistic. Finally, I was regaining control of my life again.

COMING BACK FROM a quick walk to clear my head, someone bellowed "Hold the elevator!" as the doors nearly closed. Feeling generous, and lucky enough to mash the door open button instead of the door close one, I allowed elevator refuge.

Unfortunately, the person benefiting was Asher. Crashing back into my life again like an annoying Twitter user who kept unfollowing and refollowing you.

He hurtled in just as I hit the door close button. *Damn it.*

"Oh, hey," he said, noticing me, panting from his fifteen feet of running. Not that I should say anything about that. After all, sometimes pulling off a sports bra got me winded.

Up, up, up we went in silence. The quietness between us was excruciatingly painful, but on the flip side, it was also much better than him talking.

He shifted his feet and looked over at me. "I want to apologize for taking your lead title status. My dad had sway with the board, and he and Ian are college buddies. I didn't earn any of it. It was just plain, dumb luck."

I closed my eyes and calmed my breathing. This was an

apology, but I didn't want to accept it. Sure, I had my own fair share of lucky breaks, but the difference was that people like Asher didn't get undermined, scrutinized, and second-guessed all the time. I'd proven my competence time and time again, but every day I lived with a nagging feeling that everyone was waiting for me to fail.

The elevator lurched to a stop and my eyes flew open. "Asher, what'd you do?!" I hissed.

He held up his hands like I was robbing him at gunpoint. "Nothing, I swear. I didn't touch anything."

A few seconds later, the elevator whirring sounds from the shaft above us slowed to a halt. The bright overhead lights flicked off and on a few times, before converting into a dimmer mode. That's when it hit me. The building power was out. Or maybe the elevator malfunctioned. Either way, it resulted in the worst outcome imaginable: Asher and I were stuck on this elevator together for god-only-knew-how-long.

Then all these thoughts flooded my mind.

What if the building evacuated and no one was here to rescue us?

What if it was an earthquake and this danger goes way beyond this building?

What if this was a REAL bomb threat?

What if I die here, and Asher is the last guy I will ever see? Oh god, no. "Help!" I screamed at the top of my lungs. "We need help!"

Asher paced around the elevator, swishing his ripe bro smell throughout our seventy-square-foot space. Without power, there was no airflow. No oxygen. The walls closed in around me like a trash compactor.

Above us, we could hear some muffled shouts and murmurs. Asher yelled, "We can't hear what you're saying!" The responses back were garbled and muted. He pulled out his cell, but he didn't have a signal. He tried the emergency dial on the elevator panel, but it just kept ringing. Like a caged animal, Asher yelled "Ahhhhh!" as he pounded on all four walls, forcing me to retreat and cower to the far back corner. Deranged and wild-eyed, he ran up to the sealed doors and used his meaty Hulk hands to pry them open.

"C'mon, c'mon, c'mon," he chanted, willing the doors to move. Somehow, he was able to separate them, but just by a few inches. Through the opening, we could see a bunch of our coworkers' legs and feet, as we were positioned a few feet down from our office floor. Asher tried to squeeze his body through the opening, but only his arm and leg could fit. Desperate now, I took a turn, only to find that my arm and leg were maybe the same size as Asher's, which was especially depressing to think about given our entombed state.

Asher pressed his face in the opening and yelled, "Someone call for help! I need to breathe!" Fresh air from our office floor pushed in, but because Asher was standing in the way, all I got was slightly cooler Asher-tainted air to inhale.

A familiar voice outside the doors drew me to my feet. "Hey, is that Melody back there? I've been looking for her." I had never been so happy to hear Nolan's voice.

"The fire department is on the way, Ash. Can you step aside so I can talk to Mel?"

Asher shuffled over a few steps, and I walked up to the front.

Nolan smiled. "Fancy seeing you here." He stretched out his arm to grab my hand. "Are you okay?"

I pressed my lips together and nodded, trying to fight my tears.

We held hands. "Is there anything I can help you do today? I'm a freelance intern today. I can help you."

I mustered a smile. "You'd think the stripper cosplay was my hugest favor, but I really do need your help again." Here I was, asking Nolan MacKenzie for yet another thing because everything in my life was falling apart at the seams. "I was supposed to present some slides at an investor call at one, going over the same numbers from the board meeting. You know them as well as I do, maybe even better. Can you present them and, if they ask, explain why I'm not there?" I looked at my watch. "It's in five minutes in the executive conference room."

"Oh shit, I need to go then!" He saluted me and took off down the hallway, tucking his periwinkle-and-white windowpane-patterned shirt into his baggy khaki pants.

Sue in HR squatted down a little in the doorway. "The firefighters are downstairs. They're trying to figure out what happened and get you out of there." She passed me two bottles of Gatorade and some SunChips. From deep in her pocket, she pulled out an almost-empty bottle of CBD capsules. "Can you give these to Asher? It's cannabidiol. They help me with anxiety. He's scaring everyone."

I'd been so preoccupied with my Nolan favor that I forgot Asher was behind me. Turning my head, I saw him pacing back and forth, tugging at his hair. Mumbling to himself. Falling apart right before my eyes. *Note to self: never partner with Asher in an apocalypse situation.*

I tiptoed toward him, dangling the Gatorade, chips, and CBD. When he didn't take them, I crouched down on the floor and placed them by his feet, then slowly backed away. "The firemen are here. We're going to be free soon."

Moments later, we heard shouting just as the neighboring elevator dinged on arrival. A crew of firefighters streamed out. It appeared that only our elevator was broken. Lucky us.

A flashlight beam streamed through the door, landing directly in my eyes. "Is anyone hurt?" he asked.

I turned my head and squeezed my watery eyes shut. "Well, I'm blind now, but other than that I'm okay. Asher here is freaking out, but physically, he's fine."

For nearly an hour, the elevator shaft filled with echoing sounds of banging, hammering, and electric drilling. Asher had taken two of Sue's pills and had calmed down considerably. He stopped pacing. Same with the mumbling. His eyes stayed fixed on that door. As soon as it finally opened, I knew he would bulldoze me to get through it. None of that "ladies first" bullshit.

"One. Two. Three!" Two sets of hands on each door panel pulled at the same time, forcing the part to widen enough for a body to pass through. Of course, Asher was the first to exit, pulling himself up onto the floor, stumbling directly to the men's bathroom straight ahead.

When it was my turn to exit, I whispered "Thank you" to the firefighters hoisting me up. Just past them, Nolan stood with his arms open wide, waiting for me. I collapsed into his arms, burying my face into his chest, silently shuddering and crying. He bent his head down and whispered, "Let me take you home. Let's use the stairs. No more elevators today."

Gently tugging me along, he guided me toward the back stairwell leading to the parking garage, supporting me with his arm around my shoulder as we walked side by side down the hallway. With no mental energy to overthink anything, and with Nolan so close to me, I couldn't focus on anything but him. His reassuring smile when I was inside the elevator. His warm embrace when I was freed. And now, with his body right up against mine, his firm hold around my body, all I could think about was how this was the best I'd felt in a long time. Nolan. Me. Together.

He opened the stairwell door and waved for me to pass through first. I turned around to face him as the latch clicked.

Neither of us moved down the steps. Our eyes locked and I took hesitant steps toward him. I meant to say *thank you*, but no words would come out. Instead, I put my hands on his chest and slid them up to his shoulders. My chin tilted upward and I stood on the balls of my feet so my mouth could meet his. Closing my eyes, I softly pressed my lips against his. Breathing hard, he ran his hands down my back and returned the kiss immediately, hungry for more.

Passersby chattered by the stairwell door, discussing the elevator fiasco and whether my game would launch on time. Their verdict? No fucking way. The loudest voice belonged to Ian.

Oh god. What was I doing here in the stairwell? There were no hours to spare in the day and because of the afternoon incident, I was a half day behind now. "I . . . I'm sorry. We can't do this," I muttered, dropping my hands to my side.

"Wait, what? Why not?" He raised his eyebrows in surprise.

"There's too much going on at work. And you're still sort of my intern, because you helped me out today. And I could get in trouble for this." I wagged my index finger between the two of us. "You wouldn't get fired, but I would."

Nolan's phone and mine buzzed at the same time. Mine was a text from Kat: *check your email.*

A companywide message from Ian . . . *Because of Nolan MacKenzie going above and beyond today by filling in for his supervisor on the investor call, he's being awarded this month's Seventeen Studios MVP award. Congratulations, Nolan!*

MVP awards came with a $500 Visa gift card and two free PTO days.

"Congratulations, Nolan." I sighed, trying to stifle any hostility in my voice. Yes, I was grateful he helped me out. Yes, he deserved it. But still, a little part of me was sad, maybe even angry, that I was never recognized for my work.

He stammered, "I-I-I didn't know this would happen . . . I—"

I cut him off. "It's fine." *Not really fine, but whatever.* "I'd been meaning to tell you something. My friend Jane has a strategic analyst position that opened up at her company, and I think you'd be great at it." I bit my lower lip. "If you got the job, you'd have to relocate to New York. But I think you should go for it, it's a great opportunity. I'll email you the info."

His brows knit together into a continuous, straight line. "Are you sure about this?"

"Yes. Sent it. Now we're even for you helping me with the investor call." My stomach sank as soon as his phone buzzed with my message.

He shrugged. "If you want me to apply, I will. Thanks for looking out for me."

I glanced down the stairs so he wouldn't see the tears brimming in my eyes. "I'm okay to drive home by myself now. Thanks again for helping me today. I've got it from here."

Without waiting for his reaction, I clattered down the stairs, the metal steps echoing as the rubber soles from my boots hit each one with a thud.

Once I got to my car, I had to sit there for a minute to steady myself. So much had happened that day. Mostly all bad, but I couldn't shake my constant replays of that kiss between Nolan and me in my head. Or the second one. Somehow, Nolan could make all the negativity in my life melt away, even for a fleeting moment.

Too bad it wouldn't happen again.

CHAPTER TWENTY-ONE

Jane messaged me the evening of her bachelorette party: *Whooooooooo's ready for the festivities? See you downstairs!*

Our limousine service would pick us up first and then we'd swing by Candace's place. At dinner the prior weekend, Candace said unenthusiastically, "I look like I'm smuggling a fifteen-pound bag of weed under my shirt. Can't I just stay home?"

Jane was not having any of it. "Bishes, we're *all* going in the limo. Platinum members get free champagne! Oops, sorry, Candace. I keep forgetting that you can't drink. That's more glasses for Mel and me, though!"

Before heading down to the lobby to meet Jane, I puckered my lips and turned my head upward in the bathroom mirror. I'd successfully pulled off the cat-eye look, something that took years to finally accomplish. And with a little primer, foundation, concealer, and reflective powder action, you couldn't even tell I'd been harboring all my sleep deprivation in the two deep hammock-size bags under my eyes! I'd even bought an antiaging eye cream with caffeine micropearls to perk up and stimulate my eye area and put that on for this special night. I'd need a chisel to remove all that makeup and face product later, but that wasn't something to worry about yet.

I grabbed my purse off the hall closet doorknob and stopped at the door. Did I need an umbrella, too? Seattleites never carried them and the only one in the closet was a golf umbrella with a honking Seventeen Studios logo on it. Nah.

Jane stood under the awning, wearing a scarlet minidress and bling-blinding tiara. It wasn't one of those cheesy plastic ones you got at Party City. It was more Miss-Universe-pageant-appropriate, intended to be coupled with a satin sash.

"You look very regal tonight," I said with a grin.

She touched the top of her head to confirm her perfect crown was still placed on her perfectly blown-out hair. "Oh, this? It's actually the headpiece that goes with my veil. I figured if I was spending over a thousand dollars on it, I might as well use it more than one night."

Yes. That was the fiscally sensible thing to do.

She gave me a quick once-over. "Oh, that's what you're wearing?"

I looked down. A cobalt V-neck sleeveless blouse with a black miniskirt, and a black sparkly shawl thing, plus dangly silver earrings thrown on as an afterthought. What did she mean?

Our limo pulled up right in the front of our apartment building, as planned. Or rather, just as Jane had planned. No time to change clothes now!

The chauffeur opened the back-passenger door for us. The interior, lined with plush white couches, also had a disco ball and multicolored lights that pulsed to the music. A fully stocked bar, along with a bizarre assortment of healthy snacks like quinoa chips and chickpea trail mix, at our disposal. Jane yelled over the music that she had asked for this custom assortment of treats because the VIP spread was usually "gross vending machine eats, like Chili Cheese Fritos and Grandma's Sandwich Cookies." Good lord, I would've binge eaten everything.

She poured us some champagne and asked, "So what's the plan tonight?," as if she hadn't arranged the entire itinerary a few weeks earlier and emailed it to me as "FYI."

8 P.M. Limo pickup (reservation under Jane's name). Pop champagne.

8:15 P.M. Candace pickup. Nonalcoholic drinks stocked in the back.

8:30 P.M. Dinner + Drinks at Canteen Waterfront Bistro (reservation under Jane's name).

10:30 P.M. Dancing at Saturn (VIP list under Jane's name).

"We're picking up Candace and heading to dinner," I answered cheerfully, not wanting to be a downer about her

neurotic plans. I'd never heard of Canteen, but given the shittiness of the organic snacks in the limo, I prayed to God that
this wasn't one of those overpriced hipster eateries where the
chef infused the foods with flaxseed particles and wheatgrass
flavonoids. Jane always knew all the hottest restaurants, but
her tastes lately had skewed organic-local-vegan-holistic-raw-
disgusting. She drank protein powder smoothies with ground-
up collagen and chia seeds every morning. However, since this
was her special single-woman-night-on-the-town celebration, I
needed to comply with her culinary demands.

We pulled up to Candace's townhome in Capitol Hill at 8:15
on the dot (how did Jane know?) and she waddled down the
stairs to join us. Her belly had gotten much bigger in just a
few days. She looked stunning, with her radiant skin and thick
mane of hair. I gave her a hug as she climbed inside, and our
limo continued its journey to the restaurant.

Candace tried to fasten her seat belt but it wouldn't fit over
her baby belly. "I guess they don't have a belt extender," she
grumbled, yanking hard. It took all three of us to help her ex-
pand the belt to the maximum length and it barely fit over her
midsection. But it did fit, which was most important.

Candace and I chatted away about her baby. She squealed,
"She's the size of a large rutabaga, and I can feel her kick all the
time now. My nausea's fully gone, so I won't be the first one to
throw up tonight!"

I admitted, "I don't even know what a rutabaga is. It sounds
like an old foreign car."

Laughing, Candace curved both hands and held them five inches apart. "It's a root vegetable about this size."

I tried to bring Jane into our conversation, too, but she just wasn't interested. She spent the entire ride powdering her nose, reapplying lipstick, and straightening her already perfectly placed tiara. When we arrived at Canteen, she was ready to be queen of the night.

The host opened our door and greeted us with a warm smile.

"Jane, party of three?" We nodded, and he ushered us through the foyer. "You've booked our private dining room. An excellent choice." I accidentally snort-laughed. When service workers congratulated customers for selecting their services, it always made me snigger.

Darkness had fallen outside, but the view from our private room was still spectacular. The moonlit water extended for miles, and the bobbing boats in the harbor filled me with wonder. I'd moved to Seattle three years earlier and questioned my decision so many times over the years, but this night showed how stunningly picturesque this city could be, even during the nonsummer months.

Candace pointed downward. "Whoa, look at that!" The view of Elliott Bay had diverted my attention and I hadn't looked down at the dining room floor. Our table and chairs stood atop see-through plexiglass covering a maze of minirivers, where hundreds of exotic, brightly colored fish swam to and fro.

"Oh my goodness, is that koi?" Jane jumped from her spot and landed above some coral reef.

"They're moving so fast! It's hard to figure out the fish genus and species," I said.

Candace and Jane glanced at each other, and then they looked at me. "Oh my god, Mel. Who would have guessed you were a fish nerd? This may turn out to be the highlight of my evening!" Jane giggled.

My muscles tensed as I tiptoed to the table. These fish darted around without being bothered by our looming presence, but I still didn't like the idea of stepping so closely above them. It also made me self-conscious to walk on top of living things wearing a skirt. Sure, these fish weren't capable of peering upward, but they could totally see my underwear if they flopped sideways. But maybe this was the champagne talking.

Her Royal Highness Jane had ordered the wine ahead of time, and our dedicated waiter had poured out two glasses. "The red wine had time to breathe!" Jane said gleefully as we toasted to the evening. Candace raised her glass of sparkling grape juice.

"Cheers!" We clinked glasses and, no pun intended, I drank like a fish.

It took me a while to figure out why restaurant reviewers loved Canteen, because both the ambiance and the patrons looked so pretentious. The restaurant recommended sharing all items on the menu. Canteen's culinary shtick was gourmet "mess hall food," served in wooden bowls that you passed around to your tablemates. But even though it was family-style summer camp fare, that didn't mean it was cheap. This place charged twenty-two dollars for a medium-size bowl of tater tots. The mac and cheese was double that price. The freezer aisle at the grocery store had the same thing for maybe six dollars, tops.

Jane had already precalled in our dinner order. We continued drinking as we waited for the food to come out in installments.

First, the pitcher of "Grown-Up Gluten-Free Vodka Kool-Aid Punch" arrived at our table, along with two red Dixie cups. The mini–tofu dogs and sprouted organic potato salad came next. To me they tasted fine, but Candace took a bite of each one and spit them into her napkin.

Vegan baked beans soon followed, and then for dessert we had campfire s'mores that we could roast tableside. I ate about a dozen charred s'more bites, while interspersing toasts to the bride-to-be with the never-ending supply of spiked grape Kool-Aid. Aside from the astronomical bill and the fear of floors cracking and us falling into the koi swarms, the night turned out to be much more fun than expected.

Jane fell into me with a lazy smile plastered on her face. "Our limo is outside, we should head out."

Candace whispered, "Wow, even though she's completely hammered, she's still keeping us on schedule! I need to run to the bathroom before we go. Sorry, pregnancy makes me pee a ton!"

I turned to Jane. "Are we really going to a club with a frequently peeing pregnant woman?"

"Ab-so-fucking-lutely! This might be one of Candace's last crazy nights out in a long time."

I hadn't considered this was Candace's last hurrah before having kids. Jane would be getting married soon and settling down too. And as for me, well, I took the night off and wasn't working on that cursed video game. The game that would make or break my production career. The game that put a bull's-eye on my back for all those online trolls.

More drinks, anyone?

WE JUMPED INTO the limo and I poured two glasses of champagne and made Candace a sparkling apple juice cocktail with maraschino cherries and a lime garnish.

I gave a toast. "To Queen Jane. May all her drinks be paid for tonight. And may she pass those free drinks over to me."

We giggled and clinked glasses. Candace went next.

"Cheers to my girls! We've been through a lot together." A flash of melancholy spread across her face, and then she burst into tears.

"Oh my god, Candace, are you okay?" I asked at the same time Jane yelped, "Oh my god, Candace, your makeup is running!" We both handed her fistfuls of tissues, for different reasons.

Candace blew her nose. "I'm sorry. I shouldn't be crying at a bachelorette party. I guess I'm sad that so much has changed recently. I got married, I'm having a baby soon. A year ago, my life was much more carefree. Now my life will never be the same. I think this might be my hormones talking, though." She took a deep breath and fanned her face with her hands.

I reached out and patted her arm. "Candace, we're here for you, no matter what."

Jane patted her other arm. "Well, whatever you think of your life, at least you're not getting ripped apart online like Melody, by a bunch of douchebag losers who probably live in their mom's basement."

"Yeah, Melody, what's going on with that?" Candace had stopped crying and had regained her composure.

I shrugged. "Well, I know a few things now. Like that the Seattle police don't know jack shit about tracking down trolls, so your bunch of feminist hackers are helping me figure out who the really dangerous ones are. I just hope they find something soon. Oh, I have a 2.5-star review average on my game, with over five hundred reviews, and the game still isn't out yet."

Jane said, "Yikes. That's terrible." She topped off my champagne glass.

"It's gone up from 1.5 stars last week. So there's that."

Candace asked, "Can I help with anything? I could do the publicity for your game. I'll be on maternity leave soon and bored out of my mind. I could put a PR plan together!" She seemed to be back to her old, bubbly self. Maybe she needed a friend in crisis to distract her. Or maybe it really was hormones. If Candace could help with the media outreach for the launch, then this game might actually have a chance to succeed.

"Candace, you are brilliant. I'd love your help with PR. A million yeses! Thank you!" She gave me a side hug, and we toasted again.

Jane squealed, "We're here!" as the limo slowly rolled up to the Saturn Club.

The line of patrons wrapped around the block, fully encircling the building. Jane walked right up to the bouncer, and within nanoseconds he unhooked the velvet rope and waved us through. I had to give her credit, Jane had her shit together. And that made my life easier as maid of honor.

The hostess just inside the front entrance tapped around on her iPad to look up our reservation. She walked us over to a set of tables with Reserved signs. "You can pick any open table here. The minimum table purchase is five hundred. Is it just you three?" She handed us a menu listing bottle prices of whiskey, scotch, tequila, and their own signature Intergalactic Punch made with absinthe, pineapple juice, ginger, and lime. The other tables were occupied with investment banker and corporate lawyer bro types. Our adjacent male compadres ogled as we settled into our table. Jane loved the attention and even winked at a few admirers.

I rolled my eyes. "Ugh, this place reminds me of those Korean nightclubs where the men get table service and leer at female patrons, and then ask for the pretty ones to be escorted to their table."

Jane waved down the petite Asian waitress and asked for a bottle of Grey Goose. When she left with our order, Jane motioned for us to lean in so we could hear her. "One of my firm's partners owns this club. He's done a lot of business in Korea and really liked the nightlife there. So yeah, this place is modeled after those 'booking' clubs in Seoul."

The table made a whirring sound as our vodka ascended to the center section, along with shot glasses and mixers. Jane and I poured ourselves two shots each and tossed them both back.

"Let's go dance!" Jane grabbed my hand, and I pulled Candace off her seat to come, too. With surprising steadiness, Jane scampered down the stairs and led us through the crowd. I glanced back to see if anyone had stolen the $300 bottle of Grey Goose we left on the table.

"Nice tiara!" a handsome (but barely my height) guy yelled out to Jane. She gave him a dazzling smile and kept moving toward the main dance area. Candace's belly whacked into people when she turned left or right.

Jane and I stood on our tippy-toes to see if we could find clearance in any parts of the dance floor. Some space cleared near the DJ booth, by a gigantic overhead speaker the size of the three of us put together, so that was undesirable. Jane shouted to Candace and me, "Okay, stand facing me and form a circle. When I say 'now,' slowly take a step back. Let's do that a few times to see if we can make room." She sounded like she knew what she was doing, so Candace and I nodded and awaited her instructions.

"Now!" she yelled. I took a step back and my heel clamped down on the back of someone's shoe. "Sorry," I whimpered and then turned back around cringing.

Candace bumped into a man holding a drink, which he spilled on himself. He turned around with arms cocked, ready for a fight, but looked down and noticed her belly. His face softened. "Oh man, a true party girl! Can I touch it?" She shot him an *if you touch my belly I will murder you here and now* look. He winced and scooched forward a little. Candace took another step back.

Jane's tiara caught the light and sparkled wildly as we danced, reflecting little rainbows all over the place. She slithered to the music while Candace bopped along. I took some photos, then swayed and stumbled to the beat. All the Kool-Aid, champagne, and vodka had finally caught up with me.

A drunk guy wearing sunglasses on his head came over to chat. "Helloooooo, bride-to-be. You're so pretty and sparkly."

Jane looked away sheepishly and then fixed her stare right back on him. "You think I'm pretty?"

Candace and I exchanged a glance. *Oh, please.*

He stepped closer to her. "You are VERY pretty. And I love how you dance. Any chance you want to have one last fun night before you get married?"

I cleared my throat and tugged on her elbow. "Hey, let's go back to our table. I'm feeling claustrophobic."

After a fit of giggles, she said, "Awwww, you're no fun, Mel," and then waved goodbye to her suitor. She blew kisses to all the people who shouted "Congratulations!" as we passed by.

The waitress came by our table and we ordered kimchi fried rice, fries with gochujang dip, and spicy stir-fried rice cake. Yeah, there was no doubt now that this club was inspired by the Korean clubbing scene. Half the menu was filled with the kind of bar food you ate at 2 A.M. with your Korean friends after a night of heavy debauchery.

Throughout the night, as men of all shapes and sizes stopped by our table to chat with us, did they wonder why someone dressed like Lady Diana showed up to the club with her frumpy Asian friend and extremely pregnant sidekick? Maybe they were too drunk to notice, I concluded.

When our ginormous food order arrived, we passed around the platters of fried-up goodness and laughed the night away. Just as I stuffed some stir-fried spicy rice cakes into my mouth, I received a text from an Unknown ID.

You girls look like you're having fun tonight. Congratulations to the bride.-DDay

My heart stopped. I scanned the room in slow motion. Everyone around me, smiling, drinking, dancing, eating. Jane's tiara head thrown back in laughter. People making out at other tables. Twentysomethings on the dance floor grinding so hard they looked like they were making babies right there in front of me.

No one lurked. No one stared. But someone was here, watching me.

"I have to get out! He's here!" Jane and Candace gaped as I knocked over my drink and scrambled out of the booth. "I'm sorry. I need to leave!" I grabbed my purse and ran to the entrance, bumping and elbowing my way out.

"Ow! Yeah, you better get out of here!"

"Watch your back!"

"I'll fuck you up for that!"

Hate-filled words ricocheted around the room and enveloped me as I pressed onward to the exit. Sweat and tears streamed down my face as I thrust my trembling body through the front door, straight into a downpour.

Shit. My umbrella would have come in handy now.

Shivering, drenched, and terrified, I turned around to make sure no one followed me out.

How could I stay safe now? Danger was everywhere and I had nowhere to hide.

CHAPTER TWENTY-TWO

Can you explain one more time on how this stalker found your number?" The male police sergeant on the scene looked retirement age and had kind crinkles around his eyes. Very grandfatherly and sympathetic. But he didn't know shit about troll stalkers.

Club patrons and onlookers took selfies in front of the patrol car. Wil called Nolan, his stripper BFF, who sped to the club in his green plaid pajamas and gave me his bathrobe for warmth. In any other circumstance I would have teased him about his PJs, but this wasn't the time. To any passerby, I looked pretty silly standing in front of the club with a plush blue bathrobe, but it warmed me up, and that's what counted. He opened an umbrella and held it over our heads while the sergeant took notes.

I choked back sobs and described to the officer how I'd been doxed and my phone number had been leaked. "I got my number removed from the message boards, but this stalker still has it. You can add this incident to the harassment case already open with Seattle Police." He typed my name into his patrol car laptop and couldn't find me. After a few tries, he found me under "Melanie."

Tears fell onto the robe and were quickly absorbed by the lush plush. What would Jane say about my hideous makeup now streaked down my face? I snickered inside at the thought of her backing away with her hands up, denying knowing me, and then turning and fleeing.

I leaned my head on Nolan's shoulder. "Why me?"

I'd already asked this question many times before.

I had asked myself *Why me?* with each hate-filled email I opened, read, and deleted.

Why me? I'd wondered when anonymous racists called me a chink, jap, or gook on those gaming message boards, and no one came to my defense. Some idiot had even called me a spic and no one contested him. These fools couldn't even get their racist terms straight.

I'd questioned *Why me?* when an angry keyboard warrior claimed that my silence on social media was evidence that I secretly passed judgment on those who engaged in trolling me. This guy received hundreds of likes for his post. What kind of messed-up logic was that, when silence and lack of retaliation somehow meant I was a judgy bitch?

What was motivating these haters? Competitiveness? Gender, class, or race entitlement? Jealousy, or boredom, or maybe combat for combat's sake? Perhaps just good old-fashioned caveman-with-club misogyny? Were they doing it for the laughs? Or worse, all of the above? It could be anything. Or everything.

Danger lurked everywhere now, both online and out in the real world. Even though no one had physically harmed me, yet, could anyone actually ensure my safety? Like paranoid prey, I continually checked my surroundings and flinched at even the smallest unexpected noise. How had control over my own life slipped away so quickly?

Nolan folded me into him as we waited for the police squad to check for any possible larger threats to the establishment and to the patrons inside. With my cheek against his warm, taut chest, I felt his heartbeat pulsing as hard and fast as mine. Slowly, he stroked my hair as I cried into his shirt.

Candace volunteered to take Jane home. During the sergeant's interview, she'd screamed at one point, "My maid of honor is HOT, look at her! No wonder people want to stalk her. She's HOT!" Her outburst was comical at first, but after about twenty seconds of that on repeat, it became unbearable. Candace gave me a final hug and helped put hiccupping Jane into the Liftr car. I could say with 100 percent certainty that Jane would be puking her brains out within the hour, and Candace would need to deal with that. That tiara, an unfailing beacon for alcohol donations, had earned Jane a lot of extra free drinks.

Sergeant Banks came over and wiped a handkerchief across his sweaty forehead. "Well, to me this stalking sounds like it's the responsibility of the internet companies who host those message boards. One would hope that one of the biggest technology meccas in the world would have a police department that was better at investigating cases like these. Give us a burglar or car jacker or something and we can handle that better."

"So what you're saying is . . . even though we have clear-cut evidence of stalking, death threats, and assault warnings, you can't help her?" Nolan asked.

His slight shrug said everything. "Our resources are limited—it'll take us quite some time to pull everything together."

I didn't have "quite some time." I sent WheedWacker a screenshot of the anonymous message with my text, *Can you ID this stalking asshole?*

An immediate reply. *Fuckers like these are tricky. Need more info. Dynamic IPs, IP spoofing, using relays is the norm these days for these guys but we'll hunt 'em down. We've been deleting and reporting your personal info when we see it online and on the Darknet. When you reactivated your social media accounts to post tonight's photos, we think the anon creepster wanted to spook you. Delete all your photos and suspend accounts immediately.*

I did. I deleted everything. All my social media accounts, gone. I asked the sergeant, "What if I find out these stalkers' identity? Can you make arrests then?"

He raised his eyebrows. "It would be more likely." Much more encouraging than a shrug.

Candace and Jane had already gone, and as the police entourage thinned out, it was time to leave. With Nolan's arm still draped over my shoulder, I turned to face him, to thank him for being there with me. Supporting me through yet another crisis.

His eyes gleamed, even in the cloud-covered darkness. For what felt like an eternity, we stared at each other, like we did on top of those stairs, just moments before our lips met and he returned my kiss, leaving me roused and confused. I thought back to when Candace and Jane had said I was too picky when it came to men and needed to be open to opportunities.

Well, here was opportunity standing right in front of me.

This time I knew what I wanted.

I wanted Nolan.

When I stepped a little closer to him, his lips twisted into a slight frown as he pulled his arm away from me. "Hey, you've been through a lot tonight," he said, offering me a wavering smile. "You've been drinking and under duress, and the last time we did this"—he hesitated with his next words—"you regretted it. Like, a lot." He stiffened and scratched his cheek. "The most important thing for me right now is to get you home safely. Is that okay?"

Numb from both the frigid weather and his rejection, I barely nodded. Had I missed my chance with him?

With Nolan's hand barely touching my back, we walked over to a Subaru. My eyes widened when he unlocked the doors. "You have a Subaru Legacy? I pegged you as a BMW guy."

He smirked. "Really? I don't know if I should be flattered or offended by that. I bought this car when I realized I'd be moving to Seattle. I read somewhere that it was one of the most popular cars in Washington State." His face fell instantly when he remembered something. "But I might need to sell it soon."

The early morning mist had already settled on his windshield. With his wipers on full blast, he swished away the dewy wetness as he drove me home. Biting my lip during the quiet drive, I couldn't help but wonder if he was moving to New York. If anything could ever happen between us. If this attraction was just one-way. How different would everything be if I had stopped worrying, doubting, and overthinking and had just let things play out on that stairwell?

I CALLED MY parents early in the morning after my apartment building was swept for bombs (yes, BOMBS).

"Your daddy and me still wonder how you get a stalker. Stalker usually go after beautiful girl."

"Thanks for being so supportive, Mom."

"We watch local evening news every day. All the stalkers want to be boyfriend. Maybe you have secret admire crush."

I closed my eyes. "Mom, not all stalkers are infatuated with who they are stalking."

"Well, if you choose doctor or lawyer career like we want, you not have this problem. Those job you don't have people stalk you. Unless you are psychiatrist or criminal defender, maybe that is problem."

I sighed deeply. For once, I'd have to agree with them about this. "That may be true about doctors and lawyers, but I still don't want either of those careers."

My mom asked, "So what you do now? You have a plan?"

"Of course I have a plan. Don't worry about me."

I had no plan, but there was no way in hell I'd tell them that.

My dad got on the line. "Melody, you okay? You farmer friend Nolan, he helping you?"

"Yeah, he is. A lot. He's been a big help."

"Good. Good. He is nice guy."

I laughed nervously. "Yeah, he is."

We quickly said our goodbyes. What were you supposed to talk about with your parents when you had originally called to let them know a madman stalker was hunting you down and they tell you that for once, they actually like a guy that you like, but he maybe doesn't reciprocate your feelings and you can't date him anyway while he works at your company or you'll get fired? Not exactly something Google could help answer.

CHAPTER TWENTY-THREE

First thing Monday morning, my phone buzzed with an international text from my hacker friend. *Traced UltimateDDay's IP to your company. BetaGank user login UltimateDDay changed from HashAsh four months ago. More to come.*

HashAsh?

That was Asher's college nickname.

He was the one who leaked the news to BetaGank? Why did he lie to me?

I hunted down Asher in the kitchen. Where all could see and hear, I simply lost it. "Asher, you fucking son of a bitch! *You* leaked my game info on BetaGank? You destroyed my reputation online and then you acted like we were buddies at work? Fuck you . . . you . . . fucking fuck!"

Onlookers stood up from their workstations to get a better view of the spectacle. A crowd of coffee drinkers had gathered around, like we were opponents sparring in a spectator sports arena. People had probably never seen anyone unleash fury to this level during working hours.

Color drained from Asher's face, and he took on a chalky, sickly hue.

I shouted, "You'd better not get sick on my new Chucks!" His green pallor and sad, downcast eyes almost made me feel sorry for him, but I didn't. This douchebag was my enemy. "You thought I wouldn't be able to trace it back to you, is that it? Stupid, naïve Melody? Well, I did figure it out. If you're going to troll online, at least be smart enough not to use a work IP address."

Asher looked at the crowd of people around us and said to me in a hushed voice, "Melody, I need to talk to you in private."

"Oh no, Asher, there's no private anymore!" I looked around at the onlookers. "Get your popcorn ready, folks." I turned back to Asher and poked his chest hard with my index finger. "NOTHING is private now. You made sure of that when you started posting shit about me online. Because of *you*, people are doxing me and sending my personal information around for everyone to see. Did you know that there's a picture of my mom, dad, and me eating hot dogs from the Puyallup Fair floating in cyberspace now, thanks to you? And people are now making obscene comments about me and my affinity for hot dogs? I don't even like hot dogs unless they're on a stick and wrapped in cornbread. But whatever. Anything you want to say to me, you can say in front of our jury here of gaming peers." I made a sweeping gesture toward the bystanders. Screw Asher and his request for privacy.

He shoved his hands into his pockets. "Um, okay. We can talk here then. Ian told me to leak the game info online. He might deny it now, but this was all his idea, not mine. But honestly, he didn't mean for it to turn out the way it did. And I certainly didn't. He wanted to create some buzz around the game and thought it would be interesting to give BetaGank exclusive access to insider information. But as you know, they kind of mocked the game and then things got waaaaay out of hand. Ian saw this as a marketing or PR strategy, to generate excitement around the game. It was never supposed to deliberately target you." His shoulders slouched and he looked back down. If he vomited on his own shoes, I'd be happy with that.

Was he telling me the truth? It seemed plausible that Ian had orchestrated all this shit.

He bit his lip and looked back up. "And there's more to the story. After GameCon, someone hacked into my BetaGank account and changed all the passwords. I didn't get around to dealing with that because that's the time when Ian gave me *Girls of War* and I got distracted. So if any doxing came from that account, I swear it wasn't me. I'm not smart enough to do that sort of shit."

"I believe that one," I muttered.

"And I don't have any smart-enough friends, either. All my bros are, like, cool."

I exploded. "Well, screw you! And your bros!" Too bad Asher was way too tall to put into a choke hold.

Joe the PR guy broke through the crowd and motioned for Asher to follow him. He did the same for me. Damn, busted by the principal. Guess there would be no fight after school.

We followed Joe to his office and he shut the door behind us. "Shit, you two, I could hear your yelling from here."

Asher said, "Actually, she was the yeller, not me."

My blood pulsed through my body, down to my toes. I said in a low voice, "You deserved every bit of it."

Joe gestured for us to sit down. "I could hear everything. And, Melody, Asher is telling you the truth about the game leak. That was intentional, by Ian. No one had the foresight to know this would turn into the chaos that soon followed. We are all deeply sorry for what happened to you."

I stared at Joe. "Sorry" didn't cut it. "Why didn't you run this by me first? My life is in shambles now because of your terrible plan."

Joe scooted his chair forward and took a long sip of water. Perhaps a stall tactic. "At the time, we didn't think you could weigh in on it in a meaningful way."

This seemed like code for *You were a noob, and female, so we didn't involve you in this decision.*

"Well, thank you ALL for inadvertently ruining my life." My fists clenched into two shaking balls, ready at a moment's notice to punch both their faces if they pissed me off any further. I had the element of surprise on my side.

Asher said to Joe, "Here's the thing, though—I lost control of my account access sometime last month. Someone else used it to target Melody. I'd only submitted the game leak to BetaGank and that's it. I didn't do anything else, I swear."

Joe said to me, "Can we agree that Asher should reclaim his BetaGank account and make a public statement, explaining that he is your coworker and he vouches for your work? Do you have any objection to us doing this?"

"Oh, *now* you want my opinion?" I rolled my eyes. "Yes. Fine. Can I go now?"

Joe nodded. "I am so deeply sorry all this happened to you."

"You helped cause this, you at least acknowledge that, right?" I asked.

Joe looked squeamish. Could the head of PR admit to any wrongdoing? Probably not. "Off the record? I advised Ian against this publicity stunt. But he's the guy in charge."

Ian made this decision solo. Good to know.

I hadn't anticipated reentering the gossip spotlight when I left Joe's office. Intense stares came from every direction, observing my every move as I walked to my desk. *Nothing to see here, folks.*

Exhausted from the day's events, I plopped down in my chair and buried my head in my hands. This was all Ian's doing, and the fact that he didn't take accountability for what happened to me as a result of his poor decisions really pissed me off.

A vivid memory of Nolan and me eating dinner together flashed in my mind. The night he gave me a much-needed pep talk: *You're great at your job and the company needs you. I think you should demand a raise. Your game has such visibility, I bet they'd do it.* Months had passed and I still hadn't asked for a raise, even though I deserved it. It was time to channel Sheryl Sandberg. Chin up and chest thrust forward, I stamped down the hallway and pounded on Ian's door. It creaked open with my final knock, revealing a dark, quiet office.

His admin assistant jumped up from her seat and walked around her desk. "You don't have anything scheduled."

I pushed the door wider. "That's okay, I'll wait for him." Inside, I sat on one of his guest chairs just as a shadowy figure shot upright from the sofa.

"Holy shit!" I flicked on Ian's desk lamp to see better.

From the love seat, Ian pulled himself to his feet and rubbed his eyes. "You scared me," he said, yawning.

"I'll make this quick so you can get back to your busy day." I rolled my eyes. "I know you asked Asher to leak the game info to BetaGank."

"I hear what you're saying, Melody, and I appreciate you stopping by to express your concerns. Your perspective is valued at our studio, as you know. I don't know what he told you but—"

I cut him off. "Look, I don't need you to throw your rehearsed, pseudo-pro-fem language at me. I'm not here to debate, because I'm telling you facts, not opinions. Joe also confirmed it. I just don't get why you thought it would be a good idea. It had a huge risk of failing before we even got to development."

"Okay, fine." His voice dipped ice cold. "Yes, it was a gamble. There's always risk in game production." He waved his hand toward me. "Case in point. You."

My heart beat faster as I clenched and unclenched my fists. "But you wouldn't have done what you did with our other games. Like *Zooful Nation*. Or the *UFC Fighter* one. Or even *Girls of War*."

He let out a grim laugh. "Well, it's simple. That's because I thought this game would fail. It wasn't my idea and now it's all the fucking board wants to hear about." In higher falsetto, he mocked, "Tell us about *Ultimate Apocalypse*'s subscription model! Have you thought of merch opportunities? Have you thought about the next feminist game?" With his index finger pointing at his head and thumb finger up, he pretended to shoot.

Ian had never supported this game. And clearly, he *still* didn't. But the board was all up in his business about it, so his professional success was intertwined with mine. Now *UA* couldn't fail anymore, because Ian's success directly depended on it.

This was my opportunity to seize the moment. "Ian, I want a raise."

He scoffed. "You haven't even been here that long. Don't be ridiculous."

My voice grew firmer. "The facts are clear. I've had to learn fast and I do a damn good job. I work harder than anyone else here, on the front line and behind the scenes. You need this game to launch on time. To do that, you need me to take *UA* to completion. Now that I think of it, I want double the game ship bonus, too, because I was on an accelerated timeline."

He sputtered, unable to form words.

"I'm not leaving until you confirm we have a deal."

A soft knock at the door interrupted us. His admin's head popped in. "Ian, you have your meeting with those board members who wanted a tour of the studio. They're standing at my desk. What do you want me to do?"

I jumped to my feet. "I'd be happy to give them a tour. I'm sure they'd love to know all about my experience working on *Ultimate Apocalypse*."

He glared at me, then shifted his gaze to his assistant. After flexing his jaw, he growled, "I'll be right out. Also, please draw some paperwork for Melody's five percent raise and double game ship bonus."

He stood up and looked back at me as he exited. "You better not fuck anything up, Melody." And with that, he slammed the door.

I took deep breaths and tried to calm my trembling hands by sitting on them. I got a raise! And a bonus! Without giving it any thought, I pulled out my phone and texted Nolan while I walked back to my desk. *I asked for a raise and bonus, like you suggested. It worked! Celebration soon?*

He replied quickly. *Cool! Can't though, out of town a few days, east coast. Have fun!*

With my eyes glued to my screen, I ran smack into Asher

on his way to the kitchen. "Boy trouble?" he joked as I recoiled from him.

"None of your business," I growled.

He snuck a look over my shoulder anyway. "If you want my dude opinion, it looks like he's hiding something." He paused. "Or hiding . . . someone."

I didn't ask for his opinion, but still, I couldn't shake the feeling that Nolan was on the East Coast for final interviews, or mending his strained relationship with his family to move back home, or maybe he was reacquainting himself with cropped-out-of-picture girl. For someone who just got a raise *and* a bonus, I sure didn't feel like celebrating.

CHAPTER TWENTY-FOUR

Did you see the email from Ian?" Kat barged into my office with wild eyes and a flaring nose. I hadn't even had time to put my coffee down.

"Not yet. What did it say?"

"You need to read it." She leaned over to see my screen.

"I just got in, Kat, and haven't logged in. Why don't you just tell me about the email."

"Trust me, it's better if you see it." She continued to stare at my blank screen.

Jesus Christ. I logged in to the network and accessed my mail, under Kat's intense surveillance. She skimmed my unread mail and pointed. "There. Click on that one."

From Ian, subject line: "Congratulations Asher, for your feature article in WIRED's Exclusive Game Issue!" I clicked on the link.

The article opened the way one of those interview pieces go with an actor or actress shown behind the scenes, catching him or her being "real" at home or at a café. "I met Asher, bright-eyed, midtwenties, at the low-key Jitterbug Coffee Shop on Lake Union. Ash, as his bros call him, wore a signature twentysomething striped shirt over an ironic T-shirt. I peered to get a closer look at the slogan. 'PIES B4 GUYS,' he pointed out, with a laugh. 'A friend of mine had this shirt, and I had to get one too.'" The article went on to talk about how progressive Seventeen Studios was, and how epic the *Girls of War* game launch would be, with bigger, better explosions, and strong female fighters. Gaming analysts expected the title to shatter mobile game records and put Seventeen Studios on the map. "Finally," the article pointed out, "we have an all-female first-person shooter game. Hello, twenty-first century!"

Asher, a supporter of women, with these basically nude women running around with automatic assault rifles? What a heaping load of BS. And that jerk stole my shirt idea.

Kat asked, "How far did you get before you felt the bile come up through your esophagus?"

"Not far at all. Three paragraphs. How'd he get featured in *WIRED*?"

Kat smirked. "I almost vomited at two. So, in women-bashing speak, you're asking who he screwed to get this article written?" She snorted and shook her head. "From what I hear, his dad is very well connected."

"With all the marketing resources and publicity being put behind *Girls of War*, he'll definitely have an impressive release." I slumped down in my chair. And my game? The artists had made *Ultimate Apocalypse* a visual showstopper and the writers we hired kept the story line tight and made the banter light-hearted and fun. Even with amazing graphics and a punchy story, we needed rampant word of mouth to make *UA* a success. And my indefinite social media ban didn't help matters one bit.

I straightened in my chair. "Kat?"

"Yeah? You look like you thought of something."

"I did." I smiled and rubbed my hands together. "It's time to feed the trolls!"

CANDACE'S OB-GYN PLACED her on maternity bed rest for the remainder of her pregnancy due to a potential placenta risk. Her too-active lifestyle made the doctor nervous. Bored and restless, she volunteered to help pull some strings to get my game featured on *Seattle Metropolitan* magazine's homepage. The editor in chief was in Candace's Lamaze class. I didn't know how Candace managed to pitch my story during their breathing and birthing exercises, but she did it!

We had a few late-night publicity brainstorm sessions, and we agreed that going with a nontraditional route to publicize my game would serve us best. Rather than focusing our efforts on gaming/tech blogs and game magazines, we opted to target women's interest and lifestyle publications. *Seattle Metropolitan*, *Cosmo*, *Marie Claire*, and *Jezebel* were the first to respond to our pitch. Women were my primary target, and if I'd gone with a "traditional" 18–34 male game publicity approach, my game would be DOA on launch day.

The *Seattle Met* article started off with a bold, surprising statement.

Chances are you've never heard of Melody Joo. And if you have, you've probably heard some terrible things about her from a small group of very vocal gaming hatemongers. She'd like to set the record straight.

Melody is a junior producer and creator of the title *Ultimate Apocalypse*, to be released this November, just in time for the holidays. She's been under a gag order to not respond to any attacks or harassment targeting her competency as a producer and as a living human being, but she's agreed to do a first-ever interview to address the vicious online attacks that she's been barraged with the last few months.

When we began the interview she asked, "Would it be okay to do this in a Q&A or FAQ format?" and we thought she was kidding, but she wasn't. We asked her a bunch of questions (some of them really personal) and she provided straightforward, genuine answers. We had so much fun that we didn't extend this interview much more beyond the FAQs. Without further delay, here is Melody Joo, Gamer Girl extraordinaire:

Melody, let's just get straight to it. You've been accused online of being many terrible things, one of

them being a ho. Are you a ho? *No. I've had three serious boyfriends in my whole life, and I kissed two guys in high school. No hookups. And sorry, no girl-on-girl action.*

Are you a slut? *See above.*

Are you a whore? Not the sex-worker kind, but the attention-seeking kind? *I don't like attention and barely use social media. When people sing "Happy Birthday" to me on my birthday I want to run away. But then I wouldn't get cake.*

Are you a dyke? *See #1.*

Are you a cunt or bitch? *I am a tad bit snarky, sardonic, silly, and immature. That's about as extreme as I get.*

Did you fuck your way up the ladder? *Hahaha. No. I am very much a bottom-rung plebeian. And please see #1 again.*

Are you stupid? *I was a National Merit semifinalist in high school, an eighth-grade regional algebra competition finalist, and I was placed in advanced calculus in college thanks to my AP score. I really suck at geometry and chemistry though. If you want to call me stupid at geometry and chemistry, that's fine. I'd totally agree with you there.*

RockJock33, one of your haters, asked, "Shouldn't you go kill yourself?" What do you think about that? *I get squeamish when I see blood, so no thanks to the death suggestion. Plus, I like my life.*

Are you a social justice warrior/feminazi? *I prefer to think of myself as an "Equality Evangelist."*

You're fat and disgusting, right? *I went to the doctor this morning and had to pay a $35 co-pay to help me answer this question. My BMI is 23. According to my physician, my BMI is average for my weight and height. I am disgusting when eating nachos because I always ask for extra cheese and it drips everywhere. I'm a disgusting nacho slob.*

Then you're ugly, right? *I ran my picture through the Hot or Not app. I scored a 71% hot. While I'm not a bombshell, actual data exists that suggests I am not ugly.*

Let's talk race. Are you a straight-A genius, a kung-fu master, a bad driver, a dragon lady, and good with computers? Oh, and do you speak Chinese? *No.*

Are you a chink, gook, or jap? *Slurs are stupid. It would be like me calling white people "honkies" and "crackers." That sounds stupid, right? People don't use those terms anymore, for good reason. And my ethnicity is Korean, not Chinese or Japanese, for the record, so at least consider using correct racial references when referring to my heritage. But note I'm American, just like many of your readers. I was born here, and I've paid one-third of my hard-earned wages since I was sixteen years old to the US government.*

Would you like to be ravaged by a stranger wielding a Wiffle-ball-bat-size dick? *No, thank you. I'm* *very selective of whom I ravage and am ravaged by. See answer to question #1. Also, I do not believe anyone's dick is two and a half feet long. I'd want picture proof with a yardstick of that.*

Boobs! Boobs! What's your bra size? *34B. I'm a size M in Adidas sports bras. You can buy a three-pack at Costco for $14.99.*

A question, one from us, not from those jerks who've been harassing you. What was the inspiration behind *Ultimate Apocalypse*? *This game's purpose is pure entertainment. It started off as a parody idea of all the over-the-top male power fantasy, shoot-'em-up games that have female secondary characters just to objectify and sexualize them. The* Ultimate Apocalypse *follows three male strippers who emerge from a run-down strip club without their memories, unharmed after an apocalyptic world war. At the same time, Doomsday government scientists unleash creatures on the earth, because they think it's their calling: aliens, zombies, vampires, you name it. And these strippers need to fight them to survive. They meet badass warriors along their journey, the majority of whom are female. To win the game, the men need to join forces with the women, otherwise they won't survive, because the women have complementary skills that they need.*

Who's your favorite character? *Hands down, it's Sophia. We gave her a normal, relatable name. She's* *sporty and can throw knives and axes. This kick-ass character is my favorite because we made her just like my real-life gaming heroine, Kat. But in real life, Kat is pretty clumsy, and if she tried to throw a knife it would boomerang and stab her jugular vein. Sophia is basically Kat 2.0.*

Is there anything else you'd like to say to our readers? Or to the army of vile trolls who want to see you fail? *Thank you so much for this platform. The breadth of harassing comments makes it hard to address it all. But I do want to talk about the sexualizing and objectifying comments made about me online.*

At the start of the online controversy, the fact that I was Asian, female, and worked in gaming triggered thousands of vile assholes to comment on my ass, tits, and vagina. So let me give everyone a quick rundown on my physical traits. I fart, puke from excessive drinking, and have constipation when I'm dehydrated, just like everyone else, male or female. I also have irritable bowel syndrome. I have adult acne and hairy forearms. My nose-blowing sounds like a honking goose, and it annoys people, especially my mom. I've had a muffin top since birth. One of my front adult teeth got knocked out from a volleyball mishap so I have a fake tooth, and when it's removed I look like an Asian hillbilly.

I worry every day about my parents getting older, because I'm an only child and would be their sole caregiver. I cry when I watch the movie Annie. Overall, I'm just a regular ol' person, not a slut, not a prude, but possibly a little grosser and gassier than the average human being. So, to my angry vocal gaming constituents, consider all this when you feel compelled to comment about my ass, tits, and vagina, or anyone else's for that matter. Who is the person you are trying to "bring down," and what is your motivation to do so? Think about what is driving you to harangue women like me online, and where the anger is coming from. Is it because you think your actions are anonymous and untraceable? Are you doing it for attention? For the "lulz"? Or is it really something deeper, maybe something else from your history that is compelling you to spew hateful words toward a stranger?

If we met face-to-face, could you say all the same things you're posting online while looking me straight in the eye? Think about your nieces, daughters, sisters, and baby cousins. Would they be proud of what you're saying online? What would they think of your words?

I'm not sure I have much more to say than this. I think I'll end it here, if that's okay. Thank you again, Seattle Met.

To view the game trailer, and to find out more about Melody's *Ultimate Apocalypse*, click *here*.

Candace got the link to the article before it went live and called me to tell me how much she loved it, and then she burst into tears (totally the hormones). "Why are all these haters after you?" She blew her nose. "They can go to hell! I hate them!"

Then she screamed, "Oh god!," and then more shrieking pierced through the phone.

Candace's water broke, five weeks early.

ANNABELLE YING FUNG was born at 5:50 A.M. and rushed straight to the NICU. With underdeveloped lungs and a weak heartbeat, she needed around-the-clock breathing assistance.

My eyes brimmed with tears as I sat in the hospital waiting area, rereading the same paragraph over and over from a battered *Food & Wine* magazine from September 2013. This was all my fault. Her water broke when we were chatting on the phone about game PR stuff. Tears flowed down my cheeks as I squeezed my eyes closed, wishing this nightmare would just stop.

Wil came into the waiting room and poked my arm. "Do you know where the vending machines are? I've been up twenty-eight hours straight. Breakfast isn't served for a while, and I'm starving." With his lean stature and gaunt face, he probably needed more than just one breakfast.

I stood up and hugged him. "I'm so sorry, Wil. I feel horrible. This happened because of me."

"Mel, she'd already been on bed rest for over a week, on Dr. Zach's orders. If it didn't happen while you two were on the phone, it could have happened when she went to the bathroom, or when she coughed or something. Don't put this all on yourself."

His words made sense logically, but they didn't make me

feel better. This happened while Candace and I were on the phone together. Had I been a major factor in the early delivery, if not the actual root cause?

We found the vending area down the hallway. He contemplated his processed-food options and bought a giant frosted honey bun. "I love these things. Candace won't let me eat them." He frowned. "Maybe I should have something else instead." He bought some Wheat Thins and left the honey bun behind the dispenser flap. Damn. Maybe I'd come back for that a little later.

"How are Candace and Annabelle?" I asked.

He smiled weakly. "Candace's sleeping now. They gave her a sedative because once the shock from her early labor wore off, she got a little hysterical. She needs rest so her body can recover from the delivery. Annabelle is a fighter, she takes after her mom. She's only four pounds but her vitals are strong for her size." His eyes watered but he didn't cry. "If she can make it through the next twenty-four hours, I'll feel way better about everything."

I reached out and hugged him. Their parents were en route to Seattle but wouldn't be here until later in the evening. Until then, I was the closest thing to family they both had.

"Do you need anything from me? Some clothes from home? Maybe water your plants? Go on a McDonald's run for breakfast?"

He shook his head. "Actually, Nolan offered and is helping us out with emergency apartment stuff. But if you were here when Candace woke up, that would be wonderful."

On the way to their room, the nurses on duty looked up and

smiled. No one seemed panicked about Candace's early baby delivery. A Zenlike calmness hung in the air, which seemed like a very good thing.

I tiptoed to Candace's bedside while she slept. Even though she'd been through a night of hell, she looked beautiful. Both her arms had IV tubes sticking out of them, and she wore a heartbeat monitor on her right index finger.

Beep. Beep. Beep. A steady, confident heartbeat.

"When's she supposed to wake up?" I asked Wil.

He glanced at his watch. "My guess is within the next thirty minutes." He waved the newly opened bag of Wheat Thins in front of me. "Breakfast?"

"No thanks. I'll save my calories for the bacon and eggs when the real breakfasts are delivered." He shrugged and shook the bag into his mouth. I could hear the crackers scrape against the insides of the packaging and tumble out. Next came the crumb avalanche. Then he shook it one last time for good measure before he peered in to confirm he'd eaten everything.

Candace's eyes fluttered a little, and her breathing came faster. When she opened her eyes, Wil called the head nurse, who checked Candace's pulse and scanned her forehead temperature with a digital baton.

"You're awake, dear. That's wonderful! Can you tell me your name?"

"I'm Candace." She blinked a lot and looked around the room.

"That's right! Do you recognize the people standing by your bed?"

Candace glanced at Wil and me. "That's my husband, Wil, and that's Melody." She reached out and squeezed my hand.

"Do you know where you are?"

"At a Methodist church? Or maybe school. Wait. A hospital. Because . . . oh. Oh! How's my baby? Can I see my baby?!"

The heart monitor bleeped with more urgency.

BEEP! BEEP! BEEP!

"Good, Candace. We just need you to stay calm so I can get a read on your vitals. Annabelle is fine. When you're cleared by our doctor, we'll get you to the NICU so you can see her. I need to take your blood pressure now." Nurse Nancy, who had a kind grandma face, was a pro. Candace's beeping slowed, and she submitted to all the poking and prodding from the medical team. The quicker she got cleared, the sooner she'd see Annabelle.

The doctor sent Candace and Wil to the NICU. Because I wasn't family, I couldn't visit baby Annabelle with them. The nurse invited me to stay in Candace's hospital room while they stayed with the baby, but she encouraged me to go home and get some sleep. Wil promised to call me with any new news.

ON MY WAY to the hospital garage I saw Jane standing at the information desk, badgering the poor elderly volunteer for information on Candace's whereabouts. Her hands tightly gripped a giant shopping bag and a toddler-size duffel. She ran up to me and skidded to a stop. "Whoa. You should get some sleep. They wouldn't let me in, can you believe it?! How is she? How is the baby? I texted everyone but no one replied."

A sad sigh escaped me. "We don't have any cell service in here. Candace seemed a little dazed but that's because they gave her sedatives. She and Wil are in the NICU now, and I didn't get to see the baby or see any pictures. It sounds like everything was rushed, and complicated, but the good news is Annabelle is thriving, according to the head nurse."

Jane squealed. "Annabelle? Awwww, what a cute name! Is the baby going to be okay?"

"She was born just under thirty-four weeks and had been tracking to a lower birth weight during the entire pregnancy, so there is uncertainty." I stifled a yawn, somewhat unsuccessfully. "The doctors were keeping an eye on Annabelle's weight gain, heart development, and lung maturation. Those seem to be the critical things."

She frowned and looked down at the bags she brought. "I didn't know how to help, so I went to Nordstrom and bought a shitload of preemie outfits." She opened the shopping bag to let me see. Yep, a shitload of preemie outfits. There were maybe twenty or thirty of them, and they were sooooo tiny. They looked like baby doll clothes.

"What's in the other bag?"

She looked at me quizzically.

"The duffel bag."

She looked down and then glanced away. "Oh, it's nothing. I wasn't thinking."

"Well, it IS something. It's a physical thing in your hand. Is it full of weed? Why are you acting so weird?"

"What?! No, of course not," she scoffed.

She groaned and put the duffel on a waiting room end table. I unzipped it and peered inside.

It was Candace's bridesmaid dress.

"Before you say anything, I already said I hadn't been thinking straight. I thought I'd bring the dress to show her how lovely they turned out, just to have something to talk about since babies weren't my thing." She teared up. "But then on the way here I realized we fitted it for her to be pregnant at my wedding. And . . . and that's just depressing." Her wedding was in a couple of weeks. Candace would have been thirty-six weeks pregnant with Annabelle. I wiped my eyes with a tissue and handed one to Jane, too.

"Look, Candace and Wil are going to be in the NICU for a long time, so you'll be here all day if you wait for them. Wil checks his messages every hour or so. I'll let him know I saw you outside and that we headed back home together. I have their key so maybe later we can wash their preemie clothes and maybe clean up their place so when they do come home everything will be nice and tidy."

As soon as I suggested we should clean, Jane wrinkled her nose. A cleaning person came to her place twice a week. Jane wasn't exactly the roll-up-your-sleeves-and-clean type. She pleaded, "Can I bring Helga?"

"Your cleaning person's name is Helga?" I'd never heard of

a person in this country, living in this century, with the name Helga. It seemed like the sort of name you'd give a minor character in a slapstick comedy series.

"Yes, that's her real name, and I can ask her to come to their house tomorrow. That's one of the days she normally cleans my place, but I can skip it."

"Okay, that sounds great. Did you drive here?" I'd taken a Liftr to avoid hospital parking fees.

BOOP-BOOP! She unlocked a BMW convertible just outside the sliding doors. "I did drive, and you can be my first passenger. Just bought it last week!" Ahhhh, new car smell. Far better than that antiseptic aroma permeating the hospital.

On the drive home, I casually mentioned, "Hey, did you know that Asher wanted me to convince you to abolish all maid of honor and best man dancing requirements?"

She laughed. "Asher's a disaster on the dance floor. He does this weird boxing-like arm thing and doesn't move his feet. The only way he even dances at all is if he's completely drunk."

"I'd like to ask then, as a favor to me, to make sure you DO have a wedding party dance. And could you make a big stink if he doesn't come out to the dance floor?"

Jane asked, "Are you SURE you want to be subjected to dancing with Asher for a full three minutes, smiling for the audience, with your hands and bodies touching, while he steps all over your feet?"

Tough call. Cancel the dance, or torture him while also torturing me? "Um, never mind. Let's cancel the dance." We pulled into our parking garage and took the elevator to our apartments. "Unless you really want it."

A flurry of delayed text notifications popped up on my phone when I unlocked my door.

Jane: *Where are you? I'm in the waiting room.*

Mom: *Thank you sending the Seattle article. Waaa! You famous now! You should pic different picture, this one you have double chin. Maybe ask to retake or ask them to erase.*

Nolan: *I have to tell you something! In person. When I'm back in town ok?* A wave of sadness hit me as I read his excited message. Even when he wasn't traveling, I'd managed to avoid him since the night at the club, for both our sakes. I wasn't ready to be around him yet.

Kat: *Oh holy shit you have over 700 comments on your Seattle Met article! And Cosmo and Redbook just published articles too. Your PR friend is a genius! Trolls took the bait (including someone claiming to be UltimateDDay) and are battling all these liberal Seattleites and women's rights advocates, who are rallying for you! Tallyhooooo!*

Fresh tears brimmed on my eyelashes and trickled down my cheeks. Candace had really pulled through for me. So had the *Seattle Met*, and a lot of their readers.

Tallyho, motherfuckers.

CHAPTER TWENTY-FIVE

Kat sent me a text. *Why is Asher in Sue's office?*

Had he actually reported me for not-technically dating Nolan? My pulse sped up as I walked down the HR corridor. When I passed Sue's room, I looked over as discreetly as possible, which really wasn't at all. Asher was seated in one of her guest chairs, facing her, and Sue didn't even look up when I zipped by. Usually, she waved.

After my recon work, I texted Kat. *Couldn't see anything. Nada.*

My stomach churned, jaw muscles tightened, knowing that any moment I could be called into Sue's or Ian's office to be let go. Terminated. My biggest nightmare becoming my reality. As various scenarios of getting fired played out in my mind, Kat messaged again. *Interesting email. Very unexpected. Maybe Asher's not such a horrible guy after all?*

Seventeen Studios had issued a formal statement: an incident had been reported in which an employee shared proprietary information with external media without proper clearance. Such action was not permitted at the company and warranted disciplinary action, including possible probation or termination.

At last, something was being done about Ian's deliberate actions that had directly resulted in my utter misery. Finally, he would be held accountable.

Just before leaving work at a reasonably early time, Wheed-Wacker disclosed the identities of many of my self-righteous, vicious cyberbullies. And they weren't your stereotypical basement dwelling, Mountain Dew–drinking virgins.

@ApeSht75: A white middle-aged accountant (ACCOUNTANT? WTF) from Des Moines, IA. Family man. Churchgoer with a lesbian mother and sister.

@Hi_TierX: Upper 20s neuroscience PHD candidate. White. Played a LOT of video games. Harassed a LOT of women, people of color, and LGBTQ.

@GSquad_7: This guy was always getting banned on social media and wanted to rape everything. EVERYTHING. It was all he talked about. He just turned 18.

@XBulletGamr: In his 50s, lived with his mom, a day trader who posted lots of porn pics. Mostly Asian fantasy porn.

@gravitygirl23: A black female gamer in her 20s. She
    posted about #girlpower in a sarcastic way and hated
    all women of all races. To be fair, she also hated
    men of all races. She must have a backstory, but
    WheedWacker couldn't find it.

@flipper9000: A Filipino American guy in his 30s.
    Single. He did not like Asian women. In fact, he
    hated them. All of them.

She texted: *Want me to dox them? I have cell #s, addresses, SSNs,
even banking info. I wouldn't go that far though.*
    I could have asked WheedWacker to do it, and she would
have. Posting that personal information would have escalated
this to another level, but I refused to add more fuel to the fire.
Game over. This stupid shit needed to stop.

> *Nah, no need. The harassment has really taken a
> nosedive since my Seattle Met interview, but thank
> you for everything. Justice Brigade saved me.*

WheedWacker responded: *By the way, we changed our name
to Bitch Brigade. Police and Media confused Justice Brigade with the
Justice League like all the time, and Wonder Woman was the only goddamned woman on that Justice League team. We'll go by B.B. effective
immediately.*
    Me: *Has a nice ring to it. I love this bitch identity appropriation.*

You might think about 13.13 as another way to express B.B. It's way nerdier.

WheedWacker replied: *13.13. Yes! Well, we can get you those files if you need them anytime. Just ask Candace, and she'll find me. I'm disconnecting this number now. Good luck, Gamer Girl.*

I wrote: *No, thank YOU,* but the message did not go through.

The rain had let up, and now the skies were clear, not a single cloud for miles. No bluebirds singing, though. The sun burned my eyes, like someone coming out of a dark movie theater and being thrust into direct sunlight. This momentary pause in precipitation was glorious. Pedestrians swished past me, some talking on their phones on their way home, some chatting with friends or coworkers, and a few walking alone. My body tingled all the way down to my fingertips and toes.

I had control again. What a wonderful feeling.

CHAPTER TWENTY-SIX

My phone rang at 6:15 A.M. a day before launch. All I heard were high-pitched squeals, which at first I thought was a fax machine transmission. But it turned out to be my friend Nick, shrieking with glee.

"Melody! Are you up? Wake up! Remember how I submitted your game trailer to all the advertising award festivals? Well, it won Grand Prize at the Indie Webbies for video CGI! And not just any grand prize. It was the Grand fucking Prix! We got the highest honor! How amazing is that?"

I rubbed the sleep out of my eyes. "Oh wow. Congratulations, Nick! But it's not 'we' we're talking about, it's YOU. YOU won this and you deserve this so much. I am so excited and proud of you."

I could feel him beaming through the phone. "There's more. The *Ultimate Apocalypse* trailer's been picked up by a few industry news outlets, so your game trailer is going to be featured in both *Adweek* and *Ad Age*. And the UK and other European countries and regions are also picking up this news. A video game for women, with stripper heroes? The press is already all over that shit!" More press for him meant more press for me. Good deal!

Like a guardian angel, Nick sent miracle news a day before my game launch. Newsletter subscriptions for the game nearly doubled overnight, thanks to this buzz outside of the gaming news world.

Joe our PR guy called me that morning, too, on my way into work. "We've gotten so many urgent merchandising inquiries from toy and apparel companies, and new wellness, skincare, and fitness product placement requests. Hurry up and get to the office!"

That afternoon, women's interest magazines reached out to ask for copies of the game, company press releases, and high-resolution game images so they could publish online game reviews around the holidays. I'd just finished putting together press kit mailers to send out to editors, but this influx of requests made marketing so easy because these publications and websites sought me out, and not the other way around.

In our last afternoon team meeting before the big day, all of us looked like the apocalyptic zombies we'd designed in the game, but we were in good spirits. *Ultimate Apocalypse* would be in the hands of people outside of the Seventeen Studios walls!

In an unexpected company announcement, Ian revealed that Asher's *Girls of War* game would have a soft launch on the same day of *Ultimate Apocalypse*'s release. "Our goal is to maximize our PR opportunity for Seventeen Studios by launching two of our amazing games on the same day. This is rarely seen in the game industry, and we expect exponential press coverage because of this two-for-one surprise release."

I passed Asher's office on my way to mail a few press kits. His shaggy hair, full beard, and untucked lumberjack shirt that pulled too tight on the buttons made me feel a little better about my own unkempt appearance.

"Hey," I said, shifting the leaning tower of padded envelopes in my arms. "How're you doing?"

He looked up and a smile spread across his face. "Oh good, I thought you were the finance guy, hounding me for budget numbers. Isn't he annoying?"

"I wouldn't know, I had no game budget," I said drily.

"Oh, right, I'm an asshole. I forgot . . . sorry."

"Just stopping by to say hi, wish you luck on your game launch, and to thank you for talking to HR about Ian."

"I have my own apology for you, too." He dipped his head down, so low that his overgrown beard merged with his chest hair. "I'm sorry I didn't think you could produce a video game. More proof that I'm an asshole." An apologetic asshole was way better than just a plain ol' regular asshole.

"Ash-hole apology accepted." I put the envelopes down and extended my hand.

He reached out to shake it and then hesitated. "Before we call a truce, are you sure you don't wanna talk smack tomorrow when our games launch? We'll get real-time download numbers so we can see which game, you know, wins."

I lowered my hand. "Fine then. Tomorrow we'll see whether my male stripper and female warrior game can outdo your big-boobed war-ravaged women one."

His eyes sparkled as he laughed. "Deal!"

"I need to get to the mailroom before the last pickup. See ya." I padded out of his office.

While tasked with putting postage labels on my mail, I thought through the launch-day download scenarios. If *Girls of War* came out on top, which everyone expected, I'd be okay with that. Our studio considered *GoW* to be one of their biggest flagship games. What I didn't want was for the *GoW* beta release to blow my game out of the water, though. Time had run out for any last-minute maneuvering, so we'd just need to wait and see.

And pray.

And possibly vomit.

NOLAN STOPPED BY my office while I was checking download links to make sure there were no typos in our *Ultimate Apocalypse* game description.

"Hey, stranger, got a second?"

I smiled and waved him in. Nolan was back! "For you, yes."

"Guess what?"

"I'm terrible at these guessing games."

"Try anyway."

"You're an alien life-form who wants to take me to your native planet so I can rule as queen."

"Okay, never mind, you do suck at this. I got a job offer! A few actually. One from your friend Jane's company, and another at Epicenter Games!"

My stomach sank like an anchor. Epicenter was in the Bay Area. And of course, the other position was in NYC.

"I was so inspired by our conversations. And you were right. I needed to stand up for what I wanted in life. Fight for it, even when it's hard, just like you do. So I 'Sheryl Sandberged the shit out of this,' as you say." He chuckled. "I passed on the New York job because I wanted to stay in gaming. I'm taking the Epicenter job."

"Oh. Then you'd need to move soon, right?" An uneasiness in my gut made me grimace. He would leave, and that would be the end of us. Not that there *was* an us.

But did I still want there to be?

A rolling sense of sadness hit me, leaving me unsteady enough to grab the armrests of my chair. For months, Nolan had been there for me when I needed him the most. He didn't care that I was career minded, so much so that my workaholic tendencies during a ship cycle meant eating microwaved Stouffer's for nearly every meal. Most important, he liked me for who I was, flaws and all. Damn it, here was a guy I couldn't live without, someone whose like-to-hate ratio was through the roof, and he was moving away.

He sat down on the corner of my desk and his whole face spread into a warm smile. "The headquarters is in Northern California, but I'll be in an office for their mobile games just down the street in Lake Union. This is my last official week at Seventeen as an intern." Nolan leaned toward me and whispered, "You know what that means, right? For us? Or do you not want to play guessing games anymore?" His gaze met mine and my heart melted, then burst into streamers and confetti.

Oh my god, yes. Oh my god. Oh my god.

I breathed in and out, steadily and calmly. *Must not freak out. Must **NOT FREAK OUT**.* My stomach turned happy flips as he stood up and slowly drew a card from his pocket.

"It means . . . we go celebrate!" He handed me a punch card. "I got my tenth punch at Cold Stone Creamery today! This entitles you to one free medium scoop with one topping. I thought maybe we could go tomorrow to celebrate my new job and your game launch."

Nolan MacKenzie had my whole heart. All I wanted was for him to feel the same way about me.

"Th-thanks." I put on the fakest of smiles as Nolan dropkicked my shattered heart. I'd never been so sad to get free ice cream in my life.

LAUNCH DAY TURNED out to be weirder than I expected.

People ran through the halls yelling out download numbers. Someone right outside my office screamed, "Shit! *GoW* just hit fifty thousand downloads the first hour!" Our studio had never seen numbers that high on a launch day.

In comparison, I'd gotten maybe twenty thousand downloads, but since my game included expertly integrated product placements and merchandise sale opportunities, my game would hit profitability first. The limited edition *Ultimate Apocalypse* tees sold out within an hour.

Online reviews poured in for both games. *GoW* got accolades from both critics and players, and by noon his game had a four-out-of-five-star ranking on most of the popular gaming sites. *UA* hovered around three stars overall, with a wide range of ratings from one-star gaming haters ("game is stupid and shallow, like the game producer who made it," "unoriginal and hack, unrealistic," "guys don't really look like that") to my five-star raters ("finally, a fun game for women," "hubba hubba," "great story arcs, fun characters, and nice eye candy").

Kat warned me about trying to defend my game online. "If you respond to the negative reviews, people will go on the attack, saying you're too sensitive and you're femi-nasty. Let it go. And let your fans defend your honor. Did you see your good critic reviews in the press?"

Joe emailed a launch-day PR summary to the entire company, and I couldn't believe my eyes. My game had double the number of critic endorsements as *GoW*, plus *Ultimate Apocalypse* had been featured as the lead story in tech blogs and the *Seattle Times* daily tech section, and *UA* was trending on social media faster than *GoW*. BetaGank wrote, "Kudos to Seventeen Studios for its game originality and technical mastery. With *Ultimate Apocalypse*, they've set a new high bar for mobile games. An impressive FPS mobile debut from Seventeen Studios."

Rain, one of the senior producers who had given me a crash course in production when I first joined the company, popped his head in my office. "Congratulations, Melody! I'm so proud of you!"

"Thank you, you were a great teacher."

"And you were a great pupil. Did you see the email about the company launch lunch? Or maybe it's lunch launch? Whatever. There's free food to celebrate the launches today."

My stomach muscles clenched tight. "I don't really feel like going to another company event where women in skimpy cosplay outfits offer me an assortment of gourmet pig-in-a-blanket appetizers."

Rain smiled. "When we have *Zooful Nation* launch parties, they're circus themed and have cotton candy and peanuts and all kinds of shit. I can only imagine your launch lunch will be better than that. Ian usually gives a short speech, too." He disappeared out of view. My stomach gurgled at his mention of lunch. Maybe I could get free food and then duck out.

The thumping EDM music shook the walls as I approached the ground-floor party, and the light beams moving across the floor spilled a multitude of colors into the hallway through the open double doors. Dozens of people walked out with booze, T-shirts, and bags of swag. Most of the guys leaving the event had on *GoW* tees, autographed on the back by Asher and Ian. I rolled my eyes.

A few people left wearing *Ultimate Apocalypse* shirts, mainly women and a few gay men. A handful of lanky hipster dudes wore them, too, but it may have been because most of the launch shirts for my game ran smaller.

I walked in and beelined to the freebie stations. The only *UA* shirts left were size XS, about two sizes off from what I needed. Pulling one over my head anyway, I squeezed my head through the supersmall head hole, like I was reenacting my vaginal birth. My arms pushed through next but there wasn't any room in the chest area to get both arms in there. My writhing caught Rain's eye.

"Here. Take mine. It's a men's L, but that's better than shoving yourself into a too-tight S."

"It's a too-tight **EXTRA** S, actually."

He looked mortified. "Oh my god, I'm so sorry. I didn't mean that."

I laughed and peeled the shirt off. "I've never fit into an XS my entire life, honestly. I went straight from young girl sizes to ladies' size S, and then M. Don't know why I'm sharing all this with you, by the way."

"That's okay, I grew up with sisters, and now my wife and I have three daughters. I'm used to talking about this kind of stuff. Did you get a good look around? Ian went a little overboard."

The entrance was only as far as I'd gotten. I looked up and

noticed jumbo video screens playing synchronized scene excerpts from the two launch games. It was a game mashup party: there were apocalypse-themed "survival" boxed lunches, and war ammunition–themed drinks, like the AK-47 Absinthe Cocktail, a Grenade Grenadine Cooler, and Rum Rocket Launchers.

Ian walked across the room. "Isn't this amazing? The events team did such an amazing job, right?"

I muttered, "I'd rather funnel events money into more press kits and advertising." And not on ill-fitting T-shirts or specialty drinks offered in cups shaped like grenades.

He ignored me. "The board members are here, too. They just told me they want you to say a few words."

Before I could protest, the music lowered, drawing attention to PR Joe, who stood on a tall makeshift stage in the front of the room. "If I could have your attention, everyone! Let's give the Seventeen Studios events team a huge round of applause. Lift your glasses. The food and drinks are amazing, events team!"

The crowd erupted in cheers as everyone clinked grenade cups.

Ian jumped on the stage and shooed PR Joe off. "Thanks for warming up the crowd, Joe. Or maybe it's the alcohol that's helping." More cheers erupted. There were at least two hundred people there.

He said, "Congratulations to both the *Girls of War* and *Ultimate Apocalypse* teams for working so hard to get those games launched on time. Seventeen Studios knows how to get shit done!"

More applause. More cheers. Ian really had a knack for rallying the troops. People were loving this.

"Unfortunately, Asher, the game creator of *Girls of War*, can't be with us now, because he's on the phone with Warner Bros. *Girls of War* was optioned for a TV series and a movie this morning. What a success story!"

My stomach dropped, like I was on one of those horrible free-fall rides at Six Flags. My ears and face blazed with pulsing heat. Asher's booberific game became a runaway hit overnight and *Hollywood Reporter* and *Entertainment Weekly* would announce his blockbuster deal soon. He'd hit the entitled-affluent-white-bro jackpot.

Joe walked over and offered me one of his two grenade drinks. "You look like you need it." He smelled his cocktail and furrowed his brow. "Is Ian going to ask you to speak about your experience as a woman in the gaming industry?" He took a sip and then coughed. "Wow, this is strong."

I took a giant swig, needing a little something to take the edge off. "He wants me to speak because the board is here, and of course he gave me zero notice. The expectation is to say amazing things about my opportunities here, right?"

"Shit, this tastes like paint thinner." He looked around and found a table behind us. Placing his drink on the corner, he said, "Yes, he's hoping you'll say something like that."

"And as the head of PR, do you agree? Are you here to

coach me?" Tipsy tingles hit my toes and fingertips. That paint-thinner cocktail was seriously potent.

"As someone who saw what you went through, I think you should say what's in your heart."

"And what if my heart hates everything about gaming right now?"

Kat and Rain walked by us, with two stolen trays of cookies. My heart softened a bit.

Joe looked me in the eye. "With all the odds stacked against you, somehow you managed to release that game, with no executive support. Say whatever the fuck you want." He grabbed his drink from the table and raised his glass. "Tell them all to fuck off."

Ian took the mic again and rambled off the names of everyone who'd helped make *Girls of War* a success. He paused and shuffled the index cards on the podium. "Today we also launched *Ultimate Apocalypse,* and we've reached over thirty thousand downloads as of an hour ago. We're projecting to hit one hundred thousand before midnight. Congratulations to the *UA* team!"

A healthy wave of applause filled the air. It didn't sound like pity clapping.

"I've invited Melanie . . . er . . . Melody Joo to come onstage to talk about her experience leading the production of this sleeper hit. We appreciate all her contributions as a woman in gaming, am I right? Let's give Melody, our female production superstar, a round of applause for her hard work."

The clapping continued as I made my way to the stairs. Ian gave me a firm handshake at the podium. He whispered, "Five minutes. And then we drop the balloons. It's on a timer."

I peered through the blazing white spotlights. Joe stood there right in the front, with five fingers held up. Thank god for Joe and his timekeeping skills.

A quick scan of the room revealed it was 90 percent men. Some older dudes stood in the far back, presumably the board of directors. Ian drank artillery cocktails at the bar while Kat and Rain jointly stole stacks of survivor box lunches without him noticing. And Asher remained absent, probably still on the fucking phone with Warner Bros.

I took a slow, deep breath, and then spoke from my heart.

"Thank you for that rousing male speech, Ian, from the bottom of my female heart. Speaking of females, how many of you gave reviews for the *Girls of War* game on BetaGank or some other review site today?"

About 80 percent of the audience raised their hands. Even some of the board members did. A few guys in the back even gave celebratory whistles.

"And how many of you reviewed *Ultimate Apocalypse*?"

All hands went down, except for Kat, Rain, Joe, and Kedra the receptionist. And the two dev interns. That was it. Six people, seven if you included me. No whistles.

"Right. Seven people from this company reviewed that game. It's an unwritten rule at Seventeen to have all employees honestly review every game we launch. Ninety percent of our company submitted reviews for *Zooful Nation*, which targets six- to twelve-year-olds. You aren't anywhere near that demographic, and yet, you all posted reviews for that game." I swallowed hard. "I'm not even saying *UA* should have gotten an automatic five stars from you. In fact, Kat over there is so honest, I bet she gave it only three."

She yelled back, "I gave it three and a half!"

Her comment cut the tension. The crowd laughed and all eyes moved back on me. "Okay, let's move past the reviews. How many of you downloaded *UA*?"

Again, the same people, plus a row of women raising their hands in the back. Nolan burst through the doors in the back, donning a massive *UA* T-shirt, waving at me with both arms. I nodded at him.

Moving to the front of the crowd, he winked at me and smiled proudly, fueling my confidence.

"You see, *Ultimate Apocalypse* was the ultimate underdog game. It became an incubator project that was thrust into market without any room for error. You'll remember that resources were taken away. We were moved to back burner status. And somehow, with our bare-bones team, we pulled it off. With no marketing budget. No dev resources. And a junior producer who flew by the seat of her pants but had an amazing team to support her to make it all come together. This game had been set on a course to fail, and the world expected as much. But the team of devotees, those seven people who had their hands raised high a few seconds ago, wouldn't let this game crash and burn. Because that isn't part of our company's DNA.

"Yes, *UA* was a sleeper hit. We won a coveted advertising award and got a ton of nongamer media coverage thanks to a dear friend of mine who moonlit as our publicist while pregnant on bed rest. We didn't get a movie deal or anything, though. Warner Bros. must've lost my number or something. But we got a shitload of downloads and reviews, with no help from you all."

I looked at Joe. One minute remaining.

Shit. Wrap this up, Melody. "I want to thank the core team who worked so hard to make *UA* successful. And to those who downloaded the game, thank you for that. To everyone who didn't raise his hand, please think about why you didn't feel compelled to support this game. What are your biases? What made you think, 'I'll help *Girls of War*, and *Zooful Nation*, but not this other game?' I think you know why.

"The *UA* team, despite all odds, proved itself. This game is on track to pass the break-even point this week and will be profitable. Soon, we'll be competing with *Zooful Nation* on lucrativeness. So please, go do the right thing. Download and review this fucking game."

My phone lit up on the podium with a text from Nolan. *****FIVE STAR SPEECH!*

I cracked a smile and looked directly at him with my conclusion. "Thank you for your support."

The jumbo monitors around us lit up with "Congratulations!" messages as ceremonious trumpet music blared on the speakers overhead. Thousands of balloons showered down on the partygoers, many of whom stood silent and stunned. It was kind of like the Stephen King *Carrie* prom scene, but with balloons, not blood. And no death.

A decent number of attendees snapped into action and downloaded the game. I said what needed to be said. My heart was no longer heavy.

CHAPTER TWENTY-SEVEN

Wedding day. Also known as "Bridezilla's Bitch for a Day" day.

"Have you seen my phone? I swear I just had it. Can you call it again so we can find it?"

"Can you unwrap this candy? My fingernails are drying. Just pop it into my mouth when you're done."

"Ohhhhh, maid of honorrrrrrrr! Can you call room service and ask why they're taking so long with my lunch?"

Cinderella Melody. And Jane was the evil stepmother and stepsisters combined.

This is only going to be for one day, I told myself, while waiting in the cashier line at the hotel minimarket. The morning began ominously, with my car not starting. Luckily, Nolan was nice enough to drive me to the hotel. With my blessing, he ordered room service up in the bridesmaids' suite and crashed on my pillowtop bed while we got ready in Jane's room.

I placed three bottles of cold, lime-flavored Perrier water, an apple, and a banana in a basket. All for Jane, of course.

For me, I grabbed a bag of Flamin' Hot Cheetos. My comfort food. *Mental note: do NOT touch any bridal shit with flaming red cheese dust fingers.*

Revised mental note: pour the Cheetos directly into mouth. No cheese dust fingers!

"Can I get those for you? Or at least charge them to Sean's room?"

I looked up to find Asher grinning at me. He had a fresh haircut and no beard. He also looked tan and had less of a beer gut. That movie deal had done him wonders.

"Hey, how are you, Mister Hollywood?" I asked cheerily. We'd be walking down the aisle together within a few hours, smiling fakely at the camera and at all the wedding guests. After the reception I could go back to mostly disliking him.

Asher snorted. "Yeah, you can thank my dad for that. He's the one who brokered all the film and TV deals. He and Ian go way back and had a lot of discussions already in the works before Ian told me our studio was producing *GoW*. As for hard-earned success, you win hands down. I'm just a plain, lucky white dude at a video game company. You're Melody Joo, slayer of internet trolls." He unloaded everything from his basket onto the counter and I added my purchases too. "So, the news isn't out yet, but I accepted an offer at a start-up game studio in Bellevue. I'm going to be a senior producer! I wanted to go somewhere my dad couldn't interfere. Want me to put in a good word for you there?"

"Nah, I'm good." Things at Seventeen were much better

now. Great, in fact. My raise and bonus came through, and a few weeks after the *UA* launch, I was now in charge of *Ultimate Apocalypse 2* production with my own small team.

The cashier said, "Twenty-two dollars and ten cents, sir."

"Damn, Melody, how many bags of Cheetos did you buy?" Asher laughed. "Please charge it to penthouse 1201." He turned to me. "I heard they have two Jacuzzis in there. You know, one for each of them."

He grabbed a few infant-size bottles of local artisan hand-crafted vodka by the cash register. "Add these, too, please. To celebrate."

The cashier smiled politely as she handed Asher his liquor and pushed my brown bag full of sundries toward me, with Chester Cheetah peeking over the top.

"Do you need to go up right now? We could have a . . . *pre*-party."

I couldn't tell if he was being gross or not. "I need to go up to the room or Jane will freak out. Candace will be here soon for hair and makeup, and then it's wedding time. I'm the only one here to help Her Highness."

"Sean's been a bit of a prima donna prick today too. He's stressed, but happy. Sounds like those two were meant to be."

Asher's phone buzzed. His eyes bulged as he read his message. "Holy shit, Melody. Look at this."

Sue from HR sent a shocking email on a Saturday after-noon. "It is with mixed emotions that we announce that Ian MacKenzie has stepped down from the role of CEO of Seventeen Studios. Ian will remain at the company, dedicating his time to special projects. Our interim CEO, Tope Claybrooks, joins our company in two weeks . . ."

"Isn't this great?" Asher bellowed. "Ian's getting demoted! Anyone who is assigned 'special projects' at Seventeen is basically getting pushed out. It's a bullshit thing that companies say when they don't want it to look like that person is getting kicked to the curb right away. Trust me, the only special projects Ian is working on are cover letters and updating his résumé."

"Wow, I thought guys like him were untouchable." I never thought someone like Ian could fall so mightily.

Asher grinned. "If enough people complain about you to HR, you become a liability to the company." He lowered his voice. "You remember how I went to Sue and told her about how he asked me to leak your game info? Well, my dad actually told the board. Other employees have complained about him, too. I wasn't the only one. I'm actually surprised it took this long for the company to take action."

I searched online for Tope Claybrooks. Assuming I found the correct Tope with game-related work history, she was a midforties African American woman with chunky dreadlocks. She had most recently been SVP of development at Bigfoot Studios, a huge casual game company in the Bay Area, and she got her CS degree from Spelman, the black all-women college in Georgia. I couldn't WAIT to see what changes she'd implement at our company.

"Good riddance, right?" Asher said, and held up his hand in front of me, waiting for a fist bump or something. "Hey"—he shot me a pretend hurt look—"you can't leave me hanging."

I rolled my eyes.

He put his fist down.

An appointment alert buzzed on my phone. "I've gotta go. Hair and makeup time. I'll see you on the aisle. Don't trip me."

He said, "I'm too scared of you, honestly. I wouldn't dare!" He said it jokingly, but I think he meant it.

Back at the bridal room, the hair-and-makeup artist tapped her foot as I unloaded the sundries. Candace had just finished and looked very glamorous with a half updo and loose curls cascading down her shoulders.

I squealed, "Awww, Candie!" We ran up to each other but we didn't hug. One sudden move and her makeup could smudge, or a rogue hairpin could get snagged. I awkwardly patted her shoulder. "How's your kiddo?"

"Annabelle's great! She's gaining weight so fast now." Candace teared up, and she began fanning her face and looking upward at the sky. "Oh shit, I don't want my eye makeup to run."

I sat down on the chair and the makeup artist inspected my face. "You need false eyelashes."

Um, what? "I really don't think that would be a good idea." I could barely handle contact lenses. Fake eyelashes? No way.

Jane chimed in with an opinion, of course. "Melody, I think you'd look amazing. She put some on me. It's mainly for the wedding pictures, to make my eyes pop more." She walked up to me so I could get a closer look. Sure enough, she had these mile-long thick lashes. But she looked pretty and normal in them. I never even wore eye makeup.

"Candace, did you get them?"

"She didn't need them. Her lashes just needed some mascara. Her eyes are gorgeous and so big." The makeup artist lifted her stash of eyelashes from her cosmetic bag.

Thanks for pointing all of that out. "Fine. You can try it, but I can tell you now, you might need a plan B."

She asked me to open as wide as I could, and with my Korean eyes being shaped the way nature had intended, she had to forcibly hold them open the entire time as she gently glued the lashes onto the top and bottom of my lids. My eyes watered nonstop, which interfered with the glue drying. It's not like I could help it. There were foreign objects near my eye sockets, and my eyes tried desperately to flush everything out.

After five minutes of this medieval eye torture, she handed me a mirror.

I looked . . . different. Like a hooker version of myself. And not in a good way. Every time I blinked I saw black lines.

Blink, black. Blink, black. "These are glued on, right? It looks like they might be falling off and interfering with my vision." Jane and Candace circled me, ensuring that the eyelashes looked great.

"I . . . I can't do this, sorry. I'm blinking way too much because I'm not used to having things hanging from my eyelids, and the more I blink, the more I notice the skinny black bars and it looks like I'm in jail."

Silently judging me, the makeup person unglued the lashes without protesting. I just prayed she wouldn't punish me by giving me tight poodle curls and neon-blue eye shadow.

The next time she handed me the mirror I looked much better. Pretty, in fact. Borderline glamorous. I hadn't had a makeover like this since high school prom, and the person staring back at me in the mirror looked like a froofy Melody impostor. This fanciful look was nice for a day, but it didn't feel like me. I couldn't wait to wash it all off after the wedding and go back to my normal, lip-gloss-and-a-few-pats-of-powder life.

Candace whistled. "Wow, she really enhanced all your features. You look stunning."

"Thank you," I said, beaming now.

With great care, we slid into our bridesmaid gowns and helped Jane into her wedding gown. She walked up to the full-length mirror by the bathroom door and slowly turned. A dazzling, picture-perfect bride.

She grinned at Candace and me. "Wow," she said, admiring her dress detailing on her back. "I look amazing."

Candace and I looked at each other and burst into a fit of giggles. Jane was something else.

My phone buzzed. Asher. *It's showtime. Groom and groomsmen are ready and in position. Philharmonic is playing! BTW I have a flask in my jacket if you need it.*

"Time to head down!" I yelped, and we gathered our bouquets in the hallway. Nolan peeked out of the bridesmaid suite next door. His ruffled hair had multiple cowlicks and he had pillow marks on his right cheek. "You look beautiful, Melody. All of you do! Good luck!"

"Thank you," I said, blushing as we walked down the hall.

Candace's eyes bulged at the sight of him and she elbowed me in the ribs. She whispered, "Wil and Nolan hang out all the time now. He talks about you so much."

I shushed her. "If he liked me that way, he would have asked me out already."

She responded with a shrug but no words.

A door slammed and someone yelled, "Hold the elevator! I need to ask the front desk for towels. For some reason you don't have any." Nolan barreled toward us and made it just in time.

On the ride down, I repositioned a loose curl that had fallen out of Jane's tiara. When I looked up, Nolan shifted his glance away from me, smiling to himself, like he had a secret he wasn't disclosing just yet.

When we reached the ground floor, Jane and Candace exited the elevator first. Nolan said, "Um, Melody? Can you wait a second?" Up ahead, neither Jane nor Candace noticed that I broke formation while Nolan pushed the door open button.

The doors started to beep. In a panicky whine, I said, "Oh god, you know I don't do well in elevators."

"Oh shit, I'm so sorry!" He gestured with his hand for me to walk out first. He reached out and gently gripped my arm, not letting me join the bridal party yet. "So . . . I'm not an intern anymore."

My cheeks flushed at his touch. Instant blush, no makeup artist needed. "Yes, that's right! I should have congratulated you before. Should we go get ice cream?" My heart raced and I couldn't think straight, so all I could do was kid around. "You know, I should go now. It's time for the ceremony." The bridal party had turned around and was heading back toward us.

How was it possible to feel so warm when he simultaneously sent chills down my fingers and toes? Those were some powerful pheromones he had.

He let go of my arm and rubbed his chin. "Uh, not ice cream. I was hoping for something else."

I blinked rapidly, my mind unable to process his words.

Jane walked in between us and pointed her bouquet in Nolan's face. "This is neither the time nor the place for . . . whatever this is." Lowering her flowers, she glowered at him. "I don't even know who the hell you are."

He nodded reverently. "Sorry, Jane. I'm Nolan MacKenzie." He held out his hand and they shook awkwardly.

Her face softened. "Ah, I know you. You're the intern."

"Former intern," he clarified.

She whispered to me, "I like your intern, he's perfect for you." She hooked one arm with mine and the other with Candace's, taking great care to not smush the bridal bouquet.

"Let's go, ladies." She motioned for Candace and me to start walking. "It's my big day, bishes! I'm getting hitched!"

THANKFULLY, THE CEREMONY was short and sweet, and there was so much going on I could forget about my strange encounter with Nolan outside the elevator. The bride and groom said their lines without stumbling, and no one tripped down the aisle. They exchanged a few lines of noncustomized vows and went straight into the final kiss. Sean did one of those movie kisses where he tilted Jane back, and she lifted her foot as they smooched. Cute stuff. The crowd loved it. So did the photographer.

The start of the reception was pretty typical, too, except for when the bride's dad gave a speech that sounded more like a rundown of Jane's résumé: he rattled off all her academic and work-related accomplishments. I wasn't sure what her perfect math SAT score had to do with her meeting her soul mate, or what her acceptance into Wharton Business School had to do with love.

Luckily Jane had the foresight to ask Asher and me to forgo our maid of honor and best man speech duties because she knew her dad would ramble on for the total allotted speaking time. It wasn't a huge deal to me either way whether I did or not. Whatever made Jane happy that night was fine with me. Bored to tears, my thoughts drifted to Nolan, replaying the day's events. Maybe after the wedding, he and I could sit down and talk about where things stood between us.

I had just ordered a lychee martini at the open bar when the DJ squawked on the microphone, "Laaaaaaadies and gentlemen! It's time for the best man and the maid of honor to help get this party started!" With Miley Cyrus's "Party in the USA" playing in the background, he whooped, "Melody Joo! Asher Jennings! Come onnnnn down!"

I searched the crowd for Asher but couldn't find him. The DJ continued yammering into the microphone. "It's a wedding tradition! Melody and Asher, it's tiiiiiime for you to dance! Don't be shy!" Everyone turned around in their seats, looking for me. A handful of people pointed to the bar. "Oh, we found her! Everyone please give Melody a warm round of applause for being an amazing maid of honor today, and to encourage her to come up here and *dance, dance, dance!*" He clapped along to those last three words.

"*Dance, dance, dance,*" the crowd chanted.

With a plastered smile hiding my distress beneath the surface, I waved to the crowd and made my way to the front. The wedding-goers blocking my way to the dance floor moved their legs so a clear path opened up magically, like Moses parting the Red Sea.

Wearing my dreadful toga dress, I looked at the hundreds of wedding guests, who were waiting for me to dance, dance, dance to Miley's anthem.

Asher still wasn't there. I stood all by my lonesome in front of two hundred people. Just Miley Cyrus and me.

"Paging Asher Jennings! Report to dance floor, stat," the DJ joked.

Asher, where the fuck are you?

The DJ, hired to make the night go smoothly, filled the airtime. "While we wait for Asher, everyone, this is Melody Joo, friends with Jane since graduating from college. And, gentlemen, there's no riiiiing on that left haaaaaand!"

I wanted to flee but my knees locked and froze in place. I could usually muster a quip to say in awkward moments like these, but this time no words came out. *God, please, don't let me cry up here.*

I searched the audience for Asher and found Candace, her mouth agape, with a look of pity and horror on her face. She, too, had no words.

My chest tightened and blood rushed to my face. Hotness swept across my body.

I blinked back tears.

I had about ten seconds before the waterworks show would begin. My thoughts muddled and I didn't know what to do. My choices appeared limited: I could run out the door and ruin Jane's wedding plans, or stay here and cry in front of everyone.

Jane shot a panicked look at Candace and me. She would have to change plans. And for control-freak Jane, that was just too much to handle on what was supposed to be the best day of her life.

The doors near the DJ booth flung open and Wil charged in, wearing disheveled athletic wear head to toe. He nudged the DJ aside. "Sorry, everyone, a slight change in the itinerary. Asher wasn't feeling well, but lucky for us, we have a suitable replacement."

Wil looked at me and grinned. "Nolan MacKenzie, would you please do the honor of joining Melody on the dance floor?"

A spotlight moved to the doorway and a freshly showered Nolan walked in, waving and smiling sheepishly at the wedding guests, like he was in a parade. The crowd erupted in applause as he joined me on the center of the dance floor.

He took my hands and said, "I'm wearing Wil's tux. It feels weird. Does it fit?"

The pants were too short and his jacket was too big. His silver bow tie sat askew. He looked perfect.

I nodded.

He exhaled and said softly, "Asher's passed out on a couch in the lobby." We swayed to the music as applause swelled around us. "Does this count as our first date? We look really fancy and we're dancing and there's an open bar."

Did he say . . . first date?

I nodded again.

The tears finally came. Joyful tears, mixed with a smattering of *thank the fuck* relieved ones. After all our ups and downs, back and forths, Nolan and I finally fell into place together.

Candace ran up to me with wads of tissue. "Don't let your makeup run! They're taking pictures!"

The DJ cranked up Taylor Swift's "How You Get the Girl," and a dozen or so drunk people joined us on the dance floor. The nondancing guests clinked their forks on their plates as they happily devoured their gorgonzola beet salads.

My eyes focused only on Nolan, who pulled away and shimmy danced next to me, making me giggle. "Mel, I wanted to ask you out for so long, but I was too chicken. It sounds stupid, but I thought that maybe you would ask me out if you liked me. You seemed like the first-mover type. After we kissed though, I wanted to go for it . . . but could never quite get the timing right with all the shit that kept happening to you. That, and you also somehow kept becoming my boss. And then I had to find a job and you had your game release. I even just now tried to tell you in the elevator how I felt but royally screwed that up too." He stopped dancing. "I was worried I'd waited too long. I guess that really sounds stupid."

"No, I definitely get it. It was never a good time. But, look, today we're together, and all decked out." At the song's end, he spun a full 360 degrees, showing off his borrowed tux.

He grabbed me around the waist, tighter this time. I whispered as we swayed together to the music, "It's weird to see you without any gingham."

"What the hell is gingham?" he asked, pulling his head back to look at me.

My jaw dropped. "You wear it all the time, are you serious?"

He drew in closer. "You'll have to show me what you're talking about then. No clue."

"Okay, on our next date." Tilting my head up, I tugged his noningham shirt so he'd bend down. "Thank you for everything you did today." Closing my eyes and heart fluttering with anticipation, I inhaled his clean showered scent and parted my lips. Without any hesitation this time, I pressed my mouth against his. His lips were soft, and full, and perfectly smooth. Like with two opposing magnets, it was hard to pull away from him. This was all I wanted, to be here with Nolan Fucking MacKenzie. Kissing Nolan Fucking MacKenzie. In a toga pressed against Nolan Fucking MacKenzie.

"Wow," he murmured. His eyes opened slowly, as if he was awakening from an incredible dream. "Can we do that again?"

"Yes. Stop talking." I pulled his shirt and brought his lips to mine again, pressing harder this time, sending ripples of electricity through my body. I breathed him in deeply as he slid his hands down my lower back and slowly showered me with kisses down the left side of my neck, sending my heart racing.

Candace and Wil danced over to us. "Get a room!" they cheered in unison.

Nolan and I looked at each other and burst into laughter. Maybe Candace wouldn't mind if I kicked her out of the bridesmaids' room.

The dance floor cleared, and my parents called just as we sat down for dinner. Nolan looked down at my vibrating phone. "You know, now's a good time to take it, or they'll keep calling back, over and over and over . . ."

I laughed. "You're right. Who knows what we'll be up to

later." I squeezed his shoulder and left the ballroom. In the lobby, I paced around while telling my parents about the wedding, letting them know that Nolan and I had finally gone on a date.

Drunk Asher lifted his head from the couch. "Issss 'bout fucking time." He passed out immediately.

Mom screeched, "Waaaaaaa! We so happy! Jee-jus answer our prayer! We pray every day. Every day because you single so long. SO long. Now maybe Jee-jus answer our other prayers."

"Other prayers?"

My mom yelled, "We want you to marry!"

Then my dad. "And have baby!"

Oh god. Really?

EPILOGUE

Eight Months Later

The University of Washington eSports Club held a "Women in Gaming" Q&A, and most of the questions had been easy to answer.

"What's your favorite game of all time?"
Easy. Mario Kart. *A Nintendo classic.*

"What's the hardest game you ever played?"
Any Resident Evil *title. It's hard to play when you're covering your face with a pillow because you're too scared.*

"Do you like working in video games?"
Depends when you ask me. I just got promoted to producer, so as of today, yes!

A student raised her hand, and the moderator handed her the mic. "Hi, Melody, I'm the president of the esports club, Jessie. What do you think is the hardest part about being a woman in gaming?" Jessie had dyed jet-black hair with purple streaks and wore black leather head to toe. Her bright red lipstick suited her. Such contrast and boldness.

"This is a great question. Does everyone have a few hours? It may take me a while to answer!" I took a sip of water to buy some time. The room fell silent. I could hear people breathing. Dozens of young men and women at this event waited to hear my response.

"For women in gaming, you're damned if you do, and damned if you don't. Let's take an actual game play example. A question for the female gamers in the audience, how many of you have been told that you're good, for a girl?"

A few hands crept up, from a dozen or so female gamers.

"Okay, now for those women here who aren't good at gaming. I'm one of them. How many of you have been told you aren't any good because you're a girl?"

Half the women there raised their hands. More than I expected.

"So it's sort of like that, working in games. Women working at game companies have to constantly overcome perception barriers. I argue a lot about how women are portrayed in the games we produce. Gaming is very white, and bro heavy. And the more nonwhite nonbros we have at companies like mine who can interject opinions and different perspectives, the more diverse the gaming offerings will be in the future. I would love to see more of this happen."

I looked at Jessie to see if I'd answered her question. She smiled back at me and nodded.

Whew.

"If it's okay to shamelessly plug my company's diversity internship program, I'd love to do that now." I passed out our recruitment flyers. With the help of Sue from HR, Seventeen Studios established a paid diversity summer program, created by yours truly. The board of directors approved our plan for broadening our recruiting efforts in all levels of hiring (*cough* more women *cough* people of color *cough* LGBTQ *cough*). The beauty of this program was that we weren't just limited to new college graduates. Underrepresented professionals who wanted to switch industries and work in games could apply too.

Sue and Tope, our new, wonderful studio leader, asked me to be the company's diversity show pony (okay, maybe not in those words), but I was fine with that. Nonwhite, nonmale game producers were uncommon. We needed more. With the number of female gamers growing exponentially each year, gaming could go the way of American college admissions, where the number of women surpassed the men. In just a few months, Sue and Tope had overhauled our entire hiring process, revamped our diversity and sexual harassment employee training, and implemented mandatory manager inclusivity coaching, with the goal of helping teams foster community with new diverse group members.

After the Q&A ended, students and community members

wandered to the back of the room to hoard the free cookies, crackers, cheese cubes, and soda. It reminded me of the Seventeen lunchroom after a board meeting, when all the vultures swooped in to forage the sandwich and cookie trays. The board of directors always left soggy chicken salad pita remnants, and oatmeal raisin cookies. I don't know why anyone would ever bother to order oatmeal raisin cookies. Who would ever pick oatmeal raisin over a chocolate chip cookie?

Jessie skipped the free food frenzy and beelined over to me. She handed me her résumé. "I would love to work at Seventeen. I love games, and I have As in all my CS classes."

She had the grades, and the right background. I skimmed her cover letter and résumé. "This all looks great. You have an outstanding academic record and you've had some impressive internships already." I couldn't wait to pass her information to Sue and the recruiting team. I'd even send it to Nolan at Epicenter so she had more than one company in play.

She handed me her business card. "Jessie Alvarez, Games Enthusiast." I flipped the card over. A simple logo embossed on a plain white background: "13.13."

"It would be a dream come true for me to work with you," she said, adjusting her horn-rimmed glasses on her nose.

My face beamed. "Same for me."

WHEN THE EVENT came to an end, I went down to the parking lot and unlocked my new black Fiat with my personalized

ACKNOWLEDGMENTS

When I started writing this book in 2016, I had this blob of an idea in my head that I wanted to tell a story about a woman working in the video game industry. Nerdy me went into full MBA research mode by attending industry panels, reading a ton of articles and books, and interviewing friends who worked at game companies, and I quickly came to the realization that the game industry wasn't exactly always fun and games for those who came from marginalized backgrounds. With the support of so many people, this story evolved and grew so much over the years, and through writing this book I found a stronger voice and discovered what kind of author I wanted to be.

To my MVP agent Brent, my fiercest advocate, this book wouldn't have been written (and rewritten 473,168,392 times haha) without your support. You've always believed in my stories and seem to have Suzanne ESP when you send emails or check in by phone. Thank you for everything.

To my brilliant editor, Carrie Feron, who brought out the

heart of my story (with more levity) and whose insightful comments gave my characters much more depth, thank you so much. Asante Simons, a huge thank-you for being the behind-the-scenes ingenious editing wizard that you are.

I owe a debt of gratitude to all the folks at Avon/Morrow/HarperCollins who played significant roles in the design, editing, sales, and marketing of LOATHE. Massive thank-yous to Imani Gary, Julie Paulauski, Angela Craft, Ploy Siripant, Ashley Caswell, Diahann Sturge, Evangelos Vasilakis, and Laurie McGee for your time and dedication. Ellen Whitfield at JKS, I can't thank you enough for your invaluable assistance (and infectious enthusiasm!).

I'm deeply grateful for the earliest readers of this book: Helen Hoang, I honestly don't know what I would do without you. I can't wait till we write our publishing musical! Roselle Lim, when you first asked to read my book, I was so honored . . . and now I'm honored to be your friend! To the talented Whitney Schneider, thank you for being my longtime CP and putting up with my first-draft ramblings for so many projects. Alexa Martin, thank you so much for finding time to read the pre-sub version. Ken Choy, you cheered me on through the early drafts of this book, it means so much to me.

Julia K., thank you for giving me advice along the way as I was writing this book. And thank you for reading LOATHE and sending me game production and character motivation notes that were so incredibly helpful. It's funny how far we've come since that accounting class together. Chris O. and

Adam O., your game industry expertise helped me so much in my final edits, thank you immensely. Yoko N., Jeremy M., and Elizabeth W., endless gratitude to you for giving me invaluable insight into your professional worlds.

To Kathleen Barber, Chelsea Resnick, Kristin Rockaway, Sheila Athens, Nancy Johnson, Alison Hammer, Janet Rundquist, Gwynne Jackson, Annette Christie, Judy Lin, Sarah Henning, Kellye Garrett, Liz Lawson, Jeff Bishop, my WFWA friends, and the LA WFWA gals, I appreciate you so much. To the present/past members of my MAPID writers group, especially Ken, Curtis, Michael, Jason, and Ben, I'm eternally grateful to you for all the years of helpful feedback.

Thank you to my family (shout out to the Parks and Brimers!) and my dearest girlfriends for supporting me through this writing journey. Trevor, you've believed in me since day one. Sorry about the human-size laundry backlog during my deadline season. CJ, you are the sweetest kiddo in the world, thank you for downloading my picture off the internet and making a minute-long book trailer of my face.

And finally, to my readers, there are literally millions of other novels out there, so it means the world to me that you chose mine. Thank you from the bottom of my heart.